$1.00 $1.25

"Two in a hammock?"

Chelsea's voice rose in a squeak, and she eyed Sam doubtfully as he lounged before her.

"Why not? It's worth a try." He grasped her wrist as he spoke and tugged her in. To Chelsea's surprise it worked—before she knew it she was nestled comfortably against him.

With a little more maneuvering, she managed to get her arms around Sam's neck. Then she sought his lips, fueling his hunger with her own. Before long they were both breathing harder, and the hammock rocked gently as their passion increased.

Briefly Sam pulled away from their kiss. His eyes met hers with a mingling of humor and longing as he whispered, "I think we're getting the 'hang' of it...."

Books by Barbara Delinsky

FINGER PRINTS

HARLEQUIN TEMPTATION

These books may be available at your local bookseller.

Don't miss any of our special offers. Write to us at the following address for information on our newest releases.

Harlequin Reader Service
P.O. Box 52040, Phoenix, AZ 85072-2040
Canadian address: P.O. Box 2800, Postal Station A,
5170 Yonge St., Willowdale, Ont. M2N 6J3

First Things First

BARBARA DELINSKY

Harlequin Books

TORONTO • NEW YORK • LONDON
AMSTERDAM • PARIS • SYDNEY • HAMBURG
STOCKHOLM • ATHENS • TOKYO • MILAN

Published December 1985
Second printing January 1986

ISBN 0-373-25187-4

Copyright © 1985 by Barbara Delinsky. All rights reserved.
Philippine copyright 1985. Australian copyright 1985.
Except for use in any review, the reproduction or utilization of
this work in whole or in part in any form by any electronic,
mechanical or other means, now known or hereafter invented,
including xerography, photocopying and recording, or in any
information storage or retrieval system, is forbidden without
the permission of the publisher, Harlequin Enterprises Limited,
225 Duncan Mill Road, Don Mills, Ontario, Canada M3B 3K9.

All the characters in this book have no existence outside the
imagination of the author and have no relation whatsoever to
anyone bearing the same name or names. They are not even
distantly inspired by any individual known or unknown to the
author, and all incidents are pure invention.

The Harlequin trademarks, consisting of the words, TEMPTATION,
HARLEQUIN TEMPTATION, HARLEQUIN TEMPTATIONS,
and the portrayal of a Harlequin, are trademarks of Harlequin Enterprises
Limited; the portrayal of a Harlequin is registered in the United
States Patent and Trademark Office and in the Canada Trade
Marks Office.

Printed in Canada

"I'D LIKE YOU TO FIND MY SON," Beatrice London announced, eyes level and cool.

Chelsea Ross sat across from her in the sitting room of the elegant Wellesley Hills estate to which she'd been summoned. It wasn't the question that surprised her, for she received similar ones on a regular basis. Rather, it was the age of the woman, who had to be nearing sixty, and the setting itself, reeking of seasoned wealth, that took her aback. More often Chelsea found herself in a shabby three-family house or a crowded apartment. More often she faced a young mother whose child had been abducted or whose teenager had run off.

And more often there was a note of frantic pleading accompanying the request. Not so now.

"Your son?" Chelsea asked quietly.

Beatrice London didn't blink. Her perfectly coiffed silver hair didn't bob. Her fingers, with their perfectly painted nails, didn't flutter. She sat in her Queen Anne chair with proper regality. "My son...Samuel Prescott London."

It was certainly a name befitting the offspring of as stately a woman as Beatrice London, but if Chelsea was supposed to recognize it, she failed.

"I'm afraid I'm unfamiliar with the name," she said as kindly as she could. "Most of my work involves a different class of people."

"I'm well aware of that, Miss Ross. I'm also well aware of your success rate in this line of work, which is one of the reasons I'm hiring you."

Chelsea might have thanked her for the compliment had it been offered with a semblance of warmth. But there was an arrogance about the older woman that suggested thanks were neither expected nor called for. So Chelsea simply pretended that this case was like any other, and set out to learn what she could. Unfortunately the answer to her first question was further evidence of how different this situation was from the norm.

"How old is your son?"

"He'll turn forty next month."

Chelsea ingested the information with as much aplomb as she could muster. Different from the others? This was a *first* for her. "How long has he been missing?" she asked rather doubtfully.

"Six months. And it's not a matter of being 'missing.' I have a rough idea where he is, and I know that he's well."

"Mrs. London, I'm not sure I understand—"

"Samuel left his office last December for a week's vacation in Mexico. He's still there. He's abandoned a successful business, of which he is the president, an expensive condominium on the harbor front, a membership in the country club and a charming young woman who won't wait forever. He should have long since come to his senses and returned. Since he hasn't, I'm hiring you to bring him back."

Her words, though evenly intoned, suggested an underlying anger. It was this that Chelsea homed in on. "Forty years old. He's not exactly a child. I can understand your wanting to locate him if you haven't heard from him and are worried, but to bring him back? Isn't that decision his to make?"

"You obviously haven't had children of your own, Miss Ross, or you wouldn't say that. A mother feels responsible regardless of the age of her child. Right now, Samuel is shirking *his* obligations. It's up to me to remind him of that."

At that moment Chelsea felt distinct sympathy for the poor, irresponsible Samuel. If she'd had a mother as imperious, as overbearing as Beatrice London, she'd probably have run away from home, too. But then, her own mother had been just the reverse and her younger sister had still disappeared. That thought brought Chelsea back on track.

"Tell me more about him, Mrs. London. Do you have any idea why he left?"

"He wanted a vacation, so he said. He hadn't been away in over a year and a half, and he wanted to rest. Surely he's had enough rest by now," she stated firmly.

"If you know 'roughly' where he is, I take it you've heard from him."

"Not directly. He's spoken on the phone from time to time with his office, so I know that he's still in the Yucatán."

"He passes messages on to you through the office?"

"No. I *call* the office to wheedle what little I can from his associates."

Chelsea duly noted the disdain in the woman's voice. "He has partners?"

Mrs. London raised her eyes to the ceiling in a brief show of impatience. "London and McGee is one of the largest real-estate developers in New England. Surely you've heard of them?"

"I'm afraid I haven't," Chelsea responded ever so calmly. "As I told you before, I'm used to dealing with a different type of clientele. Is London and McGree headquartered in Boston?"

"Yes. Its offices are at One Beacon Street."

Chelsea did know the address and recognized the prestige it carried. "If your son is president, who is McGee?"

"Vice-president."

"Is he the one you've been dealing with?"

"He won't answer my calls. I've been talking with one of the lesser vice-presidents, a man named Norman Schialli."

"What does he tell you?"

"Just that Samuel is alive and well and not ready to return to Boston."

"I take it McGee's running things in his absence?"

"It appears that way, and if Samuel doesn't get back here, he may find his business stolen right out from under his nose."

"You don't trust McGee?"

"Not particularly. The man may be a hard worker, but he doesn't have a bit of class. Why Samuel ever went into business with him is beyond me. Why Samuel didn't go into the *family* business is beyond me."

"What is the family business, Mrs. London?" Chelsea asked. Having already professed her ignorance, she had nothing to lose by being so blunt.

This time Beatrice London didn't need to look at the ceiling to express impatience. It was written all over her face, generously mingling with the arrogance that Chelsea had had a taste of before. "The London Corporation. We own three large theater complexes and the Winslow Arena here in Boston, plus numerous other entertainment centers along the Eastern Seaboard. My husband's father started the business. My husband carried it on. I've been at the helm since my husband died four years ago."

Beatrice London was at the helm—that Chelsea found easy to believe. The woman was a born executive, judging from the businesslike air she exuded. A born ruler. Once again Chelsea found herself siding with the hapless Samuel.

"I see," she said, her thoughts moving on. "And your son chose not to go into the family business. I assume that was against your wishes?"

"Miss Ross, I'm not sure this is relevant to the problem at hand. I'm hiring you to find my son and bring him back, not to delve into the family history."

"Everything is relevant, Mrs. London. Anything I can learn about your son will be of help." Chelsea tipped her head to the side in a gesture of skepticism, perhaps wariness. "But, to tell you the truth, I'm not at all sure why you've come to me. I'd have thought that a woman of your standing would more naturally seek out a private investigator."

Beatrice London was undaunted by the question. She had her answer fully prepared. "A private investigator might be able to locate my son, but I doubt he'd be able to bring him back."

"And you think I would?"

"Yes." Her gaze narrowed speculatively. "I do think so."

"Why?"

"Because you're a woman, for one thing. An attractive woman. For another, you're a blonde. For a third, you appear to be a good actress."

It was all Chelsea could do not to self-consciously run her fingers through her hair. Yes, she was blond, though her short, bluntly cut cap was probably rather windblown at the moment. Attractive? She supposed, in a way. But..."An actress? Excuse me, but I'm not sure I know what you mean."

"I saw you on television last week, Miss Ross. You handled yourself with dignity and the kind of style that can't have come naturally to a woman born and bred in a depressed New Hampshire mill town."

Chelsea would have angrily spit out a response, but that would only have given credence to Beatrice London's words. "We can't all be born wealthy, Mrs. London, but dignity and style aren't things you buy."

"Maybe not dignity. Style certainly is." Her eyes dropped in a blunt appraisal of Chelsea's silk blouse and coordinating skirt. "You're a good shopper. Filene's Basement on the day of the Neiman Marcus sale?" Chelsea didn't have to say a word in answer. "I don't have the patience for it myself, though I do have my share of Neiman Marcus clothes. You look very nice, Miss Ross. But then, you intended to, coming to a home in this area, didn't you?"

"There are appropriate ways to dress for every occasion," Chelsea reasoned, sounding more composed than she felt. She was usually the one to ask the questions, yet somehow she felt she was on the firing line. "How did you know where I come from?"

For the first time in the interview, Beatrice London smiled. It wasn't a smile Chelsea particularly cared for. "I hired a private investigator, of course."

That, too, was a first, from Chelsea's standpoint, and she cared for it even less than the smile, which had already vanished. "Was that necessary?"

"I felt it was. I'm entrusting you with a very serious job. I wanted to be sure I was hiring the right person. I saw you for the first time on that show last week. I'd have been a fool not to have checked you out. I know that you've been locating missing children for the past six years, that you're successful in roughly three out of four cases you take on, that you have a tenacity that can only come from having been on the other end of the stick." She barely paused for a breath, as though sufficient air was a given like everything else she owned. "I know about your sister, Miss Ross, and the fact that her disappearance was what started you in this line of work."

Chelsea didn't flinch, partly because she knew that Beatrice London would have expected her to, partly because she'd long since come to accept that certain cases, even some of those hitting closer to the heart than others, couldn't be won. It wasn't that she didn't still ache for her sister, for her parents, for herself, because she did. But she knew enough to face the facts and go on with life. Dedicating herself to helping families in situations such as hers helped.

"You must know that I don't have formal training or a license to do what I do."

"You don't need either. You're dedicated and law-abiding. You've built up a nationwide network of contacts—groups formed to locate children, law-enforcement personnel who are more than happy to have help, public welfare officials and sympathetic bystanders. You work primarily by phone, traveling when your contacts aren't enough. You very definitely undercharge your clients, and you pay taxes on every cent you make, including your salary from Icabod's."

Chelsea took a quick breath. "Your investigator earned his fee," she commented dryly. "I hope he doesn't undercharge *you*."

"He doesn't charge me; I *pay* him, and generously. Money, and the prospect of receiving it, does wonders for incentive. You'll find that out yourself when we get around to talking business."

"I thought that was what we were doing, but we seem to keep veering off the subject. I'll need to know much more about the situation with your son before I decide whether or not to take on the case."

Beatrice London studied Chelsea's face for a minute. It was obvious the woman didn't care for her independence, equally obvious that she didn't care to air any dirty laundry until she had a commitment. Still, Chelsea felt her argument made sense. Indeed, she was doing nothing more than Mrs. London had done when she'd contemplated hiring her.

Apparently Beatrice reached the same conclusion. "All right. I'll tell you what you need to know. Samuel grew up in this house, graduated from Harvard and the Harvard Business School as his father had, and then joined the family firm. He stayed with us for two years before he went out on his own."

"Why did he leave?"

"He and his father had a disagreement. I never knew what it was about. My husband refused to tell me."

"Had Samuel been living with you up until then?"

"Yes. After he left, I tried to get him to come back, both here and to the office, but he was adamant. I've kept trying, but he's remained firm."

Almost against her wishes, Chelsea found her interest piqued. Human motivations fascinated her, particularly when they involved family relationships. "Even after his father died?"

"Most vociferously then. He argued that he had his hands full with his own business and that I was more than capable of handling the corporation, but we both knew that it would have been simple to bring London and McGee in as a division of LC. Samuel wouldn't hear of it."

Chelsea was rooting for Samuel. "Have the two of you stayed close in spite of it?"

"Not as close as I'd like. Oh, we see each other often. He takes me to parties from time to time. But he won't have anything to do with the corporation, even though he stands to inherit it one day."

"There aren't any other children?"

"No. Just Samuel. That's why I want you to bring him back."

Given the drift of the conversation, Chelsea looked again for signs of softness, of maternal need, of worry, but all she saw was the aura of command the woman wore like a royal cape.

"Tell me about Samuel—his likes, dislikes, hobbies, anything that might give me a lead."

Beatrice's right shoulder lifted in what could have been a shrug. "Samuel is straight as an arrow. He likes fine restaurants and good theater. He plays golf at the club, but he was never a dedicated athlete. He works hard at his job. I guess you might call him intense."

"What about the woman he was seeing? Was it a long-standing affair?"

"'Affair' isn't a term I care to use," Mrs. London instructed disdainfully. "Samuel and Linda have known each other for years. She's the daughter of one of our oldest friends."

"Was a marriage in the offing?"

"I had certainly hoped so. Samuel wasn't considering any-one else."

"Did he *want* to marry?"

"Of course he did. He wanted a home and a wife. He wanted children to inherit from him."

"But he's nearly forty. Why hasn't he moved sooner?"

"He claims he's been too busy."

"So you have discussed it with him?"

"Of course. It's my responsibility."

Chelsea bit off a retort. There was still more she wanted to know. Struggling to put the pieces of the puzzle together, she frowned at the Oriental carpet underfoot and spoke her sub-sequent thoughts aloud. "Okay, let's see what we've got. He had a good job, a condo, a lady friend. He left the business in the hands of his partner, and the condo and lady friend in limbo, and took off for a vacation in Mexico. Six months later he's still there." Slowly she raised contemplative eyes. "What do you think he's doing there?"

"That's one of the things you'll have to find out."

"Is it possible that he's ducking some kind of legal hassle?"

"Absolutely not! Samuel is straight as an arrow. I told you that."

"Maybe there was something he didn't tell you."

"No! Samuel wouldn't do anything illegal. It isn't in his nature. He never rebelled, even when he was younger. He's as moral and upstanding as his father and I raised him to be."

Chelsea had finally gotten a rise out of the unflappable Beatrice London. She was indignant, perhaps, but sincere. Whatever the facts proved to be, Mrs. London truly be-lieved her son to be moral and upstanding.

"I'm sorry. I didn't mean any offense. It's just that I have to consider every possibility.... You said that Samuel was in the Yucatán?"

"That's right. He started out in Cancun. From there he moved inland."

"Is he still moving?"

"No."

"But you don't know exactly where he is?"

"I know that he's living in a small Mayan village somewhere."

"A Mayan village?" Chelsea echoed, wanting to laugh but squelching the urge. She saw definite signs of a time warp. Had it been twenty years before, she might have believed Beatrice London's rich and proper boy had escaped the confines of his rich and proper life to reside with a guru in India. But that particular mania had passed, and Samuel Prescott London was nearly forty years old. "What's he doing in a Mayan village?" she asked meekly.

"If I knew that, I wouldn't have hired you," Mrs. London snapped.

"But I haven't said I'd accept the job!" Chelsea retorted, helpless to stop herself. Even she wasn't immune to such snobbery after a time. But the satisfaction she felt at momentarily having the upper hand was erased with her adversary's next smug statement.

"You will. You need the money."

For an instant, silence permeated a room that suddenly seemed closed in to Chelsea. "Another tip from your investigator?" she asked quietly.

At that moment, Beatrice London appeared to be in her element. Power was obviously something she savored, which perhaps explained why her son's refusal to return to Boston rankled her. It was also a possible reason, in Chelsea's mind at least, why the elusive Samuel refused to return.

"My investigator was thorough. I know precisely how much money you earn from your searches, *and* how much you earn at Icabod's. Of course, a woman like you must do very well in tips, particularly working as a bartender in a place that caters to wealthy businessmen after hours."

Chelsea found the elegantly scrolled armrests of her chair to be wonderful braces. She promptly used them to lever herself to her feet. "I think you should find someone else to do your bidding, Mrs. London. If your son is anywhere near as presumptuous as you, I'm not sure I care to go looking for him." Purse in hand, she was turning to show herself out when Beatrice London spoke again.

"I also know precisely how much it will cost you to go back to school to get that degree you've got your heart set on."

Chelsea stopped under the archway to the hall. She didn't turn, simply dug her neatly trimmed fingernails into the crisp canvas of her purse.

"You see, I really know quite a bit, Miss Ross. I have to say that I admire you for what you want to do. You already have a bachelor's degree, but you want a Ph.D. in psychology. Hoping to treat some of those confused young runaways?"

"Actually—" Chelsea gritted her teeth "—I was hoping to counsel their families. A runaway always has reasons, and nine times out of ten they relate to the home."

The implication she was trying to make was promptly ignored by the indomitable Beatrice London, who remained sitting in her chair with her hands crossed in her lap. "I'll pay you what you need, Miss Ross. I'll give you half now and the other half when you retrieve my son. I'll cover your tuition for the three-year doctoral program, plus add a generous amount to cover your living expenses during that time. I'll even secure your acceptance in the program at Harvard."

Chelsea whirled on her heels. "I don't need your help with that, Mrs. London. I can get in on my own!"

"I know," the other said with an icy smile. "You graduated third in your class from Mount Holyoke, on scholarship all the way, which would have made my job that much easier. But if you won't let me pull strings in the admissions office, the least I can do is to give you a glowing reference."

"*If* I retrieve your son."

"If you retrieve my son."

Chelsea hadn't reentered the room; rather, she held her ground as she considered the bait Beatrice London dangled before her.

For six years she'd scraped by, working daily out of her tiny apartment and nightly at the bar, saving her pennies so that she might return full-time to school. She'd assumed it would take at least another three years to save what she needed. But if the fee on this job would cover it all, plus expenses—she made rapid mental calculations—she'd be able to use what she'd saved for investing in an office when she finally got her degree.

Chelsea had no doubts about being able to locate Samuel London. What troubled her was whether or not she'd be able to convince him to come home.

"Your offer is generous, Mrs. London," she said, "and I'd be lying if I said that I didn't want the money. But your son is a grown man. Aside from my being female and blond, what makes you think that I can get him back here?"

"You left out the attractive part. My son is a good-looking man himself. And he's not blind. You also left out the actress part. Well, perhaps actress is too strong a word. Let's just say that, between your looks and your intelligence, I think you'd be able to trap him."

Germs of suggestion were flitting through Chelsea's mind and she had the sudden feeling they might be injurious to her health. "I'm not sure I follow you, Mrs. London," she said stiffly.

"You do, Miss Ross, but if you want me to spell it out, I will. I want you to use your bloodhound instinct to locate my son. Then I want you to use your feminine wiles, and any other wiles you may have up your sleeve, to lure him back to Boston."

"You want me to seduce him!"

"I never used the word 'seduce.' I'm not suggesting anything tawdry, and even if I were, Samuel's not the type. He's far from inexperienced, but I assure you he's not a playboy. No, what I'm suggesting is something more subtle, which is where your innate intelligence comes to play. I want you to enchant him, to wrap him around your little finger, so to speak. I want you to give him good reason to follow you when you finally fly home—"

"Finally? How long do you expect me to stay in Mexico?"

"Only as long as it takes."

"But I've got a business here, and a job—"

"Neither of which you'll need, given the fee you'll be receiving from me. Of course," she went on in a patronizing tone, "it's for you to decide where your priorities lie. You're not getting any younger, Miss Ross. The way I see it, if you spend another three or four years saving up money for ever-rising tuition fees, then four or five years working for the degree—naturally, it will take longer if you have to earn your living expenses as you go—you'll be nearing forty before you'll be able to start work as a therapist. My way, you'll be barely thirty-three."

"The timing is actually perfect for you," she went on, ignoring Chelsea's cheerless expression. "This is June. You'll have the entire summer to get Samuel out of Mexico. You can be back well before classes start in the fall."

Chelsea didn't know what to say. She'd never had a proposition quite like the one she was now being offered. But then, she'd never been manipulated by the likes of Beatrice London. "You've got everything worked out, haven't you?"

"Not everything. You're the one who'll have to deal with Samuel, and I'm afraid I can't be much help on that score. If anything you do smacks of me, he's sure to become suspicious. He's *not* to know I've hired you."

"Then I'm to come up with some far-fetched excuse?" Chelsea was used to dealing with the truth, not fabricating it. Once more, doubts were surfacing.

"Not far-fetched. Plausible. It shouldn't be too difficult. You could pose as a student of Mayan culture, or a bored young lady who's run away from the city, or simply a tourist who's fallen in love with the Yucatán."

Chelsea took a deep breath and slowly shook her head. "I don't know, Mrs. London. Despite what you think, I'm really not an actress. I may have faked my way through situations in the past, but it would be nothing like this. To purposely lead a man on for days, maybe weeks—I just don't know if I can do it."

"What if I threw in a wardrobe bonus on top of everything else? You could skip the basement and go directly to Neiman Marcus."

"It's not a matter of money—"

"Isn't it? If it weren't for the money, you would have already turned tail and run." With great care, Beatrice London rose from her seat and walked slowly toward a small marble-topped table. "Don't get me wrong. I'm not criticizing you for it. If I were in your situation, I'd accept the offer in a minute." Lifting a photograph, she turned to Chelsea. "Sometimes we have to do things we don't care for, if only to get to those things that truly mean something to us. I do believe you want to be a counselor, Miss Ross. You certainly have good reason to want to be one." In the unhurried gait of the confident rich, she approached Chelsea. "Is spending a few weeks, maybe a month or two, with this man too much of a price to pay to gain the means of achieving your personal goal?" With that, she held out a picture of her son.

Chelsea studied the formal black-and-white shot. Samuel Prescott London looked as unapproachable as his name sounded. He had dark, immaculately clipped hair, a pale, lean face and glasses. Though his skin was free of wrinkles, there was a sternness about him that made him look old and tired. Had she not already been told otherwise, Chelsea would have guessed him to be at least forty-five.

"When was this taken?" she asked, taking the photo from Mrs. London's hand for a closer study.

"Two years ago. It's standard publicity fare, but I'm afraid it's the best I have."

"Nothing less formal?" Chelsea was searching the face in the photograph for some hint of character but found none.

Mrs. London hesitated for just a moment. "I suppose I must have something in the den. Excuse me, please." She sidestepped Chelsea and entered the hall.

Chelsea held the photo gingerly. It wasn't heavy, yet it weighed her down, for it represented an unexpected passkey to her future. She knew, as did the shrewd Beatrice London, that she couldn't possibly turn down the older woman's offer. Nor could she deny the bad taste in her mouth that came with the thought of what she was being asked to do.

"Perhaps these will help." Mrs. London was back then, offering three smaller unframed snapshots for Chelsea's study. The first was of Samuel in black tie and tails, standing with his exquisitely gowned mother. "That was taken at my niece's wedding four years ago." The second was of Samuel sitting with four other people on the gleaming deck of a yacht. "Those are family friends. It was taken the summer before last in Newport." The third was of Samuel with a pleasant-looking woman. "Linda," was Mrs. London's lone comment.

Chelsea slipped each snapshot behind the others, rotating them slowly until she'd seen them at least twice. In every shot Samuel Prescott London wore the same glasses, the same clipped hairstyle, the same formal expression. In none of them did he look particularly happy.

"May I keep this one?" Chelsea asked, taking the publicity shot and handing the others back.

"If it'll help."

"It should." She tucked it into her purse, then withdrew a small notebook and a pen. But Beatrice London was already returning to the marble table, presenting her this time with a slim manilla folder.

"I think you'll find all the pertinent background information here. I've included his vital statistics, plus the name and address of the hotel where he stayed in Cancun."

Chelsea tucked the folder beneath her notebook. "I'd like the names of some of his friends. It would be a help if I could talk with them."

"I...think not. They're apt to tip him off."

"I can get around that," Chelsea murmured. She didn't particularly like what she was going to do, but once committed—and she knew she was—she felt confident. "I can pose as a friend of any old friend of his. Perhaps you can give me a name—someone he may have known in college but hasn't seen since?" When Beatrice remained skeptical, she added, "I can say that I'm headed for the Yucatán and heard he was there, perhaps even that I'm a writer researching the modern day Maya. If Samuel's been there for six months, he'd be a logical contact."

"And what kind of useful information do you think you could get from his friends?"

"At best, the exact spot where he is. At least some idea where to start looking."

"And if no one knows that?"

"Then I'll have learned something about Samuel simply by meeting his friends. You'd be surprised how many subtle things can emerge from a seemingly innocent conversation."

"Is that how you usually work?"

"Not always, but often. It depends on the case. In this case, I think it would be wise for me to learn anything and everything I can about your son well before I hit Mexico. If I'm to...enchant him, as you say, I'd better find out what he likes."

Mrs. London considered for just a minute, then decided to cooperate. For the first time that morning, Chelsea was grateful she was with a businesswoman. Like a dutiful secretary she raised her pen and took dictation, albeit in scribbled longhand.

"David McGee is his partner. One Beacon Street." She dictated the phone number. "Norman Schialli is at the same address and number. Samuel's golf partner is Hal Washburn, a lawyer in the Exchange Building. Neil Grant is a longtime friend. You'll find him at Harbor Towers, but I don't know his phone number offhand."

"I can find it. What about Linda?"

"I'd rather you didn't contact Linda. She's a perceptive young woman. If she sensed too much interest on your part, she might be hurt."

Too much interest...in Samuel London? Chelsea wanted to laugh. "Not if I handle it gently. Please, Mrs. London. You'll have to trust me. Linda might be more help than all of the others combined...unwittingly, of course."

"It had better be 'of course,'" the other woman stated firmly. But nonetheless she yielded. "Linda Huntington. She has her own place in town, but I believe she's already joined her parents at their summer home in Osterville. That's on the Cape—"

"I know. Have you a number?"

"Yes." She quoted it.

"Good. Now, about the name of an old college buddy..."

"Come with me."

Chelsea followed her through the large hall and down a corridor into the family library. An ornate leather-covered desk stood at one end, surrounded by neatly filled bookshelves. Mrs. London approached one, withdrew a volume that proved to be one of Samuel's college yearbooks, and thumbed through.

"Harcourt...no, here, Ingram. Jason Ingram. This should do it. The fellow was from the West Coast and I believe he went on to graduate studies at Stanford, so the chances are good he's still out there. He and Samuel weren't the closest of friends, but they must have known each other, judging from the message Jason wrote beside his picture."

Chelsea took the book and read aloud. "'To a fellow survivor of Madame LaFarge's needles. Best of luck, J.' Madame LaFarge?"

"I believe she was a professor of French literature. Samuel was good with languages."

"Ahh. See, there's something I've learned already. If he was good with languages, he's probably been able to pick up Spanish easily in Mexico."

"I'm sure that's the case...unfortunately. Samuel is very bright."

"May I borrow this yearbook also? There may be other things I can pick up from it."

With a curt nod, Beatrice London moved behind the desk, withdrew a checkbook from one of the drawers and began to write. With a snap that rent the silence, she tore off the check and handed it to Chelsea. "I'll expect you to keep me informed of your progress right up until the time you leave. After that, I'll simply have to trust that you're doing your best."

Chelsea didn't bother to look at the check. She prided herself on being a good judge of people. Though she didn't care for Beatrice London personally, she knew that the woman wouldn't cheat her. The check would cover half of the tuition rate for the doctoral program, plus half of what Beatrice estimated to be her living expenses for three years. And since Beatrice's standard of living was far, far higher than her own, Chelsea was sure the sum would be more than she would have allowed herself.

"I will try, Mrs. London. You do know, though, that I can't guarantee success. I have no idea what I'll find when I locate your son. It may be that, short of actual abduction, I'll be unable to get him back here."

"That check," Mrs. London stated, dropping her gaze to the small paper Chelsea held, "is yours in any case—unless, of course, I learn that you made less than a serious effort to bring Samuel back. The second half of the check will be forthcoming once you both return."

"I understand," Chelsea said softly.

"I think you do. Now, if you'll excuse me, I'll be on my way to the office."

Chelsea nodded and turned, retracing her steps down the long corridor and through the hall to the front door. She'd reached her time-worn Chevette, which waited awkwardly on the curve of the well-landscaped circular drive, before she realized she was still holding the check in her hand. Without looking at it, she stuffed it in her purse, slid into the car and headed off.

Driving back to her small Cambridge apartment, Chelsea found herself in an increasing state of shock. The enormity of what she'd undertaken, of what it would do to her life, hit her with startling force. She was going to spend the next weeks chasing after a man. *Then* she was going back to school!

Among other things, she felt guilt. Searching for Samuel Prescott London, formerly of Wellesley Hills, was a far cry from looking for Antonio Rodrigues of the North End or Chastity Watson of Roxbury or Peter Kolados of Somerville. Samuel was no innocent child who'd been abducted while on his way home from school. Samuel was no starry-eyed teenager running away from home in search of bright lights and glamour. Samuel hadn't left a heart-torn mother behind, a woman who cried herself to sleep at night with worry even while she struggled to hold the rest of the family together.

Chelsea wondered if she could truly turn her back on the dozens of people who'd needed her in the past years, who'd seen her as their only hope of surviving a nightmare.

Then she thought of the degree she'd be able to get, of the work she'd subsequently be able to do, of the good in it, and she felt better.

And excited. And just the slightest bit afraid.

THE FOLLOWING WEEK was as hectic a one as Chelsea had known, and since her life had always been one of long working hours and little sleep, that was saying a lot.

She tied up as many knots in ongoing searches as she was able to, guilt-ridden when she had to explain to one client or another that a new case would be taking her out of the country for a time.

She made frantic phone calls to each of the universities in the Boston area, filing applications in person, with silent prayers that it wouldn't be too late in the season to find a single spot for a doctoral candidate in psychology. Intellectually she was on a par with the other candidates, she knew, but time was against her. She could only hope that the work she'd been doing for the past six years would strike a sympathetic chord in one admissions officer or another. Pride kept her from calling Beatrice London, on that score at least.

She did call and subsequently meet with each of the people whose names Mrs. London had given her. Though her cover worked like a charm, she learned little of Samuel London's whereabouts other than that the Mayan village in which he was staying was somewhere between Cancun and the ancient Mayan city of Chichen Itza. Given the fact that one hundred twenty miles separated the two, and that there were numerous Mayan villages along the way, she knew she would have some searching to do once she arrived in the Yucatán.

Equally discouraging was the information she gleaned from the interviews with Samuel's friends—that they were friends only in the most formal sense of the word. It seemed that Samuel's work was his life. He had few outside interests, no hobbies to speak of. He was, for the most part, a loner, as straitlaced and somber an individual as his photographs suggested. Chelsea was beginning to wonder how she was possibly going to warm up to such a man. The only glimmer of hope came from Linda Huntington.

All but breathless from the running around she was doing, Chelsea nonetheless forced herself to drive down to the Cape to meet with Linda, whom she found to be surprisingly approachable.

"So you're headed for the Yucatán," Linda said, offering Chelsea a tall glass of lemonade from the pitcher the maid had delivered moments before. They were sitting on the lawn. Behind them was a polished stone patio, before them a pool.

"The day after tomorrow," Chelsea responded with what she hoped was due enthusiasm. It wasn't that she had anything against the Yucatán; in other circumstances she would have liked nothing more than to enjoy it. Traveling for pleasure had always been impossible, given her need to save money, but it was something she desperately hoped to be able to do in the future. "As I explained on the phone, I'm writing an article on the modern Maya. Firsthand research seems in order."

"Who do you write for?"

"I free-lance. Actually, I'm not sure who the article will go to, but it's something I've been wanting to write for a while and I figured this was as good a time as any. When I heard that Samuel London had been living among the Mayas for months now, I couldn't resist trying to contact him. The only problem is that no one seems to know exactly where he is. Your name came up as the one person who was closest to him before he left."

Linda smiled warmly. "Samuel and I have been friends for years."

"I was told—perhaps I'm out of place here, but I was told you two were all but engaged."

At that, Linda laughed softly, without malice. "That's how the story goes."

"If it's true, surely you've been in touch with him. You'd be able to tell me where to find him."

Linda raised delicate fingers to enumerate. "No, I haven't been in touch with him, therefore I can't tell you where he is. And no, we're not engaged."

Deep inside, Chelsea was relieved. The deception she was practicing now, the greater deception she'd have to practice once she found Samuel, was bad enough. If Linda and Samuel were truly planning marriage, she would have felt all the more despicable. "That's strange. His mother implied—"

"Beatrice has *always* implied that. She's had her heart set on it for years. So have my parents, for that matter. And Sam and I let them dream. There's no harm to it really."

"But...why *aren't* you engaged?"

'We're not in love. Well, not in the sense that would hold up in a marriage. Sam has been a friend, a good friend. He's always been there for me, and I try to return the favor. We spent hours talking of his need to get away. He was tired and—"

Linda stopped, leaving Chelsea hanging in the silence. She was sure Linda had been about to say more, to give some concrete reason for Samuel's prolonged absence, until it had occurred to her that she'd be betraying Samuel's confidence. Chelsea had to respect her, though Linda's loyalty hampered her work.

"What do you think he's been doing down there all this time?" Chelsea asked with just the right amount of innocent curiosity.

"I hope he's relaxing. He works too hard."

Chelsea chuckled. "He's probably having a grand time for himself. A small Mayan village may be awfully quiet, but Cancun is jam-packed with tourists and restaurants and discos—"

Linda sighed. "I hope that's the case."

'It wouldn't bother you?" She studied the blond-haired woman, who was far from beautiful, though nicely groomed. Chelsea wondered why a romance hadn't ever worked out between them.

"It wouldn't bother me in the least, though I doubt that's what's truly happening. Sam is inhibited. Like me, I suppose." She laughed. "We make a very boring couple."

"I don't believe that for a minute," Chelsea heard herself say. It was almost the truth. There were couples, and there were couples. If Samuel London overworked himself and Linda Huntington could get him to relax, there had to be some merit to the relationship. Moreover, Samuel was supposedly bright, Linda well-spoken. They'd both been reared in the same privileged class. In the right circles they probably did just fine.

"Well, that's neither here nor there," Linda was musing. "I wish I could help you more, Chelsea, but I honestly have no idea exactly where Sam is."

Chelsea thought for a minute, reluctant to leave with any stone unturned. "If you were to guess, based on what you know of Samuel, what would he be doing? I take it you don't think he'd be frequenting the hot spots in Cancun."

"Hardly. If he were in London, he'd be sitting through session after session of Parliament. If he were in Rome, he'd be squirreled away in the Vatican museum. If he were in Tokyo, he'd be analyzing the workings of the nearest manufacturing plant. But in Mexico...the Yucatán...a Mayan village...? He was never the outdoorsy type. He sunburns too easily. I'm sure he's visted whatever ruins are around, but...for six months?" She shrugged her shoulders, a gesture so much more human than Beatrice London's nondisplay that Chelsea found herself liking Linda. "Your guess is as good as mine."

OVER THE NEXT TWO DAYS, Chelsea struggled to make that guess, with little luck. Of what she'd learned from Linda, the only thing that encouraged her was the fact that, in Linda, Samuel had had a friend. He'd needed a friend. And Chelsea herself was adept at such a role. She was a born listener, as her boss at Icabod's had effusively told her when she'd given him her notice.

"You're the best damned bartender we've had in years, Chels. The men love you."

"They should. I make great Harvey Wallbangers!" she'd teased.

"Aside from booze. They love to talk and have someone listen. And you answer them, giving them impartial advice. They like that. If you want work when you get back, you know where to come!"

But she wouldn't want work...she hoped. At least not that kind of work.

She thought about Samuel Prescott London constantly and too often met the stern-eyed gaze that greeted her from atop the desk where she'd propped his picture. Linda had called him Sam, yet Chelsea was unable to do so. He was a formal Samuel, from the top of his neat dark head to the tips of what she assumed would be his Brooks Brothers shoes. All six-foot-one of him. All one hundred sixty-five pounds of him. Studious, spectacled, string-bean-shaped Samuel.

Only when she was at last airborne, headed south did Chelsea admit to herself that she was frightened. Samuel London was intelligent; he was bound to see through her ruse. Samuel London was straitlaced; he'd never fall for a tourist or writer or ruins-lover or whatever she decided to disguise herself as. Samuel London was stern and one dimensional; *she'd* never be able to pretend to fall for *him*.

But Samuel London was the meal ticket to her future.

With that thought in mind, she accepted a Bloody Mary from the flight attendant, opened the book in her lap and plunged into a history of the Mayan culture.

2

IT WAS POURING when the plane emerged from the clouds to descend over the flat landscape of the northeastern Yucatán. Chelsea thought of it as an omen. She knew this was the area's rainy season, but she'd still hoped to have the sun on her side. Even the pilot's cheery prediction that the skies would brighten by the end of the day did little to hearten her.

Nor did the fact that her luggage hadn't made it. She stood waiting for a whole hour, sweating in the oppressive humidity, only to learn that it was either still in Boston or, worse, had been put on the wrong plane and was God-knew-where at the moment.

She also learned that the word "urgent" was not part of the Mexican vocabulary, Spanish or otherwise.

Simmering, she filled out forms listing the hotel at which she could be reached. Gritting her teeth, she returned the ready smiles the airport officials offered. She nodded with every *si* she received—an inordinate number—though when she finally arrived at the Camino Real some time later she was no closer to retrieving her suitcase than she'd been at the airport.

Mercifully, the hotel did have her reservation. And her room was beautiful, with its tiled floor, original Mexican artwork, decorative earth-toned bedspread, and a hammock strung on the balcony. Of course, it was still raining, which ruled out a quick trip to the beach; with her bathing suit neatly packed in her suitcase that option would have been futile anyway. And the rain was gusting, which similarly ruled out use of the hammock. Just as well, she reasoned. Hammocks had never been among her allies.

Feeling decidedly sorry for herself, Chelsea plopped down on the bed and gave a voluminous sigh. No bathing suit, no hat, no suntan lotion. No shorts, no tank tops. No change of dress. No toothbrush, no makeup, no blow dryer.

She did have her carry-on bag, which she proceeded to unpack. Its contents included travelers' checks, her passport, an envelope with additional identification plus the picture of Samuel Prescott London; a light sweater she'd brought along in case the airplane had been cool, which it hadn't been; a hairbrush, a small zippered case with lipstick, cologne, a mirrored compact and a pack of Chiclets; two weighty books on Mayan civilization, a spiral-bound notebook, two pens and a travel pack of Kleenex.

"Not much, old girl, if you were hoping to charm a middle-aged workaholic," she murmured, more than a little exasperated that she hadn't put a change of underwear in her carryon, which a sympathetic fellow traveler had quietly suggested she do when the luggage calamity had first unfolded. No, she simply had the underwear she wore, the sundress on her back, the sandals on her feet and a smile that was most assuredly in hiding.

"What do *I* know," she muttered. "I'm not a seasoned traveler. I've never lost a bag before." Of course, in the past when work had taken her afield she'd brought nothing but the small carry-on case. This was the first time she'd anticipated staying in a place long enough to need more.

Impatiently she picked up the phone to call the airport. But with the language barrier and the uniformly laid-back air of each of the four people she was in turn switched to, she discovered nothing. Anywhere from one day to six before her suitcase was located and rerouted, they'd originally told her. She simply couldn't wait around that long!

Knowing from experience that idleness was her own worst enemy, she snatched up the envelope with Samuel's picture inside and set off. He, too, had first stationed himself at the Camino Real. Its front desk was as good a place as any to start her search.

Each person to whom she showed the photograph had a broad smile and a gentle shake of the head. Yes, indeed, a Samuel P. London had stayed at the Camino Real, said the manager in stilted English after he'd waded through his files. But said Samuel P. London had checked out after ten days, paid his bill in full, and taken off, presumably for home.

Braving what thankfully amounted only to a drizzle now, Chelsea dashed from one hotel to the next along the island strip, cornering managers, bellboys, tour group representatives, to no avail. She raced across the street to El Parian in hopes that one of the storekeepers might recognize the man in the photograph, but it was a pipe dream. Samuel Prescott London had the kind of face people would turn away from even before looking, she knew. Suddenly she wished *she* had. Oh, how she wished she had!

With her damp dress clinging to her clammy skin and her short hair coiling in precisely the way she despised, she couldn't begin to focus on the long-range personal rewards of this case. Cambridge, graduate school, financial solvency—all seemed light years away.

Dispiritedly she returned to her hotel, where she found that there was still no word on her luggage. She contemplated running back to the shopping center to buy the essentials, but decided that she'd no sooner spend that money than her suitcase would show up. So she settled for buying a toothbrush in the hotel shop, returning to her room to bathe while her dress dried, then, when it didn't, ordering her first Mexican dinner from room service.

As she ate, she plotted her next course of action. There was nothing she could do about her suitcase for the moment, she reasoned. The airline officials had assured her they'd notify her as soon as there was any word on it, and she sensed that all the badgering in the world wasn't going to get her bag to Cancun any sooner.

Regarding Samuel Prescott London, she was not as hamstrung. First thing in the morning she'd go to the local police. Chelsea knew that tourist cards were a necessity in Mexico; she had her own safely tucked inside her passport. She also knew it was a relatively simple matter to obtain a tourist card for a stay of up to six months in the country. Samuel, though, was fast approaching—if he hadn't already passed—that deadline, in which case he would have had to register in some other manner.

For her part, she felt no need for secrecy, given the story she'd settled on. It was, in fact, the same one she'd offered Samuel's friends at home, consistency having been a consideration. She was a free-lance writer intent on studying the Maya. Samuel had been recommended as a contact, and his mother had said that he was here.

Yes, his mother. Beatrice London had told her not to tell Samuel that she'd hired Chelsea to fetch him. There'd been no injunction—perhaps a simple matter of omission, but Chelsea didn't care—against using the woman's name with others. And the closer to the truth she stayed, the better off she'd be, Chelsea felt. Any slips she made when she was finally with Samuel would be better covered that way.

AFTER A RESTLESS NIGHT—a strange bed, Chelsea told herself, and the fact that she'd been either freezing or boiling and had spent half the night adjusting and readjusting the air conditioner's thermostat—she set off.

For convenience's sake, since she'd be traveling inland in search of Samuel, she rented a car. It was a weathered Volkswagen beetle, the kind no longer sold in the States, and it made her Chevette look like a late-model luxury sedan. When Chelsea questioned the beetle's durability, the rental agent smiled—actually he'd been smiling all along, a habit Chelsea was finding second nature to the Mexicans—and assured her that it was perfect, that it would take her wherever she wanted to go, that it had many years of life left in it. Realizing her choice was between it and an open-topped Jeep, and given that, though the sun was shining through broken clouds today, it had been raining through much of the night, she took the beetle.

The police in Cancun city were thoroughly attentive, though they had no visa form listing the name of Samuel Prescott London. It seemed that Cancun was in the state of Quintana Roo, while Chichen Itza was in Yucatán. If Samuel was somewhere between the two, his form might be registered either in Chetumal, the capital of Quintana Roo, or Merida, the capital of Yucatán. From the wealth of Spanish words swirling around her, Chelsea managed to sift out talk of a permit, but beyond that the best she could do was to leave the police station with phone numbers to call in each capital.

Back at the Camino Real once more, she set to the task. Actually, she was feeling better. The process of searching for a missing person was familiar to her. Like an intellectual treasure hunt, she found it exciting.

That was until the language barrier once again reared its head. In Cancun, which had been specifically built to cater to tourists, the majority of Mexicans had at least a minimal understanding of English. Not so in either Chetumal or Merida. After several futile attempts to make herself understood to the person at the other end of the line, Chelsea gave up and ran down to the hotel store to buy a phrase book, only to discover that the questions she needed to ask were a far cry from the more typical, "Where is the bus stop?" or "May I see the menu?"

One phrase and one only justified her expenditure, and this she promptly used when she redialed the first of the phone numbers. "Is there anyone there who speaks English?" she asked in a choppy Spanish that she was sure bore a German accent, since that was the language she'd studied both in high school and college. But it seemed to work. Though the woman who came on the line spoke an equally choppy English, prompting numerous repetitions and reclarifications, Chelsea was at last able to make herself understood—only to learn that if Samuel had extended his stay beyond the six-month limit he would have had to file for a permit, in person, in Mexico City.

Chelsea had no intention of going, in person, to Mexico City. Rather, she tempted the fates once more by picking up the phone, this time to dial the number the woman in Chetumal had readily—gratefully, if Chelsea had correctly interpreted the other's linguistic frustration—given her.

Once beyond the switchboard at the Secretaria de Governation in Mexico City, Chelsea struck gold. Samuel London had indeed made an appearance there, and though he hadn't listed a specific spot at which he could be reached, he had given the name and address of a Mexican sponsor, a Professor Paredes from the University of Yucatán in Merida.

The professor was out all day. Chelsea discovered that by phoning him every hour on the hour. In between calls she walked the beach, which was hot, phoned the airport to check on any progress in locating her luggage, of which there was none, wandered in and out of the local shops with a thought toward buying some clothes, which she eventually vetoed. Her luggage was bound to show up, she reasoned, just as was the professor in Merida.

Professor Paredes proved to be the more obliging of the two. She reached him early that evening and decided that the wait had been worth it when, in commendable English, he told her that Samuel was presently residing in the environs of Xcan, roughly ninety minutes from Cancun. When she asked him what "in the environs" meant, he explained that there were many unnamed *pueblitos* and small farms scattered along Route 180, the sole road connecting Cancun and Chichen Itza. The best he could do was to suggest she go to Xcan and start asking.

That was precisely what she set out to do when she awoke the next morning. Having washed her clothes the night before, she felt as fresh as could be expected, given the fact that again she hadn't slept well. Oh, she'd mastered the air conditioner, and the bed was no longer as strange, since it seemed she'd spent half her time in Mexico sitting on it with the telephone cradled in her lap. No, it had been the image of Samuel Prescott London that had kept her awake.

She no longer had to stare at his photograph to see his pale skin, his stern glasses, his lean cheeks. His face had become all too familiar to her, though that in itself wasn't unusual when she was working on a case. What was unusual was that she felt so very much in the dark as to what made him tick.

Theoretically, he'd had everything, and from what she'd learned, he wasn't a rebel. It was possible he'd simply cracked under the pressure, yet she found herself wondering just how much pressure he'd had. Certainly not financial, she mused with the slightest bit of envy. Perhaps his mother had gotten to him; Chelsea could believe that. Yet why it had taken him nearly forty years to react was a mystery, as was the nature of his interest in the Yucatán, given everything else she'd learned about his character.

Then again, perhaps he was simply taking a prolonged vacation.

As the beetle pulled away from the Camino Real, Chelsea realized that her heightened obsession with Samuel London related to her conviction that she was close on his tail and getting closer by the minute. She knew it, could feel it in her bones. Perhaps it was the bloodhound instinct that Beatrice London had spoken of, but Chelsea felt assured she'd have a hold on her prey before the day was done.

Of course, first she had to get out of Cancun, a task easier said than done. When she'd asked at the front desk how to get to the highway, she'd received no less than three sets of directions from the solicitous trio of clerks. In the end she'd chosen what sounded the simplest, yet she found herself making turn after turn, pausing at street corners to search for signposts. On the positive side was the fact that traffic was negligible, something she'd noticed even during the drive in from the airport that first day. Likewise, the drivers were not the impatient types she'd found in Boston, or worse, New York. Impatience, as she already knew, was not part of the Mexican character, and for once she was grateful.

At long last, and only after several stops to seek confirmation that she was indeed headed in the right direction, she hit Route 180 and stepped on the gas. When the beetle hesitated for a second as though reluctant to leave the city behind, she wondered if it was trying to tell her something. But the lure of Samuel London was too great for her to heed any such warning, so she pressed on.

Within fifteen minutes she was cursing the car, most notably the fact that it had no air-conditioning. Though it was chugging over the road at a commendable speed, the open windows brought in nothing but dust and hot air. Moreover, the stunted jungle landscape had grown quickly monotonous, so she had nothing to look at but the equally monotonous image of Samuel London, which persisted in flitting before her eyes.

Then, with the abrupt appearance of several small huts, she passed her first Mayan village. She slowed the car, but the minuscule settlement was already behind her. Though sorely tempted to make a U-turn on the highway—in actuality little more than a two-laned road cutting a straight and narrow swath through the lowlands—she tempered the urge, telling herself that there would be other villages to come.

Indeed there were. On the lookout now, Chelsea slowed the beetle in time to examine the next one more closely. She was intrigued. The tiny hamlet consisted of five or six small huts whose walls were of lashed-together sticks and whose roofs were thatched. Front doors stood open, if there were doors at all, but Chelsea was unable to see much of the dim insides.

She kept a steady foot on the gas—a miracle, given the dubious condition of the pavement of Route 180—and waited patiently for the next *pueblito* to appear. This time she saw more—children playing in an open area at the center of the cluster of huts, chickens and an occasional scrawny dog. Beyond the huts were other houses, those sided with concrete and painted in bright pinks, greens and blues.

Enchanted, she drove on, slowing at each small enclave, adding features she'd missed at the last. A woman with a pot of water balanced on her head. A small table inside one of the huts. A battered bicycle leaning against another. Orange trees, banana trees, pigs. And electrical wires. *Electrical wires*. Chelsea chuckled at the anachronism, then realized that the huts were anachronisms in and of themselves. The clock had seemingly stopped at a time long past for these people whose homes were nearly primitive.

Yet before she could begin to feel sorry for these modern-day Maya, Chelsea realized something else. They looked happy. Bemused, she passed two more *pueblitos*. The people *did* look happy. Where poverty in the States seemed invariably accompanied by grimness and dirt and sorrow, there was nothing remotely sad in the copper-hued faces that broke into smiles at her passage. There was nothing grim in the beautiful eyes of the children. As as for dirt, Chelsea couldn't begin to guess how the women kept their white dresses so clean—for they were clean, every one of them, loose expanses of white cotton broken only by collars and hems embroidered in a wild array of color.

Suddenly the settlements were behind her once more and, momentarily lost in wonder at these innocent, peaceful people, Chelsea had to forcibly remind herself that she was here on a mission. With the reappearance in her mind's eye of Samuel London's face—so startlingly different in almost every imaginable way from the faces she'd just passed—she concentrated on looking for the names of the occasional small towns she passed through.

She approached a gas station on the edge of such a town and brought the beetle to a sputtering stop. The attendant, a boy whom she guessed to be not more than twelve, was quite adept at filling her car, but he gave her a blank look when she mentioned Xcan. She figured she hadn't pronounced it properly—the professor had only said it once before spelling it for her—so she tried several variations on the theme. One of them must have hit home, for the boy pointed down the road, which didn't tell her much more than she already knew. By then two girls had approached from the roadside stand across the way and were smiling at Chelsea—at her blond hair, at her yellow sundress with its delicate spaghetti straps, at the white sandals which, Chelsea realized, were biting uncomfortably into her heat-swollen skin.

"Hello," Chelsea said, offering a smile she hoped looked less parched than she felt. Her gaze dropped to the basket of fruit one of the girls held out, then even more covetously to the glass of juice the other offered. "Is that for sale?" she asked quickly, then realized that the girls couldn't possibly understand her. She was about to turn back to the car for her phrase book when the taller of the two spoke.

"One dollah."

Chelsea wasn't about to bicker. Suddenly it seemed that her survival depended on a cold drink. Fishing a dollar free of the pesos in her pocket, she handed it over in return for the glass of what turned out to be fresh grapefruit juice, not terribly cold but wonderfully wet and refreshing. She drained the glass quickly, then returned it. "Thank you... Muchas gracias." When the girls giggled, she wondered just how bad her accent was. But there was no ridicule on either of her attendants' faces. They simply stood back, staring at her as they'd done when they'd first approached, and smiled.

Beginning to feel like something of a spectacle, Chelsea crawled back into her now-sweltering car, started its reluctant engine, and steered back onto the road. She passed more groupings of Mayan huts and several small towns before her eyes lit up. Nuevo Xcan. She had to be close!

That thought was the brightest one she was to have for many hours.

Somehow—she was later to realize that her attention had been diverted by a truck full of children, which had been bouncing precariously along the road—she missed the sign for Xcan. When, bleary-eyed from scanning every signpost in sight, she arrived in the largest town she'd seen since she'd left Cancun, she discovered she was in Valladolid. The fourth person she approached on the street was able to tell her that Xcan was pronounced "Shcan" and that she'd long since passed through it.

Hot and discouraged and hungry, she treated herself to lunch in the bougainvillea-rich courtyard of a hotel in the main square. Then, putting off as long as possible a return to the stifling confines of her car, she wandered around the square with Samuel London's picture in hand. Headshakes were becoming as common as smiles, she decided morosely. Oh, yes, she loved the hunt, but the heat was very definitely slowing her down, as was the fact that she hadn't had much sleep for two nights running.

Knowing that the day wasn't getting any younger and that she wanted some concrete progress before nightfall, she returned to the beetle, only to find that one of its tires was flat. She'd never changed a tire before. She didn't even know if there was a spare in the trunk.

There was. But the directions for putting it on were written in Spanish. She studied the diagrams and removed the spare. She found the jack and stared at it for a time, wondering somewhat hysterically where AAA was when she needed it. She glanced frantically around the square, but the few people in sight seemed intent on ambling toward wherever it was they went for siesta.

An hour later, she and the beetle limped out of Valladolid. The knuckles of her right hand were badly scraped, smudges of dirt decorated her once-fresh sundress and her sunburn-pink arms, and her back hurt. But the spare tire was on, she reasoned with grim satisfaction, and the beetle was moving. The fact that she felt sweaty, grubby and tired was a minor problem, one that would be readily solved when she returned to the Camino Real that night. Her suitcase would be awaiting her, she dreamed, as would air-conditioning, a bath and a nice, clean bed.

First, though, she'd find out where Samuel Prescott London was hiding. If it killed her, she'd smoke him out, and before the sun set!

Then the beetle died. It sputtered and choked and lost all capacity for acceleration before stumbling to a halt at the side of a forlorn stretch of road. Furious at its betrayal, Chelsea angrily switched the key on and off, jiggled the shift, pumped the clutch, slammed her hand against the steering wheel. Then, not knowing what else to do, she swore.

The beetle was beyond hearing.

Fury was quickly replaced by panic when she climbed from the car. There wasn't another vehicle in sight, much less sign of human habitation. Frantically, she imagined herself stranded, marooned, left to the wild boars and snakes and whatever other fearful beasts were sure to inhabit the surrounding bush.

And it was all Samuel Prescott London's fault!

Chelsea closed her eyes, took a deep breath and counted to ten. By that time she felt in control once more, or in as much control as a person could be under such circumstances. She looked east, then west, either of which held her only hope, since north and south led into the jungle. She could walk, she decided; the last sign of civilization she'd passed had been ten minutes away. Of course, on foot that would be close to an hour, and she was exhausted to start with. No, she decided, she'd wait for another car to come along. If its driver couldn't pinpoint the beetle's problem, at least he'd be able to transport her to a town.

Raising the beetle's hood, she leaned against its door and waited. And waited. She cursed the sun, which responded by slipping behind a heavy cloud. She cursed the practice of siesta, which had to be the reason why the road was deserted. She cursed a mosquito, which bit her anyway. But most of all, she cursed Samuel London. His face loomed large in her mind and she saw him smile, but it was the icy smile of Beatrice London and it didn't even cool the heat of her skin.

She'd been standing for little more than five minutes, though it had seemed like hours, when an old pickup truck appeared on the horizon. It approached at what seemed to Chelsea a crawl, slowing all the more as it neared, mercifully coming to a full halt behind the VW. Chelsea hadn't even had to raise her arms to flag it down, a good thing since she doubted she had the energy.

Two men climbed from the cab of the truck. They wore baggy brown pants, loose white shirts, hats and sandals. They were small of build, as were so many of the natives, and had the same bronzed skin and friendly smiles.

Chelsea's dilemma was obvious, a fact she was grateful for when, chattering softly in Spanish, the two men bent over her engine. The situation was equally obvious when they pushed and poked, then straightened and shook their heads first at each other, then at Chelsea.

"Xcan," she said. "I need to go to Xcan." She enunciated each word with care, as though it might help the men understand her English, which, of course, it didn't. But they both nodded, repeated the name of the town and pointed east. It was the direction they'd been headed when they'd stopped to aid her. She tried again. "I have to get to Xcan. Can you take me there?" She accompanied her words with exaggerated gestures, pointing first at herself, then the men, then their truck. "Xcan." She repeated the gestures. "Can you give me a ride?"

When the driver of the truck smiled and nodded, Chelsea breathed a sigh of relief. In a burst of motion she might not have been capable of, had she not feared the men might leave without her, she scooped her bag from the seat of the car and climbed into the cab of the truck.

The beetle had been luxury compared with the fitful motion of the pickup, not to mention the worn, unpadded seat Squashed between the men, Chelsea bumped along with them, clutching her bag to her chest for all she was worth. It was her trusty carryon, minus the sweater and the heavy books, and being her sole link to the real world, she suddenly treasured it.

Xcan was three towns down the road. By the time the truck reached it, Chelsea knew her bottom would be bruised for days. With multiple nods and a profusion of *gracias*, she gingerly eased herself from the truck and watched it disappear. Only then did she turn to inspect the small town in which she'd been left.

It wasn't much of a town, at least by American standards, though Chelsea saw that it was on a par with most of the other towns she'd passed through that day. There was a food store, a machine shop and a small church. Set farther back from the road and framed by huts of the concrete-and-thatch variety was a school.

Unsure as to which should be her first priority—the beetle or Samuel London—Chelsea let her thirst guide her. Entering the food store to an audience of curious eyes, she grabbed for the nearest Coke and guzzled half of it before sheepishly lowering the bottle and dipping into her pocket for money. When she was done with the Coke, she dipped again, this time into her bag for the picture of Samuel London.

One man, three women and two children stared in turn at the photograph. They talked among themselves, frowned and talked more. Chelsea held her breath. Though she couldn't understand a word they said, she sensed some difference of opinion among them and hoped that it would be resolved in her favor. But soon assorted shrugs circled the group, and one of the women handed the photograph back, her apologetic eyes saying all that was necessary.

Chelsea let out her breath. Discouraged, she murmured her thanks and headed for the machine shop. She was well aware that she might be out of luck if no one there reconized Samuel. The church looked closed, the school in a like state of abandonment. She could go from house to house, but if none of the people in these two shops knew who or where Samuel was, she doubted the others would. And, of course, there was the language barrier to contend with.

There was only one man in the machine shop, lounging in a chair balanced on its rear legs. He didn't shift position when Chelsea entered, other than to offer her a pleasant smile.

"¿Habla usted ingles?" Chelsea asked hesitantly.

"Si. A leetle," he said.

Intensely relieved, she began to speak. "I had an awful problem with my car a few miles back on the road—" She stopped when she saw the young man's utterly dumb expression, and began again, more slowly this time. "My car stopped. Down the road a little." She was encouraged when he nodded. "Is there someone nearby who can fix it?"

"Ah...si, senorita. Een Valladolid."

"But I just came from there and it's not nearby!" Chelsea cried. "I can't possibly get there without my car...oh, I'm going too fast again." She slowed down. "I have no way to get there, but I need my car fixed. Maybe *you* could just...just take a look at it?"

Unhurriedly, the young man pondered her words. Chelsea wasn't sure whether he was trying to decipher them or whether, having understood her, he was merely considering the possibility. When he spoke, it was obvious that the latter was the case.

"I don't theenk eet. I work."

She could see how hard he was working. "It wouldn't take long," she pleaded. "Just a look?"

He shrugged. "I haf no car. I would help eef I could, but...how do I say...bery important be here."

Chelsea took another tack. "Maybe someone else can look at my car. Someone else? Nearby?"

To this the young man shrugged, but he did rock forward until the front legs of the chair hit the floor. "Maybe two hours. Three. Mi padre...my fader be back."

"Two or three hours?" She moaned. Two or three hours loomed like an eternity given the fact that she was already thoroughly frazzled. But she'd never been one to beat her head against a brick wall; it appeared that in this case she had no choice but to wait. And in the meantime...

She lifted Samuel's photograph and held it out. "Do you know this man?"

The machine shop attendant studied the photograph, frowned, tipped his head, squinted. He darted a gaze at Chelsea before looking at the picture once more.

"Si. Maybe."

Her heart skipped a beat and her fatigue momentarily eased. "Have you seen him?"

"I theenk. An Americano ees leeving near here. Maybe theese one."

Though Chelsea had heard the same news from the professor in Merida, the fact that a local was now comfirming it—albeit guardedly—was gratifying. No, exciting!

"Where? Can you tell me where he is?"

The young man rubbed a lean forefinger across the broad bridge of his nose. "Down the road. Maybe five or ten meenutes walk time. There ees a path on the—" he pointed to one side, then the other, then came back to the first "—*izquierda*. The left. At the end of the path a *pueblito*. You ask there."

Chelsea was busy making mental calculations. Ten minutes walking. A path to the *pueblito*. She certainly had enough time to follow this lead before anything could possibly be done to fix her car.

She gave the young man a wide smile. "Thank you. Gracias. I will be back to see your father."

With that, she turned and headed down the road as the young man had indicated. Though each step took her farther from her car and from Xcan, her thoughts were now solely on Samuel London. As indeed they should be, she told herself. He was the reason she'd flown to Cancun in the first place. It was because of him she'd lost her luggage, had spent hours on the phone trying to make herself understood to people she'd found equally difficult to understand, had been saddled with a car that had conked out on her at the most inopportune moment. It was because of him that she'd missed Xcan in the first place and had wound up in Valladolid, that she had a sore backside, that she was at this very moment trekking along the side of a narrow Mexican highway, sweating profusely, batting at mosquitoes, biting her lips each time her ankle twisted on the uneven shoulder of the road.

Samuel Prescott London of the stern, pale face and glasses. Tall, skinny Samuel Prescott London. Samuel Prescott London, whose sole interest in life was his work.

For just a moment she thought about the fact that he was a real-estate developer. Somehow, given the image she'd formed of him, she'd have assumed him to have been an accountant or a computer hermit, communicating not with people but with ledgers or disks. Perhaps he was the paper man behind the operation, leaving his partner, McGee, to handle the interpersonal aspects of the business.

Pushing a damp strand of hair from her forehead, she walked on. At least the sun wasn't shining, she reasoned, glancing upward. The blanket of clouds seemed to be compressing the heat toward the ground. The air was thick, stifling her as she trod onward, and her dress was clinging uncomfortably to her damp skin—all because of Samuel Prescott London.

Five minutes passed, then ten, and Chelsea saw no path. Several cars and trucks had roared past, but none were going slow enough for her to ask. She kept her eyes peeled for some opening, any opening in the forest, on either side. Perhaps in his confusion the fellow at the machine shop had given her the wrong directions.

But there was nothing. No road or path. No break in the jungle whatsoever.

Swatting at a mosquito as it sampled her neck, Chelsea finally stopped. Disgruntled, she debated turning around and traipsing back to the machine shop to await the reincarnation of her car. Reincarnation? She'd never been a believer of reincarnation. Perhaps revival. Yes, the machinist's father might be able to revive her car, but she'd have quite a bit to say to the man at the rental agency!

And to Samuel Prescott London!

Suddenly she hung her head and took several shallow breaths. She couldn't tell Samuel London off! She was supposed to *charm* him!

A high laugh bubbled from her throat. If she'd thought herself at a disadvantage without the rest of the clothes from her suitcase, she was positively pathetic now! She was covered with dust and dirt smears, made all the worse by perspiration. Her knees wobbled, her arm and neck itched, she hurt all over, and her hair had to resemble a rat's nest—if rats did live in nests that were blond and damp and scraggly.

Her only saving grace was that she had no intention of actually confronting the stodgy Samuel London today. No, she was simply following her hottest lead. If she arrived at this *pueblito* and was told that the man in question was very definitely living there, she had every intention of hightailing it back to Xcan, to Cancun, to the Camino Real to await her luggage and set herself to rights before swooping down on the unsuspecting Samuel.

If she arrived at the *pueblito*. *If* she was told that the man was there. *If* she could find the damned path!

Inhaling deeply, she plodded forward once more. And she found the path. On the left. Actually, had it not been for the jungle growth all around and the fact that the path took off at a perfect right angle from the road, she would have seen it before she did. It was actually more than a path, though less than a road. A single car could have maneuvered it rather harmlessly.

Forcing herself onto the path, though, Chelsea felt decidedly at risk. Her sandals held to the stone-strewn earth even less surely than they had to the shoulder of the highway. Her skin prickled as she thought of the wildlife that had to be peering out at her from the stunted jungle on either side. She felt she was in a tunnel, whose sides would provide instant torture if she neared them and whose end was somewhere far in the distance.

So she stuck to the center of the path, scratched the mosquito bites that were beginning to swell and walked on. And on. The bag cut into her shoulder and grated against her damp back, but she ignored it. Samuel Prescott London was out there—or in there—and she was going to find him.

A blister opened on one heel, another on a toe where the strap of her sandal rubbed. Sweat trickled down her cheek, and she swiped at it with a grimy arm. Her lungs ached from inhaling the thick, hot air, and she would have given anything for the faintest hint of a breeze. But there was none. Nor was there any *pueblito*.

Chelsea glanced back the way she'd come, then turned her sights forward once more. It seemed senseless to go back now. She had to be close. She *had* to be. She didn't feel it in her bones anymore, because her bones were numb, which was a blessing since the rest of her itched and ached. But she remembered the way the path had simply materialized, and she told herself that the *pueblito* would do the same. Unless she'd taken the wrong path. Unless the young man in the machine shop had been wrong. Unless...

She felt one drop, then another. She stopped in her tracks, looked at the sky, then the ground. Stunned, she held out a hand. Not that she'd never seen rain before, but on top of everything else... And she was totally exposed. Unless she chose to duck into the jungle, which she absolutely couldn't...she couldn't...

Within minutes it was pouring and Chelsea was soaked. Standing there in the middle of a jungle path, miles from civilization, she began to laugh hysterically. Then, exhausted and uncaring, she sank to the ground and cried.

Hunched over her bag, which lay between her limply folded legs, she let her tears flow. Tears, rain...there wasn't much difference. She was hot and drenched and positively miserable. So miserable that she didn't hear the thunder of running steps until they were nearly upon her. Then, with visions of jungle cats and wild boars flashing through her brain, she jerked her head up in terror, only to find herself being engulfed by a group of men, one of whom deftly scooped her up, bag and all, and continued with the others on their way.

Her tears stopped instantly. "What are you doing?" she squealed and started to squirm. Though the man's arms were gentle, they held her firmly.

"Going somewhere dry. I won't hurt you."

One, then another of the men tossed unintelligible words their way, laughing occasionally, jogging on all the while. The man who carried Chelsea answered them in their native tongue, his voice deep and smooth and kind in a way that reassured Chelsea. Further reassurance came from the fact that he'd spoken to her in flawless English. Not only flawless, but utterly natural.

Through the rain that plastered her hair to her forehead, she looked up at his face. He was, she was sure, American. Though his skin was deeply tanned, its hue was markedly different from the muted brick shade of the Mexican faces she'd seen. His hair, too, was different—every bit as thick as that of the natives, but a lighter brown, even soaked as it was, and longer. but it was his mustache—thick and well-trimmed, brown with a lighter sheen—that caught Chelsea's eye, and his gray eyes—holding hints of both mischief and warmth—that set her at ease.

She felt she was in the arms of someone from home, someone new yet familiar, and she relaxed and let herself be trundled along in the pouring rain.

Within minutes the men turned in at what had to be the *pueblito* Chelsea had been searching for. They scattered then, and through the droplets that pelted her face she was able to catch the briefest glimpse of an enclave of huts before she was carried into one and very gently set on her feet.

Her rescuer turned away from her quickly and disappeared into the back room of the hut, returning momentarily with two towels, one of which he gave to her. She stood for an instant holding it, watching him mop his arms, his face, his hair. He stopped with his hand on the towel on his head and smiled.

"Go ahead," he urged softly. "I've got more."

Chelsea was filled with questions, the most notable being who this man was, but she found herself momentarily tongue-tied. Whoever he was, he was magnificent. She saw now that he was much taller than she, much taller than the other men he'd been with. She also saw that he was perfectly made. His wet pants did nothing to hide the narrowness of his hips, nor could his saturated short-sleeved shirt hide the breadth of his shoulders or the strength of his arms. But it was his face on which her attention focused—lean brown cheeks that bore just a hint of a shadow, a firm lower lip that curved ever so slightly beneath that wonderful mustache of his, a straight nose, laughing gray eyes.

"It's okay," he said when she blushed at being caught staring, "I like you, too. In fact, I think I love you. You've saved my life."

"Saved your life?" Chelsea echoed dumbly. "I…isn't it the other way around?"

"No way. You'd have survived that rain. I'm not sure I would have survived the fate in store for me if you hadn't shown up, though. Come on...dry off. You're dripping all over my carpet."

Chelsea glanced down to see that she was indeed dripping, but there was no carpet underfoot, simply a hard-packed dirt floor. "Oh," she said, going along with the game. "Sorry." Gingerly she set her bag on the ground and, raising the towel, started at the top. "What *would* your fate have been if I hadn't shown up?"

The man was scrubbing at his hair again. The motion made his answer slightly choppy. It also emphasized the muscular twists of his forearms and the veins carrying his life's blood through his body. "One of the fellows I was with has a daughter he's been trying to pair me with. I've put him off for a good long time, but I was beginning to run out of excuses."

"Is she that bad?" Chelsea asked, bemused.

"No, no. She's sweet and pretty and more than capable of keeping a man well-fed and happy. She also happens to be fifteen years old."

"Oh," Chelsea said. The man before her looked to be in his mid-thirties. She could understand—even respect—his hesitation. "I see what you mean.... Do they still do that here? Marry young?"

"You bet. Juana's sister is a year younger than she and has a husband and baby already."

Chelsea's towel, which had been doing little more than inching over her hair, stopped moving altogether. "My God. Fourteen. That's phenomenal!"

"Not really. Not here, at least. Extended families live in villages together. Children, grandchildren, great-grandchildren—they're welcomed and adored. It's a marvelous thing to see. These people have very little by way of material wealth, but when it comes to love they're richer than any people I've ever known."

Chelsea was enthralled by the look of admiration, of awe on his face. But as she studied it the look altered, seeming to leave the Maya behind and grow more immediate, more specific, more personal. She felt a different kind of enthrallment then, a tingling in the pit of her stomach that fanned out until her aches and pains and itches and fatigue were momentarily forgotten.

Without taking his eyes from her, the man draped his towel over his shoulder and approached until he stood a mere breath away. Her body's awakening increased with each step he took, and she had to struggle to keep her knees steady. His size was striking, appealing, and there was something elemental about him, about the way he walked, the way he held himself. It was as though he'd experienced all of life and knew the here and now to be the most vital part.

The physical warmth he exuded was far different from the summer's heat. The masculine scent of him rose above the earthy smell of the rain-soaked hut and its jungle environs.

"I have two questions to ask," he murmured as his eyes gently, hungrily, roamed her face. "Are you single?"

Stunned into silence by the potent maleness that seemed to be reaching out, enveloping her, drawing her in, Chelsea simply nodded.

His dark lashes lowered a fraction before he posed his second question, as quietly, as intensely. "Are you free?" This time there was a husky timbre to his voice.

No other thought could have possibly intruded in Chelsea's mind at that moment. Nothing in the world existed but the devastatingly appealing man before her. Barely breathing, she gave a second nod.

Then he touched her. His hands framed her face with a tentativeness in keeping with the slight trembling of his fingers. Her own hand, which had held the towel clasped to her wet head, dropped to her side, the towel to the floor, forgotten.

His fingertips examined her lightly, skimming her nose, her forehead, her eyes. His gaze held curiosity and wonderment, as though she were an apparition he wasn't quite ready to believe in. And she could no more have moved than she could have denied her own curiosity and wonderment.

As lightly as he'd touched her, he lowered his head and brushed her lips with his, but there was nothing light about the intense, hot wave of desire that shot through Chelsea. Eyes closed, she swayed, but he'd taken a step closer so that his body bolstered hers, and his hands steadied her head while the pressure of his mouth slowly increased.

Beneath the sensually abrasive tickle of his mustache, his lips moved surely, slanting and caressing, leaving hers and returning at just the right moment and with a persuasiveness that had her hungering for more. As masterful as his kiss was, there was nothing programmed about it. Chelsea felt it was tailored to fit her shape, her taste, her needs. By the time he slid his tongue into her mouth, she was starving for it, and her fevered response matched his greed. Mindless, totally dominated by the moment's passion, she twined her fingers in his damp hair, urging him closer, deeper, taking everything he offered.

Never in her life had Chelsea felt what she did now. She'd been kissed. She'd been loved. But never had she known as instant and electric an attraction as she felt for this stranger. She wanted to breathe his name, but she couldn't. She wanted to *think* his name, but she couldn't. It was that reality that finally gave her rein over her abandonment.

Her fingers formed fists in his hair and pulled, not sharply but firmly. When neither pairs of lips heeded the unwelcome intrusion she repeated the action. Then he raised his head and looked down at her. His breathing was as uneven as hers, his skin as flushed, his gaze as puzzled.

"My God!" she whispered, astonished by the force of what she'd felt seconds before. Both her mind and her body wanted to know more of this man. "I don't even know who you are!"

His puzzled look grew less disturbed, then slowly melted into a heart-rending smile, a crescent of white in his tan face beneath his mustache. He brushed the pads of his thumbs over her throbbing lips, then, with a sigh that mirrored her feelings exactly, withdrew his hands, dragged one through his hair, and took a step back.

"That's never happened to me before," he murmured sheepishly, massaging the back of his neck in a gesture that, coupled with his gaze dropping to the floor, spoke of embarrassment. "I'm sorry. I...it's just that...well, it...oh, hell, I don't know."

"Who are you?" Chelsea asked softly but more directly this time.

To her consternation, he took a minute to think about it. Then he raised smiling eyes and shrugged. "After today, I believe I'll be your servant for life." He stretched out his hand. "My name's Sam London, and I'm very, very pleased to meet you."

3

CHELSEA WAS UTTERLY DUMBFOUNDED. *Sam London?*

It suddenly hit her that since the moment she'd been scooped from the rain-drenched ground she hadn't given a second's thought to the man she was supposedly tracking down.

Now she stood staring at this stranger who'd breathed his name. Her awareness of him hadn't diminished even with the small distance he'd put between them. To put her hand in his, she knew, would be to lapse again into sensual madness. But...he was the one who had to be demented. Sam London? *The* Samuel London? Samuel *Prescott* London?

"Sam?" she gasped. "You're Sam London?"

He nodded, but his puzzlement was back, bringing tiny furrows to his brow. He slowly lowered his hand. "You're familiar with my name?"

Familiar with it? She'd been all but living and breathing it for the past week! "I...I've been looking all over for you, but..." She scrunched up her face as she studied his. This had to be a ruse, a would-the-real-Samuel-London-please-stand-up farce. "You can't be Sam London," she finally protested. "I've seen his picture. He doesn't look anything like you!"

An easy laugh met her ears. "I've been away from home for over six months, so any picture you've seen would have had to have been a 'before' shot. I've changed some."

"*Some?* It's...impossible! His hair—"

"Has grown longer. Too long?" he asked cautiously.

"No, no, but it was darker in the picture."

"It had never been in the sun long enough to lighten before." Indeed, now that it was drying, she could see the same sun-bleached sheen she'd earlier noticed in his mustache.

"And the mustache—"

"Grew."

"And the pale skin—"

"Tanned."

Chelsea slowly shook her head, unable to believe that the Samuel Prescott London of her waking nightmare and this acutely virile man to whom she was phenomenally attracted were one and the same. "But Samuel London wears glasses—"

"When he works, which was all the time back home. He needs the glasses for reading, which he hasn't done a helluva lot of lately. Things are different here. Very different."

She was still trying to mesh the two men. "He was *skinny.*"

One corner of his mouth twitched in amusement and he held up a hand in mock protest. "He was slim. Not skinny. Slim. And he's had six months of healthy living to fill him out. Honest physical labor can do that to a man." He drew himself to his full height and straightened his shoulders. "Whaddya think? Is it an improvement?"

Chelsea's eyes flared at the expansion of his chest. "It's...it's wonderful," she stammered, unable to lie or play coy. "I...this doesn't make sense. I was expecting someone totally different!" Her gaze narrowed. "How do I know you're not an imposter?"

His eyes narrowed in return. "How do *I* know you're not my mother's spy?"

That left her mute once more. She feared she'd gone pale, that guilt was written all over her face. So she forced herself to speak, choosing offense as the best defense. "Tell me about yourself," she ordered quietly. "Convince me that you're Samuel London."

He didn't hesitate. "I come from Boston but grew up in Wellesley Hills under the eternally watchful, if dictatorial eye of my mother, Beatrice London, and the more gentle and loving, if meek eye of my father, Thomas. My father died four years ago, at which point mother stepped in to formally wear the pants she'd been wearing on the sly for years. Needless to say—" he glanced down at himself, then returned his gaze to Chelsea's face "—I wear my own pants. I have a condominium on the waterfront and a firm called London and McGee. I'm a real-estate developer. I play golf at the country club once a week when the weather permits.... Enough?"

The raw facts she could argue with; the man had only to read Samuel London's résumé to know where he'd been born and raised, where he lived, what he did for a living. But the editorial content of his speech convinced her. After all, she'd met Beatrice London herself.

Plus there was the matter of his eyes. And his nose. When she superimposed tension on the relaxed features before her, she could buy the idea that they were the same as those in the pictures she'd seen. And his height fit. As did the arguments he'd made concerning those aspects of his appearance that had changed.

"Enough," she said softly, then shook her head again. "But it's going to take some getting used to. I had such an indelible image in my mind..."

"I'd like to know the why of that, but you're still soaking wet and you must be uncomfortable. How about a shower?"

She grimaced. "Wasn't that what I had?" Then she looked down at herself and her grimace intensified. "I look awful! My dress will never be the same!" Considering that it was the only piece of clothing she had to her name at the moment, she was appalled.

He glanced at her bag, which lay on the ground where she'd dropped it earlier. "Have you anything to change into?"

Her laugh was high and short. "Not here *or* at the hotel. The airline lost my luggage." She gestured with her hands. "This trip has been a disaster from the word 'go.' First my luggage, then the crazy language thing, then the car the rental agent foisted on me, then the rain and the bugs—"

Sam interrupted her with a chuckle. "Whoa. One thing at a time. First off, that shower. No, I take it back. First off, your name."

"My name?"

His eyes danced. "You do have one, don't you?"

Her mouth had dropped open; she promptly forced it shut. It seemed impossible that he didn't already know her name, when she knew his and much more. And there had been that kiss..."It's Chelsea. Chelsea Ross."

"I'm pleased to meet you, Chelsea Ross." This time when he held out his hand, he reached with his other as well. His clasp was warm, familiar, heady, and her stomach maὐe a series of feathery pirouettes. "And now that the formal introductions have been dispensed with, you can take your shower. Need another towel?"

Towel? She searched dumbly for her first, saw it lying on the ground and used it as an excuse to take her hand from his all-too-captivating grasp. She scooped up the towel and pressed it to her breasts.

"This, uh, this should be fine. I didn't really use it much before." She looked toward the back room. "The shower's out there?"

"All the way. Just go on out the back door and turn right. You can't miss it."

Avoiding his gaze as she was, she missed the twinkle in his eyes. Then he turned away, going to the room in back and returning with one of his shirts. "Not exactly a *huipile*," he mused, holding the white shirt up by its shoulders, "but it's clean and it's the best I can do at the moment." He sent a calculating glance down Chelsea's body. "Yup. It'll do."

Accepting the shirt with a self-conscious "thanks," she followed his directions, hastening through a room smaller than the first until she reached the back door. It stood wide open, as had the front door; the two were perfectly aligned

so that looking from the outside one could see straight
through the hut.

Peering cautiously through the raindrops and to the right,
she saw what appeared to be a tiny shed. Head down, she
dashed the few feet through the rain and let herself into what
was, in essence, an outhouse with a primitive shower head
rigged at one end. She had no illusions about a hot water
heater, and she didn't mind that there wasn't one. The outhouse was as muggy as the hut had been, and she was more
than hot enough to welcome cold water.

It was quite effective. By the time she'd washed her filthy
clothes, showered the dirt and grime from her body, dried off
and donned Sam's shirt, she was thinking clearly again.

All personal feelings for Samuel London aside, she had a
job to do. She'd found the man. Now she had to lure him back
to Boston. Theoretically, given the way he'd kissed her, she
had a head start on her task, though she realized his kiss
might have reflected his simple hunger for a woman, *any*
woman. Chelsea gave no credence to what he'd said about
loving her and being her slave forever; those surely were the
words of a man who'd been in near-isolation for six months.

No, she sensed that the hard part would be to convince him
to leave. Sexual hunger, even infatuation, would mean
nothing if he felt the free choice that dictated his prolonged
stay in the Yucatán was being threatened. She still didn't
know what he was doing here or, indeed, why he'd remained
so long. Those were things she was going to have to discover
before she could begin to convince him to return home.

First, though, she had to give *him* some answers. Finger-
combing her hair—she was sure it looked awful but there was
absolutely nothing she could do about it—and checking to
make sure that her shirt was securely buttoned from throat
to thigh—she'd never been prim, but then she'd never come
face to face with a man as decidedly male before—she reentered the hut.

If she thought she'd regained control of her emotions, she was mistaken. But then, she hadn't anticipated finding Sam as she did.

He was silhouetted against the front door, his back to her. One arm was raised, elbow bent, forearm against the frame of the door. The other hand was anchored in the pocket of a pair of denim cutoffs, the only piece of clothing he wore. His legs were long, the backs of his thighs and calves firm and deeply tanned. His shoulders were broad and well muscled, though not in the inflated way of a weight lifter, and his back was a solid expanse of dark skin tapering to a delightfully lean waist.

As Chelsea stared, she felt telltale tremors whisper through her. For an instant she contemplated turning and running. It simply wasn't right for her to be so attracted to him. He was a case, and personal involvement would only complicate things. Samuel Prescott London was supposed to be boring and stiff. It wasn't *fair* that he should turn out to be breathtakingly virile.

But virile he appeared to be, all the more so when he turned his head and caught sight of her. Grinning broadly, he pivoted on his heel and came to meet her. Chelsea could only swallow hard as his solid, bronzed chest neared.

"Better?" he asked gently, stopping directly before her.

Her gaze shot guiltily from his chest to his face and it took her a minute to understand what he meant. The shower. "Uh—" she cleared her throat "—yes, it was fine. Felt good." She glanced down at herself and blushed. "Thanks for the shirt. I left my...my things hanging in the bathroom. I hope you don't mind."

"Of course not. Once the rain stops we can hang them on the line. They'll dry faster that way, though nothing dries particularly well in this humidity."

"I'd read that it was the rainy season. How long does the rain keep up?"

"Anywhere from an hour to twelve. The mornings are usually bright. It's the afternoons you've got to watch out for."

She gave him a facetious look. "Now he tells me."

"I'd have told you sooner if I'd known you were around. But I'm thoroughly in the dark—" he took her elbow and guided her toward a low bench "—which is something you're about to remedy." His voice returned to normal. "How about a beer? I'm afraid it's the best thirst quencher I've got right now."

"Beer's fine," she answered. She'd seen a small icebox in the back room and relished the idea of holding something cold, really cold, between her hot palms. So intent was she on the image—a far safer, saner one than that of Sam's big, beautiful body—she overestimated the height of the bench and landed low and hard. "Ahhh!" she cried and shifted gingerly. "Am I sore!"

"You've also done something horrid to your knuckles," was Sam's grim reply, and within seconds he was on his haunches, taking her hand in his to study the bruise.

"That's from changing a tire. *This*—" she shifted on her bottom again "—is from hitching a ride in a vintage pickup truck. These—" she scratched her arm, her leg, the side of her neck "—are from the mosquitoes, and these—" she pointed toward the red blisters on her feet "—are from my sandals." She scowled. "When they talk of Montezuma's revenge, they ain't whistlin' dixie."

Sam gave a full-throated laugh. "Let's hope that's the worst of it," he said, rising again and padding from the room.

Amid the muted patter of rain on the thatched roof, Chelsea heard the clink of bottles, then the thud of the icebox closing. Filled with anticipation—she told herself it was for the beer and not Sam—she waited for him to return. When he didn't, she diverted herself by examining her surroundings.

The entire hut was dim, the only natural light—what there was of it, given the heavy rain clouds that obscured the sun— filtering in through the doors and through tiny cracks between the sticks that formed its walls.

The front room was wide, though not deep, perhaps twenty-five feet by fifteen, and nearly empty. A round wooden table seemed to be the focal point; it was low, little more than two feet off the ground. Benches, similar to the one on which she sat, squatted at intervals around the table and the room.

"Here we go," Sam announced, reappearing with two narrow-necked bottles of beer dangling between the fingers of one hand and an armful of medicinal supplies in the crook of his opposite elbow. Straddling the empty half of her bench, he lowered himself, set the bottles on the floor and took up her injured hand. "It's an antiseptic salve," he explained as he spread warm cream over her bruises. "Should make it feel better."

What made it feel better was the gentle way he spread it on and the fact that his other hand craddled hers in support. Chelsea noted the difference in size between their hands and suddenly felt delicate, a fact that annoyed her. Being delicate implied the need for protection, something she'd never felt before.

"I'm sure it'll be fine," she said more gruffly than she intended, though she made no move to withdraw her hand until Sam placed it carefully on her thigh. At that point she wished she'd retrieved it herself, because his fleeting touch seemed to burn through the fabric of her shirt, leaving her entire leg tingling. And that was *before* he treated her blisters and bites!

She was grateful for the bottle of beer he gave her at long last and took an immediate and lengthy chug.

"Okay, Chelsea Ross," he declared after he'd set the supplies aside and taken a healthy swallow of his own beer. "Tell me who you are and why you've been looking all over for me."

Chelsea took another drink. She sensed she'd need it. Not that she feared she'd trip over her story, rather Sam's closeness was doing fearful things to her nerve ends. He was straddling the bench...*straddling* it...in his cutoffs. His long legs were bent at the knees, one of which actually brushed her back when the motion of raising his bottle shifted his body that tiniest bit.

She pressed her thighs together and leaned forward to prop her elbows on them, hoping the pose looked casual and not like the cowardly move it was. "I'm a writer," she began. "I thought I'd do a piece on the modern Maya. When I heard that you'd been living down here, you seemed the perfect one to speak with."

"A writer for whom?" he asked conversationally.

"I free-lance. I'm not quite sure where I'll sell the story, though I'm sure it will sell. Even the little bit I've seen since I drove out here has been fascinating."

She'd been hoping to fast-forward the discussion to the Maya themselves, but Sam wasn't about to be rushed. He'd been in Mexico too long, she mused grudgingly, or perhaps he was simply too sharp. He tipped back his head to take another more leisurely drink of his beer, and she was suddenly fascinated by the strength of his neck, by the muscles in his tan throat as he swallowed the cool liquid. Ironically, every drop of moisture within Chelsea seemed to heat.

"Who told you I was here?" he asked.

She cleared her throat, wanting to take another cool drink herself but fearful that her hands would be trembling. "An old friend. I believe he went to school with you. Jason Ingram?" Resting her chin on her shoulder as she looked over at him, Chelsea thought she saw a moment's surprise in his eyes, so she rushed on to make her story more palatable. She'd gotten the impression from Sam's mother that Sam and Jason hadn't seen each other since college. Sam was probably asking himself how *Jason* had known he was in the Yucatán. "I saw Jason when he was in Boston last month. When I said I was thinking of writing this article, he mentioned that he'd accidentally bumped into someone who'd heard from someone else that you were here."

Sam looked pensive. "A name from the past... Jason Ingram. How is good old Jason?"

"Just fine. He sends his regards."

Sam nodded—somewhat guardedly, Chelsea thought, and she wondered whether the two men had been even less of friends than the yearbook inscription had suggested. But she wasn't about to ask. Taking sentimentality into consideration, it was plausible that an old college friend, or acquaintance, perhaps even enemy, might have indeed sent his regards. Evidently Sam reached the same conclusion.

"Return them for me when you see him.... So he'd heard I was here—but you mentioned seeing photographs. All he had was an ancient yearbook, which I doubt he'd have carted East."

"No. I called your mother to verify what Jason had heard. She wasn't sure exactly where you were, but she gave me several other names to call."

"I'm sure she did," Sam muttered under his breath.

Had Chelsea been as innocent of the situation as she was supposed to be, she would have asked him what he meant. But the last thing she felt was innocence, and though she wanted to probe, she felt that a more appropriate time would come. Too intense an interest in something so personal might sound suspicious, particularly where her relationship with his mother was concerned. The sooner she moved from the topic of Beatrice London, the better.

So she ignored his muttered aside. "Anyway, I saw the photo from your Annual Report. And one of the men in your office told me that you were living somewhere between Cancun and Chichen Itza. When I got down here and started asking questions I was put onto Professor Paredes in Merida, who told me to start looking in Xcan."

She ended her story breathlessly, convinced she'd done it right. Theoretically, she was covered from every angle. If David McGee or Norman Schialli wrote that she'd been asking around, Sam would already know. Linda Huntington and the rest would fall among those "other names" Beatrice London had given her to call. Her general reference to "asking questions" in Cancun would cover her contacts with the Mexican authorities, and the good professor from Merida would have nothing to tell Sam that he hadn't already heard.

Rather pleased, she tipped the beer bottle to her lips and savored the cool brew. Her timing was perfect, for Sam seemed to be deep in thought. Almost absently he began to stroke her waist. Far from absently she struggled to contain her urge to lean back into his hand. Then it stopped moving and he sought her gaze.

"Who *are* you, though?" he asked very softly.

Chelsea wasn't sure how to respond. On the one hand, he looked almost mystified, and she wanted to believe that he, too, was stunned by the strength of the attraction between them. On the other hand, if he doubted her story and suspected something...

"What do you mean?"

His eyes cleared. "Where do you come from? How long have you been writing? What else were you doing with your life before you popped into mine?"

Relieved by the apparent innocence of his curiosity, she smiled at him, then sat up straight. "I was born in a small mill town in New Hampshire, where I lived until I went off to college. I graduated with a major in English Lit and taught for a year at a junior college in central Massachusetts."

"Only a year?"

"I didn't really like teaching. I guess I don't have the patience for it. No, maybe patience is the wrong word. I guess I just found I wanted something more...personal."

"I'd have thought teaching was personal."

"Not at the place I taught. The classes were large and the kids didn't particularly want to be there, so they never sought me out on any kind of personal level."

"Did you switch to another school?"

"I thought about it," she mused, absently scratching a mosquito bite on her neck until Sam set down his beer and pulled her hand away. "But I felt I was floundering. I wasn't sure what I really wanted to do. And if you're not committed, particularly when discipline is a problem since the students aren't much younger than you are, you're in trouble. I was very definitely in trouble."

"So...you turned to writing."

Chelsea was momentarily jolted. Up until then she'd been telling the truth. She'd been lost in it actually, as though it were the most natural thing in the world for her to be spilling her thoughts to Sam. Concentration hadn't been necessary. In fact, she'd been looking at his hand holding hers, at his fingers, which were well formed, long and strong. Now, though, the fabrication had to begin and she needed all of her wits. Taking her hand from his, she wrapped her arms around her waist.

But he instantly spread his large hand over her back. "You're not feeling sick, are you?"

"No, no. Of course not."

He relaxed. "I wasn't sure. When you clutched your stomach. . .people often do get sick when they first come to Mexico."

"Not me," she announced. "I've got an iron constitution. I never get sick."

"Glad to hear it," he said with the same slash of a grin. "Go on then. Tell me about your writing career." He was fingering her damp curls, which barely reached the collar of the shirt she wore. He was evidently a toucher, another cause for surprise. She'd assumed Samuel Prescott London to be physically remote. At the moment, she almost wished he were, because she was having trouble thinking with his hand touching her and his thighs spread that way.

"What do you want to know," she managed in a slightly garbled voice. Between her guilt and his touch, her composure was next to nil.

"Were you successful right off the bat?"

"No." She swallowed. "Writers have a pathetically low average income." She'd read that recently in the newspaper. "I had to find other means of supporting myself."

"And...?" he prompted.

"I took to tending bar."

His hand dropped away from her and she began to breathe more easily. "Tending bar? You were a *bartender*?" His eyes lit up so brightly that Chelsea's cheeks flushed.

"Uh-huh. I was a bartender."

"That's terrific! What a different thing to do with your life!"

His enthusiasm was contagious and she smiled. "'Different' was one word for it. There were nights when I cursed it, when I'd get home at two in the morning smelling like an alcoholic, with nothing but aching feet to show for ten hours' work."

"But there must have been fun times too. I'd think you'd meet some pretty interesting people. Where did you work? What kind of places?"

For a minute Chelsea couldn't answer. It struck her that an hour before she never would have dreamed Samuel Prescott London would be carrying on such an animated conversation with her, on such a topic, no less. But...this wasn't Samuel Prescott London. This was Sam. Funny how she couldn't think of him now any other way.

Realizing she was staring at him, she blinked and shifted her gaze to the far wall. Then she squinted. "Is that a light fixture?"

Sam glanced fleetingly to where she was looking. "Uh-huh. There's one in each room."

"I saw electrical wires leading to some of the huts I passed on the highway today. Electricity...plumbing...yet the huts themselves are so primitive."

"They're not much different from those the Maya built fifteen hundred years ago," he informed her, a note of respect in his voice.

"I've read about the people of the past, but it's strange. Surely, with radios and all, today's Maya have some idea what's going on in the outside world. You'd think they'd want to improve on palm leaves and sticks."

"What's to improve on when palms keep out the rain? They provide natural ventilation for the heat, and they're free for the taking. The same thing's true of sticks. It's not as though we need insulation down here. The air never cools that much."

"But there is electricity and plumbing."

"Only in the most elementary sense, and even then not universally. Fifty percent of the huts do without both. I guess I just lucked out. It gets pretty dark at night, and I wouldn't exactly trust a kerosine lamp. Nor would I care to traipse across camp to the john."

"How did you get this place?"

"The old man who'd been living here died shortly before I arrived, so it was empty. I hooked up the shower myself, but the rest of the, uh, amenities were intact."

"You'd lived in other villages before this one?"

"A couple. I've been here for four months though. It suits me just fine."

"Don't you miss the comforts of home?"

"Nah. Well, maybe just once in a while. But this life is so simple, so *basic*. I've learned a lot by being here. I took a hell of a lot of things for granted and in so doing missed out on some of the greatest joys of life."

"Like...?"

"Simple survival. Eating food that you've grown yourself. Drinking water from the well." He shot a glance at the roof.

"Taking shelter from the rain. Lots of things, some small, some not."

"Don't you miss work?"

"I do work, harder in some ways than I've ever done before but much, much more pleasantly."

With this statement, Chelsea knew she had her own work cut out for her. She would have argued further, but she didn't want to sound pushy. And she was supposed to be studying the Maya, not criticizing their way of life. "Tell me more about these people."

He shook his head. "Tell me more about you. We were talking about your bartending adventures. Where was it you worked? In Boston?"

She hesitated for just an instant. Her gaze had fallen to his chest, to the faint swell of one breast, to the dark nipple that nested amid a whirl of tauntingly soft hair.

Blaming the sudden heat of her cheeks on the beer, she set the bottle aside, then shifted on the bench and clasped her hands around her knees. "Yes," she murmured, still slightly distracted. "I work at..." She had to think for a minute. "I worked at Icabod's. It's on Park Street..."

"I know just where it is. Terrific place. I'm told they make great Harvey Wallbangers there."

Chelsea couldn't help but laugh, remembering the parting discussion she'd had with her boss. Sam's innocent comment brought her fully back to reality. "That's Icabod's, all right. But I'm sure I've never seen you there...well, not in your present form, at least." She teasingly dropped her eyes down his body again. This time her gaze landed on the small birthmark that lay on the inside of his thigh, perilously close to the ragged hem of his shorts...and his sex...

"No," he said huskily and took a sharp breath, which mercifully drew her attention upward to his ribs. But he was suddenly cupping her chin and she next met his gaze. "If you keep looking at me that way, my present form will change all the more. And if that happens I can't be held responsible for my actions," he warned softly.

"Like...the Hulk," she stammered, trying for a joke but failing badly because his lips remained parted, warm and inviting, and she was mesmerized and her heart had begun hammering....

"Not quite," he murmured seconds before he captured her lips. He slid his fingers along her jaw, through her hair and to the back of her head, where he held her while his mouth stroked hers to full response.

It didn't take much. Chelsea felt she was drowning in a sea of fire and the only way she could save herself was by clinging to Sam's lips, taking the moisture of his mouth, letting his breath fill her lungs with life. She was weak all over and trembling by the time he released her lips to whisper against her cheek, "What is it with us, Chelsea? I've never been so damned hot before." One hand continued to hold her head, the other roamed her back and her hips, slipping beneath the hem of the shirt, coming to an abrupt halt on her bottom. "My God, you're not wearing a stitch under this, are you?" His touch seemed to burn her skin, but the sensation must have been mutual because he quickly jerked his hand away.

Needing something to hold, she nervously retrieved her beer. "Everything was...was dirty and sweaty...maybe I shouldn't have, but I wanted to be clean..."

He hauled her against him then, pressing her face to the chest she'd so helplessly admired moments before. His skin was warm and man-smelling, and its spattering of hair was a gentle cushion. Nothing, though, could cushion her from the hardness she felt at her hip. And nothing could free her from the arms wrapped around her. In turn she clutched the neck of her beer bottle for dear life.

"We're gonna have to do something about this," he rasped. "I mean, I've never laid eyes on you before but you make me want you like there's no tomorrow." He pulled her head back and commandeered her gaze. "I don't do this all the time,

Chelsea. I swear. I don't come on to women this way. There's something in you...something in me too...something between us..."

"I know," she breathed shallowly. "I know. I don't understand it, but it gets out of control. I've never felt this way. It scares me, Sam."

"We hardly know each other."

"I know." Her gaze was locked with his and she could see the dilation of his pupils.

"Maybe we should see where it leads." His voice was thick and his chest pressed her breasts when he took an unsteady breath. "Maybe we should let ourselves go." He put a hand to the pulsing vein in her neck, then slid it down her throat to the point where her shirt parted. "I could undo this button, then the next. But I don't think I'd be satisfied until I'd seen *all* of you, and then I wouldn't be satisfied until I'd touched you and tasted you, and then I'd want—ah, hell, I want it now—to be inside..."

His words were as inflamatory as everything else about the man. Chelsea reeled under the sensual onslaught. Samuel London was supposed to be *inhibited*, at least that was what Linda Huntington had said. This Sam, though, was saying it all. He was about as uninhibited as any man she'd ever known or imagined. But she was too caught up in the moment to begin analyzing the change.

"We...can't," she said, feeling more frightened than ever. It was heady knowledge that Sam shared the need that coiled deep in her belly, but it didn't absolve the fact that they were practically strangers. Or that she'd never been loose. Or that she'd been hired to come here.

He sighed and rested his forehead against hers. Her skin bore the same fine sheen of perspiration as his. "I know. It's not the right way for us.... You will stay though, won't you?"

"Stay?" Her eyes widened and her voice rose and her gaze skittered past Sam toward the door. "My Lord, the car! I was supposed to be back in Xcan to see about getting it fixed!"

Sam loosened his hold on her. "What happened to it?"

"It just...stopped. I hitched a ride to Xcan but there wasn't anyone there who could help me right then. But he should be back by now."

"In the rain? I doubt it. You can't go back out in that, Chelsea. I mean, you could, but it'd be silly. The car will be okay. It's a rental anyway. Let the rental agent worry about it."

"I can't do that!" she cried, gesturing wildly with the hand that held her beer. Fortunately the beer splashed out in the opposite direction. "It's my responsibility."

Sam retrieved the beer bottle from her hand and set it by his. "Now it's mine. I'll get a message to Xcan, and the rental agent can pick it up there."

Needing to be free of the lure of Sam's strong body, she stood up and walked toward the door, staring glumly at the rain before turning back to him. "I have to go back to Cancun. My suitcase should have arrived by now—"

"There's nothing in your suitcase you'll need out here."

"But my clothes—"

"I can easily get you some. And you look super in my shirt."

"But I don't even have a change of *underwear*—"

"Don't remind me. I'm trying to forget that little fact."

"Think of how *I* feel—practically naked..."

One side of his mustache curved up with his half smile, half grimace. "I am thinking about how you feel—practically naked—and it's driving me mad."

Chelsea approached him, her expression beseeching. "I have to get back to Cancun, Sam. Tonight."

He thought about that for a minute, then slowly pushed himself to his feet. "Give me one good reason why. I can have the car taken care of. I can get a mesassage to your hotel and they'll hold your suitcase. For that matter, I can have them check you out and hold anything you might have left in your room. We can drive in another day to pick everything up. It's silly for you to be paying for a hotel when you can stay here for nothing."

"I can't stay here." She glanced frantically around. "I don't even see where you sleep. Where would *I* sleep?"

"I have a hammock in the next room. I can sling up another one for you."

"A hammock? I can barely *sit* in one of those things...forget sleeping."

He chuckled. "That's what I said when I first got here. But all the natives sleep in hammocks. They're much cooler than a bed and, once you get used to climbing in and out, far more comfortable. Besides, you're probably exhausted. You'll sleep."

"I don't know, Sam. I'd really be better off in Cancun." Something he'd said moments earlier registered. "You have a car?"

"A Jeep, but if you're thinking what I think you're thinking, you can forget it. *I'm* not going out in this rain."

"Then *I'll* go. If you'll just loan me the Jeep—"

"No way. It doesn't even have a roof. You'd get soaked, and more tired, and then sick. Besides, it'll be getting dark soon and these roads are bad enough at night without the rain. With it, you'd be asking for trouble."

She looked away. "I'd be asking for trouble if I stayed," she murmured softly, but he heard her and took the few steps necessary to cup her shoulders with his hands.

"You really are scared, aren't you?" he asked quietly, with neither criticism nor mockery.

"Yes. I'm scared." She was terrified of the power of what seemed to be an irrevocable magnetic attraction. Even now, though the hands resting on her shoulders might have been those of a good friend or a brother, she felt her blood heat. Forget the case. This was sheer survival. She was on the verge of going under, of losing what little control she still had over her senses.

But she couldn't forget the case, she realized. And at that moment, despite what arguments she gave, she knew she had to stay. That's what the woman Beatrice London had hired would have done—stayed to get to know Sam, to worm her way into his thoughts and understand them, then alter them without his realizing it until he was on a plane bound for home. Her entire future was at stake, she reminded herself. She had to stay.

Something in her expression must have conveyed her surrender because Sam spoke softly, gently. "Look at it this way. If you live with me for a time, you'll have one fantastically authentic article to take back home with you."

She pouted, in part against the lie she perpetrated. "And you'll have been spared poor Juana."

"That too," he admitted, smiling. "Whaddya say? Will you room with me for a bit?"

"Will you give me more of that stuff for my bites? They're itching again."

His smile broadened. "I've even got insect repellent. You must taste damned sweet. Lucky mosquitoes—"

"Sam?" she interrupted, feeling she had to say something more. "About the other—"

He was right on her wavelength. "I won't rush you, Chelsea. We'll take it one step at a time. If something happens, it'll be because we're both ready."

"You aren't worried that. . .I mean, if we're living so close...well, we'd be sleeping in the same room..."

"I've never made love in a hammock. I wonder how it works."

"The floor is probably safer," was her dry retort, then, appalled, she covered her face with her hands. "I can't believe I said that."

But Sam was laughing, drawing her into his arms, hugging her. "You're precious, Chelsea. Has anyone ever told you that?"

No, no one ever had. And for a minute Chelsea let herself feel good. She adored Sam—what she knew of him. Not only was he physically superb, but he had to be the gentlest, most easy-going man she'd ever met. There was nothing macho about him; he'd taken on her case with persuasion rather than force. There was nothing arrogant or spoiled about him; he seemed to feel that his past was irrelevant, which indeed it was at the moment. He was open and warm. He was considerate and concerned.

He was also, very possibly, schizophrenic, but in his present frame of mind he was everything she'd always wanted but never found in a man. So she gloried in the feel of his arms around her and decided that, when all was said and done, even if they returned to their separate lives in Boston, the pleasure she'd known here would have made it all worthwhile.

And he was right. She'd certainly have a fantastically authentic article to sell...if she decided to take up writing.

"First things first," Sam announced, rubbing his hands together. "I'll bet you're hungry."

Chelsea was wandering around the main room of the hut somehow expecting to find things she'd missed during her earlier examination. He'd turned the light on, which helped, since the skies were darker than ever and the rain continued to fall. But though the room seemed more cozy, there was little to see.

"I ate lunch in Valladolid," she answered, folding her hands together as she turned to face him. "Something or other with chicken in it, but I was so hot and annoyed at the time, I doubt I did it justice."

"Okay. Then you're hungry. And probably tired. Want to go back and lie down while I get some things for us?"

"What things? Where are you going?" She wasn't sure if she liked the idea of being left alone. She felt strange in this strange place, somehow disembodied without Sam's arms around her. "You said you wouldn't drive in the rain."

"I won't. At least, not today. I'm just going to dash across the way to Aldana's. His wife will have an extra hammock and some clothes you can borrow. She also happens to be the best cook around. I usually take my meals there, but since you've just arrived," his eyes twinkled, "I'm sure she'll understand if I ask her to pack up some goodies for us to eat here."

"I can cook," Chelsea offered quickly, choosing to ignore the meaning behind the twinkle. Then she paused to cast a frowning glance over her shoulder. "Uh, I don't think I...saw a stove...."

Sam confirmed it. "There isn't one. The cooking is done on a small stone hearth out back, at least in this heat. During the winter months it's a little cooler so the Maya pile stones in the front room and build their fire inside."

"Like the old days." She wanted him to know she'd done her research.

"Exactly." He came closer and lowered his voice in sincerity. "It's a different way of cooking, Chelsea. I don't expect you to do it."

"But I can't impose on your friends all the time," she protested, "and I like to cook. I have to pay for my keep somehow." She wished she hadn't said that, because as soon as she heard the words she anticipated Sam's response. She was surprised—and relieved—when he took them in the spirit in which they'd been offered.

"Don't worry. We'll give you things to do. It'll be the best way to see how these people live. But for now, indulge me. You're my guest. Don't forget, you're doing me a favor being here."

Chelsea was thinking of the fifteen-year-old who would now find someone closer to her age, but Sam's pensive, almost puzzled look made her curious. "What is it?" she asked gently.

He scratched his head, then raked the hair back from his brow. It promptly fell forward again and Chelsea marveled that it could look so wonderful, so full, so dashing when he hadn't seen a stylist in months.

"I'm not sure," he began. He walked to one of the walls and slid down until he was sitting on the floor with his knees bent in front of him. "It's odd. I thought I was perfectly happy living here by myself. I mean, it's not really by myself because the doors are always open and there are always people around, and they're wonderful people, Chelsea. Quiet, but warm and sincere and generous. But...I really *am* glad you're here. I feel excited. It's like...like I was missing something without realizing it." His eyes held gentle apology when they ventured to meet hers. "Maybe I shouldn't be saying that. I'm not doing it to pressure you. But for the first time in my life I really do want the company."

Pleased that Sam was opening up to her, Chelsea knelt before him, then sat back on her heels. "You must have always had people around you," she reasoned softly, thinking of the thriving business in Boston, the weekly golf game, the social affairs a man with the stature of a Samuel Prescott London would have been invited to. Then she remembered that he'd been a loner and she tried to envision a life filled with people...but not.

Sam helped her understand. "There were always people around, but it was like I was in a shell. I went through all the motions, but my heart was never in it. I don't think I've ever been really *close* to anyone—except maybe Linda." He gave a crooked grin. "She's my partner in crime, so to speak."

"Partner in crime?"

"She was the only one who knew how miserable I was back there. She was the only one who gave me encouragement when I decided to take off. I'm sure she's the only one who understands why I haven't returned."

"I talked with her," Chelsea said, feeling an urgent need to be as open as possible. "She was concerned about you."

"You talked with Linda?"

"Hers was one of the names your mother gave me. She's very lovely, Linda is. She wasn't able to tell me where you were, but she was hoping you were happy."

He flicked at a stray thread hanging from his cutoffs. "I *have* been happy. I needed a total break, and I got it. That's why...it's so strange that I'm so glad you're here." His eyes widened when he looked at her. "It has to be you, Chelsea. If anyone else from home—someone I'd known—had come down here I'd have been furious. I know they want me back, and it should be flattering and ego boosting but it isn't. I don't want to return to all that. I don't think I can."

"No one's going to force you to do anything you don't want," she heard herself say. Her hand was on his arm and she knew she was speaking as a friend because that was what she desperately wanted to be. The fact that she'd been hired to get him back to Boston seemed totally irrelevant at the moment. "When you're ready to go back, you'll know it. And you'll do it on your terms."

Absently he kneaded the back of her hand. "The problem is that I don't yet know what those terms are. I seem to be seeing things in black and white. There's the life back there and the one here, and they're as different from each other as night from day. I haven't really given much thought to what might lie in the middle."

You will, Chelsea thought. _That's why I'm here._ "Well," she said, feeling a surge of unbidden tenderness in spite of the reminder of her task, "if you want to talk, I'm here. I'm told I'm a good sounding board. At least—" she grinned "—I've never had one of the guys throw a drink back in my face when I offered my two bits' worth along with the booze."

Sam smiled, but he looked vaguely embarrassed. "You must be a good sounding board. I'm talking more than I have in months. I've picked up Spanish and Mayan, but it's not the same. Maybe it's just that the people here can't relate to my problem. I'm not sure you can, for that matter. You probably think I'm a wealthy, self-indulgent son of a bitch."

"You got it," she teased. "Wealthy and self-indulgent. That's why you're living down here in a hut with no hot water, no television, no Ralph Lauren clothes."

He threw an arm around her neck and drew her face close. "I've got some terrific Mexican liqueur stashed away. _That's_ high living. Want some?"

"Before dinner? Are you kidding? I'd be higher than the palms on your roof." She felt pretty high just then, even without the liqueur, but she didn't want to say so. Sam would think she had a one-track mind, which she didn't, or did she? When he was close to her, she could think of nothing but him. Maybe she was as crazy as he was!

"I can take a hint," he was saying, pushing himself to his feet, hauling her up with him. "You relax. Make yourself at home. Tussle with the hammock in private if you want. I'll be back."

Then he was gone and she was alone. For several minutes she stood where she was, looking aimlessly around, wondering what she should do. Her mind seemed filled to overflowing; she couldn't quite grasp all that had happened in a day, and the more she reflected on her adventures since she'd left Cancun that morning, the more overwhelmed she became.

If she'd been in Boston, she would have had her work to keep her busy. There had always been plenty of that. If she wasn't running around or using the telephone at home, she was at Icabod's. Here there was nothing to do, and she felt at loose ends.

Yes, she was tired. She was also stiff and sore and hot. The humidity was oppressive and her skin was damp. She wandered to the front door, peered out through the rain for sign of Sam. There were half a dozen huts visible, laid out in a rough square. She saw movement in several of them, but the early evening light was too dim for her to see more.

With a sigh she turned back into the room, then crossed through to the bedroom, if one could call it that. When she switched on the wall light and looked around, her gaze was quickly drawn to the hammock that hung to one side. Several large pillows lay on it at random angles.

Sam's hammock. The place where he stretched out and slept each night. She approached it and fingered its sturdy open weave, wondering if silk sheets could have felt more intimate to her touch. The simple thought of Sam's long, lean body occupying this space was enough to stir her senses.

She eyed the hammock and its pillows with a combination of longing and hesitation. She *was* exhausted, but strangely exhilarated. On the one hand it would be heaven to rest her weary bones. On the other she knew she'd never be able to sleep. And that was *if* she managed to wedge herself into the hammock without falling to the ground.

Turning abruptly away, she scanned the rest of the room. There was a small table, similar to the one in front. She knelt beside it to read the spines of three books that lay there. One was an archeological textbook, the other two novels. Beside them was a pair of glasses. These she recognized easily and smiled. She assumed that at some point she'd see Sam wearing them, and she hoped she wouldn't burst out laughing. There seemed something totally incongruous about the Sam she knew wearing Samuel Prescott London's specs.... She drew her hand over her smile, erasing it, practicing.

Standing up, with a groan she didn't bother to smother when her legs protested, she caught sight of a chess set resting atop a large wooden trunk. Board and pieces alike were carved of onyx, swirls of gray and tan and white, exquisite. Equally fine were the items that stood on an open shelf above the trunk. There was a wood carving of what she assumed to be a Mayan god and several other onyx pieces of similar style. Triangular faces with hooked noses. Plumed headpieces. A variety of bodily coverings, some of which resembled armor. There were several clay pieces as well, one painted gaily, the others in their natural earth-toned state. Though the pieces represented varied levels of accomplishment, each in its own right was beautiful.

Chelsea lifted a small piece that resembled a bird, one that had a row of holes in its body. On impulse she put her lips to the open beak and blew softly, rewarded when a raw but definitely musical sound emerged.

Replacing the whistle, she once again stood with her hands clasped at her waist. Her eye was trained on the wooden trunk and she wondered what was in it. She glanced back through the main room to the door and saw no sign of Sam, so she quickly shifted the chess set to the floor and opened the lid of the trunk. Sam's clothes. Soft pants similar to the pair he'd been wearing earlier, shirts like the one she wore now, a pair of weathered jeans. She would have dug further—touching his things was pleasurable—but she felt like a sneak as it was, so she closed the lid and replaced the chess set.

With a sigh, she resumed her visual exploration, but there was little left to see. The only other items in the room were the small icebox and—she peered more closely because the corner was dim—a suitcase that stood against the wall. She walked over to it, studied its finely engraved S.P.L., lifted it, found that it was heavy. Filled. Sam's "other" clothes. Those he'd brought with him from Boston for his vacation in Cancun.

Strange, but she wasn't in the least bit curious about these things. Samuel Prescott London was worlds away in so many respects. Before long she'd have to give him thought, but if she managed to help Sam find that middle ground they'd spoken of, Samuel Prescott London might not be as forbidding.

She took a deep breath, then let it out as she stepped back and skimmed the room a final time. It was a spartan existence Sam led here, so very different from anything even she had known. She wondered if she'd be able to make it, if she'd be able to settle into as bare-boned a life. Even now she felt restless. She was used to activity. If only Sam would return— "Chelsea! Chelsea, help!"

With a rush of adrenaline, she raced into the front room just as Sam came lumbering through the door.

"Hot!" he cried. "Damn it, these plates are hot!"

She was by his side instantly, not sure where to begin. One of his arms was piled with a conglomeration of cotton goods and henequen, the other balanced two dishes steaming with a brown concoction out of which stuck what she recognized to be tortillas.

Her hands hovered. "What should I take? Uh, here, let me have the dishes." She grabbed for one, then sucked in a breath. "You're right! It's hot!" She barely managed to get the dish to the table without dropping it. When she reached for the second one, she grasped it carefully by its edges.

Sam's relief was immediate. "Ahhhh. That's better. Tonia wanted to be sure they were warm when we ate, but I think she overdid it. So help me, the stuff sizzled when I ran through the rain." He lowered the pile of dry goods to the table and began to present them to Chelsea one by one. "A *huipile*," he said, shaking out the fine white dress and holding it up against him. "Tonia's sister embroidered it."

Chelsea beamed, her restlessness of moments before having vanished. Sam's presence was exciting in and of itself, not to mention the gifts he'd brought. "It's beautiful," she said, then, unable to resist, added, "And it looks like it'll fit you perfectly."

He grinned back, then winked—winked!—and Chelsea's insides crinkled up. "Someday I'll show you," he said as he pressed the dress into her hands and piled two more on top of it. "Tonia said she'd find a couple more tomorrow."

"Three is plenty! I feel guilty taking them from her."

"Don't be silly. She's thrilled you're here. Hmm, maybe she wasn't so keen on pairing me up with Juana either. Juana's her niece, by the way. Julia's daughter." He pronounced the 'J' like an 'H' in true Spanish fashion. "And she insists you have more. The women down here have a thing for cleanliness. They change their dresses several times a day."

"I read about the cleanliness thing. Even the people I saw on the streets looked immaculate." She was still smiling. "They must have one super Laundromat nearby."

Sam arched a mischievous brow. "You'll see it one day.... Here. A hat." He plopped it on her head. "Actually it's Felipe's—that's Aldana's cousin—and the women don't usually wear hats but I don't want you to sunburn—"

"Sunburn!" She took off the hat and added it to her pile. "It's been raining most of the time I've been here!"

"It won't be all the time, and when the sun comes out, it's strong. You can't see your nose right now, but it looks like you've had a small taste already."

Chelsea fingered the item in question. "Oh, God. A red nose to go along with blisters, mosquito welts and frizzy hair."

"It's pretty," Sam said softly. His gaze grew tender as it caressed her blond hair. "Not frizzy. Just curly, very natural and unadulterated." His eyes met hers, but just as Chelsea was beginning to tremble, he shifted to the one item remaining. "And last but not least," he added the bulky item to the collection in her arms, "your hammock.... I'm afraid that I can't offer you any, uh, underwear." He rubbed his mustache and wouldn't look at her. "Actually, I didn't have the guts to ask."

"That's okay. My own will be dry pretty soon."

"I hope so," he mumbled feelingly, then made to take the pile of things from her and put them in the back room.

"Wait!" She grappled for the *huipile* at the bottom. "I'm putting this on."

"I kind of like you in my shirt."

"I can sleep in your shirt. While we're dining," she drawled the word, "I'd like to look a little...nicer." She was going to say more feminine, but she could see from Sam's expression that he knew what she meant.

"You really do look great that way," he insisted, but he relinquished his hold on the *huipile* and let her precede him toward the back of the house. "Don't be long. If that food gets cold, Tonia will have my neck."

"Fat chance," Chelsea quipped, meaning it on both scores. She had a strong feeling that Tonia, Aldana, Julia, Felipe, Juana and everyone else in the *pueblito* adored Sam. And there was no way those steaming dishes of whatever-they-were were going to cool in the heat.

Feeling absurdly light-headed, she dodged the raindrops and made for the outhouse, where she checked to see if her underpants were dry—they weren't—and drew on the *huipile* anyway.

Had she been held captive and naked for a full year, she wouldn't have appreciated the dress more. It fit her well, if not as loosely as some of those she'd seen. The neckline embroidery fell gently to the upper swell of her breasts. Her waist was undecipherable, but her hips filled the fabric with room to squat—she experimented, then prayed she wouldn't be doing much squatting because her thighs and calves ached so—and the hem skimmed the tops of her knees, leaving her legs bare. She half wished she had more of a tan to show off against the white, but her busy days back home hadn't left time for sunbathing. What little color she'd picked up since she'd arrived was pink.

Well, she reasoned, pink was feminine, too, and it matched several of the threads used in decorating the *huipile*. Tucking her chin in to study the embroidery more closely, she marveled at the skill it entailed.

"Chelsea? Are you still there?"

Smiling, she opened the outhouse door and sprinted into the hut.

"I was wondering if you'd fallen in," Sam said worriedly. "There isn't a problem, is there? You look great!"

"Thanks. I guess I got caught up admiring this thing. Did Julia really embroider it herself?"

He was ushering her toward the front room but his eyes didn't leave her for a minute. "Uh-huh. The women all do their own stitchery. It may be a forgotten art back home, but here it's alive and well." He gave a half bow as he eased her onto the bench by the table. "Dinner is served, Senorita."

She gave a shy smile as he lowered himself onto the bench opposite her. She almost wished he'd sat closer—there was plenty of room on her bench—though with a round table and a long bench only one person could comfortably rest his elbows. And, of course, there was the matter of sanity. A small matter. Actually, a moot one, since facing Sam was nearly as delicious as sitting next to him. He was delicious, all right, she decided, then looked at the food before her.

"Looks...interesting. What is it?"

"A kind of pork stew with black beans and all kinds of other lovelies in it." He extracted a tortilla and made to dig in. "Go ahead. Tell me what you think."

Chelsea followed his example and reached for a tortilla, then, again following his lead, used it to scoop up the thick stew. There was a certain irony in her ignorance of the eating style, she mused; had she met Samuel Prescott London, she'd probably have had to let him lead her through small forks and medium-sized forks and large forks.

"Mmm. Not bad," she said, thoughtfully licking her lips. "Actually, it's pretty good." She dipped the tortilla a second time, using it as a spoon to carry the stew to her mouth.

"You picked a good night to come. Chicken and pork are the two major meals here, but we don't have them all the time. Often dinner consists simply of *frijoles*—beans mashed into a stew—which isn't to say that it's not good. You build up an appetite when you've been working all day, so *anything* tastes good, but pork or chicken, even venison when someone's lucky enough to get it, makes things special."

"I take it the Maya still grow everything themselves."

"Just about. There's a certain pride to it." He grinned. "A couple of times I've driven into Cancun and brought back full meals for everyone from one fancy restaurant or another. It wasn't that I wanted the food—I've eaten French and Italian and Polynesian enough to last a lifetime—but I thought it would be a treat for my friends here. And I wanted to see their reaction to it."

When he paused, deep in thought, she prodded. "Well? How did they react?"

He snapped from his reverie. "Much as I'd expected, actually. They smiled and laughed and finished every last bite and complimented me and thanked me profusely."

"And...?"

"They were smiling and laughing with every bit as much enthusiasm over their *pollo pibil* the next day. The first time it happened, I was surprised, which goes to show what a snob I was. The second time I was relieved." He grew thoughtful again, though this time he shared his thoughts. "I wouldn't want to change a thing about these people. They're beautiful. I mean, *really* beautiful. They're not ambitious or grappling, and they wouldn't begin to know about selfishness. They've chosen this way of life. *Chosen* it. They're happy. And healthy." His jaw flexed. "They don't have tension headaches or high blood pressure or nervous breakdowns."

Something about the way he'd spoken at the last prompted a soft inquiry from Chelsea. "Is that what happened to you?"

He gnawed on the inside of his cheek for a minute before answering. "I didn't get as far as the breakdown, but I was on my way, I think. I had the headaches and the high blood pressure. I was a jumble of nerves behind a polished facade."

"Why? What caused it?"

He sighed, took another mouthful of stew, then rested his arms on the table. "I was driven. I had to make good at everything I did. But 'good' is relative. You attain it only to find that it's not what you thought, that something else is better, so you push yourself on and on. I didn't seem to have a touchstone, someone or something to put it all into perspective, someone to tell me, 'Hey, man, *enough.*' And I didn't have an outlet for the tension roiling around inside."

If all of her future patients were as intelligent, as perceptive, Chelsea mused, she'd be collecting unemployment. "But now that you know what you need, isn't it possible you could find it at home?"

"I don't know. I'm afraid I'll go back and get caught up in the same rat race again. It's a treadmill. You slow down or lose your footing and, bam, you're off."

"But would that be so bad? 'Off,' for you, may be higher than most other people ever aspire to—unnh, I'm sorry, I shouldn't have said that." She promptly took Sam's side. "We all have dreams and aspirations, most of which are instilled in us from birth. It's hard to change basic perceptions of success."

"Precisely. I'd have to totally overhaul my life, and when it comes to the business, at least, there are other people involved."

"You could always sell out—"

"But it's *my* business," he cut in, and Chelsea watched with slow-growing horror as his features transformed. "I started it from scratch and built it to what it is today. Sure, David's done his thing, but the biggest and the best of the projects we've taken on have been won through sheer grit on my part! The business wouldn't die if I left, but it sure wouldn't stay ahead of the others. I'm telling you, there's a war goin' on out there, and only the smartest and the fittest survive!" His voice, which had risen steadily, suddenly dropped. "Chelsea? What's wrong?"

"Oh, Sam," she whispered, stricken. "You should see yourself. The tension's back. All of it. I can see it around your eyes and on the bridge of your nose. Just like in that picture I saw. You were all but gritting your teeth when you talked just now, and...and...look at your hands!"

He did. Very slowly and consciously he unclenched his fists. Then he closed his eyes and hung his head. "You see? I can't go back. Nothing would change. It'd be suicide."

She ached for him, and for herself. "Maybe if you found that touchstone..."

He shook his head for a minute, then suddenly snapped it erect. "Hell, I'm getting morose in my old age. This was to be a celebration dinner. Your arrival is *definitely* worth celebrating." He met her gaze, hesitated, then slowly smiled. "Better?"

"Much," she said. "The other man scared me."

He accepted the dichotomy. "I thought *I* scared you."

"What you do to me scares me...like getting me to go around with frizzy hair, to eat pork stew with a tortilla for a spoon, to sleep in a hammock...I'm not sure if that's going to work, Sam. If I'm sore now, just think of what it'll be like to tip onto the floor every few minutes!"

He laughed then, and he was once again the Sam she adored. "You're just hung up on that backyard-swing variety—no pun intended. These hammocks are different. Larger and deeper, but more giving. They envelop you like a cocoon. Trust me, Chelsea. You won't have any problems. Especially after you've had a glassful of that liqueur I was telling you about."

"You're planning on getting me drunk?"

"Me? I'd never do a thing like that, especially since tomorrow's a work day. You'll have your first lesson on how the Maya live...as a matter of fact, shouldn't you be writing down all the things I've been telling you?"

"I will," Chelsea said in a teasing tone that deftly masked the guilt she felt. "I'm going to let it all—" she gestured appropriately "—stew around in my mind for a bit. Once I've digested it, I'll make notes. If I have questions, or can't remember something or other, I can ask you."

"Please do," he invited, then glared at her dish. Now eat! The entire population of this *pueblito* is looking forward to meeting you tomorrow, and if you show up looking skinny—"

"Unnh! Slim. Not skinny. Slim." They shared a chuckle, then dipped into the stew. But Chelsea was thinking about the "entire population" Sam had mentioned. "How many of them are there?"

"Twenty-six by last count, though there's another expected any day now. Hey, don't look so scared. They'll love you. They wanted to meet you tonight, but I told them you'd melt in the rain—"

"You didn't!"

"I did." Quite nonchalantly he continued eating, talking between bites. "I think the men actually believed me. They remembered how we found you crumpled on the ground this afternoon."

"I wasn't melting," she argued, thrusting a tortilla at a particularly large piece of pork. "I was just...just frustrated and angry and tired and sore. I was convinced right then that I was lost forever in the jungle and that it was only a matter of time before wild beasties would come out and devour me limb by limb."

Sam threw back his head and laughed. It was such a hearty sound that it dissolved Chelsea's crossness, which had been half put-on anyway.

"*Are* there beasts out there?" she asked cautiously.

"Some, but not this close to the settlements, and in any case they don't attack unless provoked. You weren't trying to steal some mommy monkey's baby, were you?"

"Of course not."

"So you were safe."

"That's good to know."

"Of course, you have to keep an eye out for rattlesnakes. The ancient Maya worshiped them. Did you know?"

"I didn't," she stated with distaste.

He finished chewing what was in his mouth, then gestured with a tortilla. "And another thing. Watch out for *garrapatas*."

"*¿Garrapatas?*" She mimicked his pronunciation, though she was feeling slightly wary and purposely exaggerated the roll of her 'r's.

"Mmm. That's a type of tick that lurks in the growth at the side of the road. Don't brush against them if you can help it. They come right off when you take a bath, but, man, do they itch."

"Thank you for the warning." She curled up her lip. "Are there any *other* things you'd care to tell me about?"

"Just the rats, but they do their foraging at night and are usually gone by sunup."

Chelsea dropped her tortilla in the remains of her stew. Had it been a fork, it would have rattled against the plate. "Rats. That's great. On second thought, a hammock must be nice. You can pull it around yourself and pray."

Sam reached out and gently touched her chin. "I'm teasing you, Chels. It's not all that bad. For what it's worth, I haven't suffered a single bite in all the time I've been here."

"Very reassuring."

She didn't know if he caught her sarcasm because he was looking at her dish, his own being quite empty. "Are you done?"

"I believe so."

He reached out. "May I?"

She shoved the dish forward. "Be my guest." Then she couldn't resist. "Of course, God only knows what kinds of germs I've got. There was a rash of flu last month, and some fellow at the bar last week was coughing in my face, and you can never tell if you're carrying some other kind of ugly disease."

Sam was already dipping into the dish. "I've kissed you, so I'm already exposed. I'll take my chances." With that, he put a huge chunk of stew-laden tortilla into his mouth and chewed with relish.

Elbow on the table, hand beneath her chin, Chelsea took pleasure in watching him. He looked almost boyish, eating enthusiastically, grinning at her from time to time. But he was manly as well, always manly. She wondered if every woman found him such, or whether she was just...smitten.

She was still pondering that question when he gathered the empty dishes together, piled them outside the front door, and went to fetch the liqueur. She wasn't sure where he'd stored it—perhaps at the bottom of his trunk—but he returned not only with a bottle but with two glasses, and pillows stuck under each arm. He dropped the pillows by the wall and nudged them with is foot until they were propped up, then sank down and motioned for her to follow. She'd no sooner seated herself beside him than he'd poured the liqueur and offered her a glass. She took it, staring at its dark contents.

"Is this something else I should be wary of?" She raised the glass and peered distrustfully through the liquid at the bottom. "There isn't a worm in here, is there?"

He laughed. "No worm. That's mescal, from the maguey plant. This is *xtabentun*."

"*Xtabentun*." She tugged a tidbit of information from the file in her mind. "In ancient days it was given to virgins before they were sacrificed. Since I'm not a virgin, I guess I'm safe. What's it made of?"

"It's a derivative of honey. And it's flavored with anise. We cultivate the honey here. You'll see it for yourself tomorrow."

"Oh God. Bees."

"Not to worry. They're stingless."

"I don't know, Sam. At the rate I'm going, even a stingless bee might raise welts."

"You'll be fine," he soothed, relaxing back against a pillow.

With care Chelsea sampled the *xtabentun*. In spite of a slightly bitter aftertaste, it was suprisingly good. She nodded her approval, then took a less guarded sip. Taking her cue from Sam, who looked exquisitely comfortable, she lay down against the pillow he'd set for her, stretched out her legs and propped the glass on her stomach.

"Tell me what you did when you first got to Cancun, Sam. I know you stayed at the Camino Real; that was the only stop anyone in Boston knew of. Did you go there with the intention of staying a week and flying home, or had you planned all along to move inland?"

"When I left Boston, I only knew I had to get away. My reservations were for a week. The hotel was able to give me a three-day extension, but even then I'd barely begun to relax." He raised his glass to his lips, took a measured drink, then turned the glass in his hand. "Relaxation doesn't come easy when you've never really had any practice at it. I used to prowl around Cancun looking for something to do. I *had to have something to do*. Lying on the beach wasn't *accomplishing* anything—so my mind said, even though I was physically exhausted and could have used five straight days of sleep." He gave a soft snort. "I'm afraid I didn't get much out of Cancun. I've been back for several hours at a stretch since, and I do like the place. Maybe when we drive in to pick up your things, we can see a little more."

"I'd like that," Chelsea said. "I'm afraid I gave it about as much of a chance as you did. I was so preoccupied with finding my luggage, then finding you...I don't think I took even five minutes to just sit and relax. I'm not a relaxer, either, so I know what you mean."

"You'll learn," he responded smugly, and for a minute Chelsea wondered if he intended to force-feed her the technique, but she didn't want to think of it. She wanted to think of him. He seemed very relaxed at the moment, and very open.

"Did you know where you were going when you left Cancun?"

"Only that I didn't want to go home. I decided to drive to Merida, maybe see if it had something for me that Cancun didn't."

"Did it?"

"In a roundabout way. The city itself is much larger. It was interesting enough, but what really intrigued me were the little villages I saw on my way there, *pueblitos* like this one. Then I happened to bump into Rafael—Professor Paredes— and we hit it off and started talking. He knew all about the Maya and got me hooked. It was at his suggestion that I moved to one of the villages, but at the first one I was sharing a hut with a family of six, and at the second, the family my hut belonged to returned from visiting relatives in Belize. So I came here. And stayed."

"The Maya welcomed you from the first?"

"They did in each of the places I stayed. Maybe it helped that I insisted on paying rent, but I think it was more than that. I learned their language. I did my fair share of work. I think they saw me as a friend, rather than a spectator. And what I got in return, well, no amount of money could have bought that."

Chelsea tipped her head on the pillow until she faced him. Their voices were quiet, the air intimate. She felt surprisingly relaxed and wondered if the *xtabentun* was responsible. There was a certain lethargy to her limbs. She doubted she could have stood up and walked away if she'd tried.

"What did you get, Sam? How did it come about?"

With his cheek nestled in the pillow, he let his gaze flow into hers. "It was like culture shock. One day I was wearing designer shorts and shirts, the next I wore no-name pants and a *guayabera*. I locked up my suitcase and haven't opened it since. I think I needed it that way, cold turkey."

"Was it hard?"

"Was it ever! For a couple of days I didn't really know what was going on. I couldn't do anything but sleep, and when I woke up I walked around like a zombie, not knowing what to do, not having the strength to do much anyway. The Maya I was with at the time just let me be. They saw I was fed, but they didn't ask a thing of me. In time, partly out of boredom, I guess, I started chipping in with the work. It was the best medicine in the world. Being outdoors all day, using muscles I hadn't known were there—"

"You must have burned."

"Hmm?"

"Linda said you sun-burned easily."

He sent her a mock scowl. "How personal was that talk you two had anyway?"

"Not very. But we were trying to imagine what it was you were doing down here, and she mentioned that you'd never done well in the sun."

"Like too many other things, I'd never given it a chance. Sure, I burned at the start, but then my skin became conditioned. I don't have to think about it now."

Chelsea shifted her cheek against the pillow. Her gaze broke from his to slowly glide from one to another of his features. "Your tan looks nice. You look younger than your pictures.... It's odd, actually."

"How so?"

Her eyes continued to roam his face as she struggled to put her thoughts into words. "In the pictures I saw, your skin was perfectly smooth. Now I see creases," she traced them with one finger, "on your forehead, at the corners of your eyes and in your cheeks when you smile. You look more mature, but *younger*." She scrunched up her nose. "Does that make sense?"

"I don't know," he said softly.

"It's like...like your face is alive now and the lines are from living. Like you're *experiencing* life, and the satisfaction shows up on your face." She blushed, but something drove her on. "I like the mustache, too. It makes you look adventurous."

Recapturing her gaze, Sam held it for long moments. Then, with a nearly inaudible moan, he slid his arm beneath her and drew her close to rest in the crook of his shoulder.

"Sam, I didn't mean—"

"It's okay, Chels," he soothed. He took the glass from her fingers and set it on the ground behind her, then snuggled her more comfortably in his arms. "Just lie here. Let me feel you against me. It's been a long, long time since I've felt at peace this way."

There was no way on earth Chelsea could have argued with him. His chest was a far better pillow than the real one, and his long arm encircled her, making her feel wanted and needed and protected. She, too, felt at peace. Comfortable. Languorous.

"You okay?" he breathed against her temple.

"Mmmmm." She put her hand on his chest, resting her fingers on the fine cushion of hair there. It wasn't a sensual kind of contact, nor was the way he held her. Rather, it was a quiet closeness, a comfort, an unspoken statement of the beauty of human understanding.

Within minutes, Chelsea was fast asleep.

When she awoke, it was morning. The sun shone through the cracks in the wall, but she didn't notice, because the first thing that struck her was that she was encased in a fully closed web. Groggy and disoriented, she panicked.

5

REACTING PURELY ON INSTINCT, Chelsea began to struggle. She kicked out at her webbed cocoon, elbowed it, shoved it away from her face. When it seemed to be closing in on her she began to claw at it, to no avail. Finally she blinked, half-expecting to find herself eye to eye with an oversized tarantula, then blinked again...at which point she grew absolutely still. Only her eyeballs moved then, tracing a slow, cautious arc.

Letting out a ragged breath, she sagged limply against the pillow beneath her head. "I don't believe it," she muttered. "He's made his point.... Sam?" she called. "Sam!" The point, of course, was that she wouldn't be falling out of the hammock. Point made, the problem had reversed itself. "How do I get *out* of this thing?" she wailed, but no one answered, no one came running. It appeared that she was on her own.

Part of her was grateful that she'd been spared the embarrassment. Sam would have laughed, and rightfully so. She must have looked like an absolute fool, writhing the way she had. Her *huipile* was twisted in wrinkles around her hips, her hair curled wildly about her face, her fingers were taut against the weave of the hammock—even *she* would have laughed, had it not been for the task ahead.

Carefully she studied her webbed cage. The hammock rose high on both sides of her, but mosquito netting had been drawn fully around and over it, creating the cocoon-effect she'd found so frightening. After close examination, she located its seam and cautiously peeled it back. Then, determined to take the hammock by surprise, she quickly swung her legs over its edge and stumbled to her feet.

With a sigh of relief Chelsea flexed her back and stretched gingerly, then bent forward and braced her hands on her knees. She felt weak and distinctly logy—an aftermath of the *xtabentun*? No, she'd had too little. Her hangover, she decided, was simply from the excitement and exertion and tension of the day before.

Straightening, she slowly looked around. The hut was empty, though a glance toward the front door revealed several children playing beyond, in the clearing at the *pueblito's* hub.

It was then that she recalled her imminent debut.

Looking frantically around the back room, she spotted the spare *huipiles* folded on the table. Grabbing one, she made a beeline for the shower. By the time she returned to the hut, she felt vaguely presentable.

"You're up," Sam said, grinning from his post by the door to the front room. He wore the garb of the Maya—loose pants, untucked shirt and sandals—and looked magnificently rugged. In Chelsea's slightly biased view, he also looked disgustingly awake. "Sleep well?"

"Aside from waking up in an absolute panic at being caught in a grotesque spider's web, yes." She tried to sound annoyed, but didn't quite make it. She was too self-conscious, too aware of Sam.

"You found your way out."

"Eventually.... I fell asleep on you last night?" she asked more timidly.

"Sure did. It was nice."

"I...don't remember much."

"You closed your eyes and were out like a light. Feeling better today?"

"Still tired, and a little sore, I guess, but I'm okay. I, uh," she hesitated, "I helped myself to your stuff. You know, soap and shampoo and comb. I hope you don't mind."

His eyes were sparkling and he hadn't stopped grinning. Chelsea wondered whether he'd had something intoxicating for breakfast. "Of course not. Feel free to use anything you find.... Are you hungry?"

"I'm not a breakfast eater. What time is it, anyway?"

"Eight-thirty."

She looked amazed. "I thought for sure I'd slept till at least ten or eleven! How long have you been up?"

"Since dawn. I was out with the men checking on some of the corn fields. Tonia should be ready for us by now, though. All set?"

Chelsea looked down and rocked back on her heels. With her sandals—which she'd wiped as clean as possible, given the dirt they'd collected the day before—in place on her feet, her underwear fresh beneath the clean *huipile*, and her hair as neat as it could be, given the sultriness of the air, she felt as ready as she'd ever be.

"Guess so," she sighed.

He came forward and draped an arm around her shoulders. "You look terrific, Chels. You'll knock 'em dead." He ushered her gently toward the front door. "Just relax and remember that these are some of the most friendly and unpretentious people on earth. There's nothing to be nervous about."

"I don't know why I'm nervous," she began, grateful that Sam seemed to understand. "I meet new people all the time, and they're usually pretty demanding." A case in point was Sam's mother, yet Chelsea hadn't been half as nervous when she'd entered the Wellesley Hills estate and confronted that formidable woman as she felt now. She guessed it had something to do with the culture warp here, and perhaps the fact that these people meant so much to Sam.

"Will you interpret for me?" she asked, raising beseechful eyes to his. "I don't know much more than *muchas gracias*, *por favor* and *habla usted ingles*."

"I'll be right beside you. Relax. It'll be fun."

"I wish I had my blow dryer," she mumbled as they emerged from the hut into the morning sun.

"You don't need it," he stated, gently but firmly, and gave her shoulder a squeeze. "Chin up. You'll do fine."

To Chelsea's surprise, she did. As it happened, the villagers were nearly as shy with her as she was with them. They seemed slightly in awe of her, and she wondered how much of that was because she was with Sam. She didn't object, though in other circumstances she would have readily exerted her independence. She sensed this to be a different society, one in which women's liberation was unknown, so she gratefully let Sam lead the way.

Breakfast, which was taken on benches not far from Tonia's stone fireplace, consisted of tortillas and fruit. "Tortillas are a staple," Sam explained, then corrected himself, speaking softly while those around them continued to eat. "Actually, corn is the staple, but more often than not it's soaked and softened and grilled into tortillas."

"I read about the ancient Maya doing that."

"It's still the same.... The oranges come from the trees over there." He tossed his head toward the far end of the *pueblito*. "Other mornings there are bananas or pineapples or papayas."

"And tortillas."

"Always tortillas."

They shared a smile, then set to eating. But Chelsea couldn't keep from looking around at the gathered group. "They *are* beautiful, Sam," she murmured. "The children especially. Such burnished skin. And large eyes—they've all got such large, gorgeous eyes." She smiled at one little boy and he promptly smiled back.

"Better be careful of that," Sam warned teasingly. "He'll follow you around for the rest of the day."

"I don't mind. He's precious."

"You like kids?"

"I love them. They're so fresh and innocent. It's kind of scary to think what awful things can happen to them as they get older."

"You mean physically?"

"More...emotionally. The world is big and dangerous and confusing, and there are so many choices to make—" She caught herself. "But I suppose it's different here. Maybe these people *are* better off." She caught the eye of a young girl who'd been staring at her. Shy, the girl looked away, but not before she too had smiled. "She's got a gold lining on her front tooth. Several of the others have the same. Didn't I read something about that?"

"Probably. It's a form of decoration, very prestigious. Both sexes do it; they've been doing it for centuries. Gold, silver...I'm told the ancients even used jade."

"I think I'd die. I hate the dentist."

"Dental decoration is the least of it. Though it's not done as much now, it used to be that crossed eyes were considered a mark of great beauty. Mothers used to hang jewels between the eyes of their daughters in hopes they'd become cross-eyed." He chuckled. "When I was a little kid I had to wear a patch over one eye to strengthen the other so it *wouldn't* cross. Boy, did I hate that."

Chelsea tipped her head and studied him, a dangerous thing to do. He looked so thoroughly male that for a minute she nearly forgot the purpose of her study. "I don't know," she said at last. "I think you'd look rakish, like a pirate, if you wore one now."

"Pirates turn you on?"

"I don't know. I've never met one."

"They say there used to be scores of them over in Isla Mujeres. You haven't gone there, have you?" Isla Mujeres was a short ferry ride from Cancun.

"I haven't gone *anywhere*."

"Not even to the ruins?"

"Nope."

"Then I'll have to take you. They're fascinating. The ancient Maya were positively brilliant. Astrologers, mathematicians, engineers. Wait till you see."

She knew she'd look forward to it. She knew she'd look forward to *anything* she'd do with Sam. "Do the people today still worship the ancient gods?"

"Some do, but the majority were converted to Christianity years ago. It's really a shame, but I probably know more about the ancient Maya and their accomplishments than the average present-day Maya does. When the ancient civilization died, its records and books were destroyed along with it. Glyphs have been found in many of the ruins, but we haven't been able to fully translate them."

Chelsea would have asked more, but at that moment their breakfast companions were starting to rise.

"Come," Sam said, "I want to introduce you to Reni. She lives across the way and speaks a little English. When she heard you were here, she all but begged me to let her show you around."

Chelsea had hoped Sam would do that. "Where will you be?" she asked, feeling a resurgence of that strange insecurity.

"I'll be working around and about. Not far. A little later I'll stop by Xcan to see if your car's been returned, and make sure the hotel's checked you out."

"Maybe I should go with you," she offered hopefully.

He shook his head, but his upper lip—and in turn his mustache—was toying with a smile. "The women will expect you to be most curious to see what they do, so let's indulge them. Don't worry. I can take care of things on my end, and you'll be fine."

"I know." But her tone wasn't overly confident. Given her choice, she would have opted to go with Sam. Either that or go right back to sleep. She couldn't seem to shake her muzziness, and her limbs didn't feel completely coordinated.

"Just think of the stuff you'll be able to pick up for your article," he reminded her, and she forced a smile.

"You're right. I get so caught up in things, that I seem to keep forgetting that." Better she should say it than he, and she knew it to be true. If she'd been a legitimate writer, she'd have been scribbling notes, asking non-stop questions, eagerly anticipating any and every exposure to the day-to-day living of the Maya. She wondered if Sam suspected she was less than dedicated to her work. He should only know...

"Reni will remind you," Sam quipped. He'd taken her hand and was leading her toward the spot where Tonia and two of the other women stood talking.

Chelsea listened as he conversed in Mayan with them for a minute. She could see that whatever he'd said pleased them, and she added her own grateful thanks for breakfast, which Sam translated easily. Then they left Aldana's hut and made their way across the clearing.

Reni was waiting, at least Chelsea assumed the young girl standing patiently in the shade of the hut to be she. She was definitely a girl, with smooth skin and long black hair, and as the other women did, she wore a brightly decorated *huipile*.

Her eyes glowed and she broke into an open smile when they neared. Chelsea guessed her to be in her late teens.

"Reni, I'd like you to meet Chelsea. Chelsea, Reni."

Chelsea smiled back at the girl, whose eyes hadn't left her for a minute. This surprised her, since Sam had to be far more exciting, indeed drool material. "I'm pleased to meet you, Reni," she said, then shot a hesitant glance at Sam.

"It's okay. She wants you to speak English. She's been learning as much from me as she can, but she's probably thrilled to have a second teacher. Go on, Reni," he said very gently. "You know what to say."

"I'm...pleased to meet you too...Chelsea," the young girl responded. There was a shyness to her voice, but a quiet dignity as well, a trait Chelsea was coming to associate with the Maya. "I'm very glad...you're here." She rolled her 'r's slightly more than necessary, but otherwise, Chelsea realized, her accent was excellent. "If you come with me," Reni went on, "I will show you...ar...around."

"I'd like that," Chelsea said with a smile.

"Then I'll leave you two," Sam injected. "Reni, thanks. Chels, I'll catch you later."

Chelsea nodded and watched him leave. He walked in an unhurried fashion, looking almost as though he was going off to spend the day doing nothing. She tried to conjure an image of him in a three-piece suit, striding quickly down the corridor toward his office, but the image was faulty at best and she soon abandoned it. Aside from that one relapse last night, the Sam she knew seemed totally alien to that other life. For the time being, she was content to leave things that way—particularly when, in a thoroughly endearing gesture, he returned to her moments later with the hat that had been appropriated for her use and a palmful of lotion that he very gently spread on her nose, arms and legs. Chelsea protested that she could do it herself, but Sam seemed to take such enjoyment in doing it—and Reni in laughing as he worked—that she gave in. It was all she could do, though, to hold still under his ministration, which left her warm and tingling all over. When he departed with a devilish grin and a wink, she decided she'd take this Sam over any other man.

Reni proved to be a pleasant guide and companion. Once her initial shyness wore off, she was enthusiastic and eager to please, acting as though it was a high honor to be allowed to serve as Chelsea's guide.

She and Chelsea quickly found a comfortable pace of communication, asking for and repeating words without hesitation as they walked leisurely through the *pueblito*. Since Chelsea was aiding Reni with her English, she felt it only fair that she herself should learn Mayan. If she was to be here for a time, she wanted to be able to communicate on some simple level with the natives.

Theoretically it should have been a leisurely day for Chelsea. Though one activity seemed to flow into the next, each was undertaken slowly, without hurry. No one rushed. Time seemed a limitless commodity. Aside from the ongoing endeavor of cooking, if a particular activity wasn't finished one day, it would be the next, or the next, or the next.

Chelsea wasn't one to sit still and watch, or perhaps her system simply refused to slow down. She chipped in with grinding the leaves of the henequen plant, which Sam and the other men had harvested, and helped spread the results to dry into the fiber from which rope would be made. She took her turn at weaving. She even tried her hand at embroidering. She walked with the women to where racks of corn had been left to dry. Filling a large woven bag with ears, she hoisted it onto her back and, bracing the bag's wide strap on her forehead as the other women did, carted the corn back to the huts. Once there, she followed the others' lead and scraped the kernels off, setting them to soften in a pot of water and lime.

Reni readily explained what was being done, translated instructions and answered her questions, though there were long periods of silence during which everyone worked comfortably. The silence was golden; it was warm and gentle and companionable. Though the women stopped from time to time to chat softly in Mayan, they obviously felt no need to make conversation for conversation's sake. It was also evident that they thoroughly enjoyed what they were doing. Smiles were ever-present, as were nods of gratitude and encouragement for Chelsea, who was inevitably placed in the center of activity.

Sam reappeared with the men at lunchtime and stayed around during that quiet time in the middle of the day when the sun was at its height and the heat made work not worth the effort. He took Chelsea for a walk then, telling her how he'd spent his morning, asking her what she'd seen and learned. Chelsea enjoyed their time together because she was tired and Sam's nearness seemed to give her energy. But he was gone again before long—into Valladolid in the Jeep with Felipe this time—and she didn't see him until several hours later when he fetched her and led her back to the hut. There he presented her with a new comb and toothbrush, an oversized T-shirt with Cancun emblazoned in hot pink on it and a pair of matching shorts, plus several pairs of underwear.

"I thought you didn't have the guts to ask," Chelsea teased.

Sam's neck grew red beneath his tan. "They were sitting right there on the shelf, so I didn't have to ask," he countered defensively. "They're probably not as pretty as your own, and to tell you the truth I kinda like the idea of your going without—"

"Thank you, Sam," she enunciated pointedly, then her tone softened. "Thank you for all of these things, but you really shouldn't have. My luggage is probably already in Cancun, and—"

"It's not there yet. I called. I'll try again in a couple of days."

Chelsea was more annoyed at the thought of her missing luggage then actually missing the luggage itself. What with the things Sam had bought, and those she'd been loaned by Tonia, she had everything she needed, and, oddly, the luggage seemed a stark reminder of a life she didn't really want to think about.

"You look tired," Sam commented, studying her closely.

"I am," she admitted, though his scrutiny did wonders for her energy level. "It must be all the excitement—I take that back. Excitement's the wrong word to use in describing life here. It's fascinating to me, but very quiet, easy-going, almost serene. I always thought sheer survival had to be a struggle. But these people take it all in stride. *Slow* stride. They're unhassled, very comfortable. They seem to work at will. I think I'm beginning to understand what you were saying. I do envy them, in a way."

"Was Reni a help?"

"Oh, yes. Just knowing that she could help me communicate was a comfort. I like her.... She's very curious about the outside world, isn't she?"

Sam arched a brow in amusement. "You got that impression, did you?"

"After a while, you can't miss it. Oh, she carefully spaces her questions, but they still come. Do you think she's planning on leaving one day?"

"I'm not sure." His expression grew troubled. "She was married two years ago to a fellow from Chetumal. He was one of a group of *chicleros* who'd wandered in this direction on a spree."

"*¿Chicleros?*"

"They gather chicle—you know, the stuff chewing gum is made of. It comes from trees, like sap. *Chicleros* have traditionally been thought of as being the most violent of men. Fights erupted among them at the least provocation, and murder was a fact of life. Things have eased on that score in the last twenty years, but from what I understand, Reni's parents weren't terribly thrilled when Rufino swept her away. She returned alone, a widow, three months later."

"He was *murdered*?"

"He died when his truck overturned on the highway."

"Poor Reni! She didn't mention anything about it today."

"She wouldn't. It's behind her. These people don't dwell on the past—that's another thing I admire about them, though it's a shame they don't know more about their heritage. They live for the present, one day at a time. Except Reni. I think she dreams of different things, maybe about things she saw during the short time she was with Rufino. It was during that time that she learned a little English—whether from Rufino or someone else, I don't know. I wouldn't be surprised if there'd been an American somewhere in the picture. And I wouldn't be surprised if Reni has her sights set on the States."

"Do you think she's in touch with someone there?"

"No, no. I'm sure she's not. But I think she may have visions of something larger, something not more glamorous but certainly more, shall we say, exciting, for lack of a better word." He shook his head sadly. "I'd hate to see that. She'd be in for a fall."

"Not necessarily. I suppose it would depend on where she went and what she did."

"Come on, Chelsea. A simple girl like Reni would *die* up there. She's totally ill-prepared to do anything relative to that kind of life!"

"But she's bright. She could go to school and learn."

"And then what?" He propped his hands on his hips. "She'd be alone. Here she's surrounded by people who love her. Always by people who love her. And even *aside* from the emotional isolation, she'd be starting at the bottom of the barrel—not that life at the top is much different from the dregs."

"I think you're biased," Chelsea argued quietly.

"Damned right I am!"

"So why are you encouraging her to learn more English?"

That took him aback, and his scowl slowly eased. He shrugged, then ran a hand through his hair. "Maybe," he murmured, "maybe because it's fun and because...because education, broadening oneself, has been ingrained in me." His eyes hardened once more. "Which is not to say that it's necessarily right. Life is good here. I don't think she'd find anything better."

"Life here is *different*. Yes, it's good. But that doesn't mean the other has to be bad. You're thinking in terms of black and white again, Sam—all or nothing. But that's not the way it is. There are many people back home who are happy with the lives they've chosen. Sure, they may be a little more hassled, and there may be worries and demands that people here don't have. But that's all part of a more sophisticated life, and the reward of success is all the greater."

"*That* is a debatable point," Sam declared, gray eyes flashing.

Emerging from her own involvement in the argument to realize what she'd provoked, Chelsea grew quickly silent. For one thing, she sensed she'd come on too strongly; if she hoped to convince Sam to return to Boston, it would have to be done gradually and subtly. For another, she saw the lines of tension on his face, and the realization that she'd helped put them there pained her. She dropped her gaze and began to pick at her thumb nail.

"Anyway," she said softly, "I don't think Reni's going anywhere yet. She's very young—"

"She's eighteen," Sam snapped, "and most of her peers are wives and mothers. If that's not an adult job, tell me what is."

Chelsea tucked her thumb into her palm and closed her fingers around it. She didn't want to fight with him, especially not now. Their friendship was so new, precarious in spite of the physical attraction linking them. To chance blowing it all—her stomach was in knots just thinking of it.

"I, uh, I think we're expected for dinner," she murmured without looking at him. The last thing she felt like doing was eating, but she didn't know what else to do or say to defuse the air about them.

For a minute there was silence. When at last Chelsea looked up, she found Sam eyeing her strangely. Quickly he looked away. "Right," he muttered, and promptly started off for Aldana's hut, leaving Chelsea to follow.

Dinner was no more silent than any other meal had been, yet for the first time Chelsea was uncomfortable. Sam said little, other than to occasionally offer pleasant comments in Mayan or respond to those directed his way. He smiled, but not at Chelsea, who did the best she could with the thick corn soup that had been served. As soon as she could politely do so she excused herself to return to the hut.

Sam remained behind, which didn't bother Chelsea because she was thoroughly exhausted and wanted nothing more than to shower and change into Sam's shirt, now her nightgown, and go to sleep. Her stomach was upset and she had a headache. Climbing into the hammock seemed like child's play compared to the challenge of relaxing.

Actually, she fell asleep quickly, exhaustion prevailing over her stomach and head. But she awoke in the middle of the night feeling positively ill.

The hut was pitch black, though the platinum moon did a passable job lighting her way to the outhouse. By the time she returned, feeling her way to her hammock and tumbling into it, she was too uncomfortable to think about Sam. The night sounds of the jungle—the rustle of leaves, the anguished call of the *tapacamino* bird—might well have drowned out the sound of his breathing, even if the pounding in her head hadn't.

She shifted on the hammock, tucking her knees up to alleviate the ache in her stomach, but the night felt stifling, so she soon stretched out again and tried to cool off.

It didn't work.

She threw an arm over her eyes, which hurt even though they were closed. Then she shifted once more, shoving at the pillow beneath her head, trying in vain to get comfortable. Before long she was headed for the outhouse again.

She never knew how she made it back to the hut, but she must have because the next thing she knew she was huddled in her hammock, clutching her stomach, wanting to die.

"Chelsea—"

With a loud gasp, she spun around. "Sam! My God! You scared me!"

"What's wrong, Chels? You've been up twice now. Are you sick?" He smoothed her hair from her forehead and left his hand there instead.

She could barely make out his dark form, but his voice and his touch was proof of his presence. "I feel awful, Sam! I'm sorry, I didn't mean to wake you—"

"Hush." His hand had left her forehead and was gently stroking her hot cheek. "Where does it hurt?"

"My stomach. And my head. And, oh Lord, my arms and my legs and my back—"

"Shhhh. Stretch out for a minute. Let me feel."

She moaned. "Any other time, but not now. I'm really not in the mood—"

"I want to touch your stomach to see where it hurts. Very clinically," he specified with a hint of indulgent humor. He was already easing her bent legs down, and his fingers began to gently probe. "Does it hurt here?"

"No."

He moved his fingers. "Or here?"

"Uh-uh."

He tried several other spots with like results. "So there's no localized pain."

Her eyes were closed and she was lying limply in the hammock. "No. Just a huge cramp."

"Good. Stay put. I'll be back."

Chelsea rolled to her side again and curled into a ball. "I'm not going anywhere," she muttered, but Sam had already left. When he returned, he slid an arm beneath her back and sat her up, then sank into the hammock behind her and leaned her back against him. Without further ado he began to unbutton her shirt.

"What are you *doing*, Sam?" she wailed. Of all the times she'd wanted him to touch her, this was not one.

"You're burning up, love, and this shirt's soaked. I'm going to sponge you down, then put you into something dry."

She had neither the strength nor the will to respond. She felt so sick—hot and sweaty—and the cool cloth Sam pressed to her forehead felt like heaven. So she lay her head back against his shoulder and let him take off her shirt.

Soon he was stroking a cool cloth over her fevered flesh, and she sighed. "That's better," she murmured. "Is it the heat of the night, or is it me?"

"It's you." He drew the cloth over her throat and gently bathed her shoulders.

"What is it? Do you think I have the flu?"

"I think," he stated slowly but with conviction, "that it's Montezuma's revenge. *Turista*, they call it."

"But...I thought that was just...and what about the fever? And I feel so nauseous..."

"You've got it bad, that's all." He ran the cloth down one arm, then the other. "It can happen like this when someone is overtired and overworked. What did you do to yourself before you flew down here?"

"Overworked and got overtired. But I don't understand it. I'm never sick. I have an iron—"

"Constitution. I know. And you insisted on doing your share today."

"I couldn't just sit and watch," she protested weakly. "I'm not used to being a spectator, and I'm not used to being idle."

"Sounds familiar," he murmured. Holding her carefully, he leaned over to rewet the cloth. "It probably wouldn't have happened if you'd stayed in Cancun. The food there's pretty safe. You can even drink water from the tap. Once you get off the beaten track, though, you're in trouble." He was speaking softly, almost in a croon, and Chelsea would have been lulled had it not been for the sudden intensification of the cramping in her stomach. Without wanting to, she moaned, and the cloth came to an abrupt stop over her navel.

"Need to use the john again?"

"Uh...no...I think it's okay." She was grateful when the cramp eased because she was beginning to feel more than a little embarrassed. "What were you saying?" she asked, wanting desperately to redirect Sam's thoughts from her intestinal system.

Supporting her with an arm beneath her breasts, he turned her sideways and began to bathe her back. "About what?"

"What causes this...thing."

"¿*Turista*? It's caused by bacteria. Purification systems are practically nonexistent out here, and newcomers just don't have the antibodies to fight them off."

"How long does it last?"

"That depends on you. If you fight it and insist on getting right up and doing things, you'll be sick longer. On the other hand, if you're willing to take it easy, to just lie here and rest, you should be fine in a day."

"Right now," she sighed, "I don't think I could do much of anything even if I wanted to." She let her head fall back to Sam's shoulder when he returned her to her original position. Again he shifted, again the cloth returned fresh and cool. This time it smoothed over her stomach to her waist, then slid higher, around and over one breast, then the next.

"Clinical, Sam. Please. Be clinical."

"I'm trying, I'm trying."

The cloth was thin, little more than a light, wet glove on Sam's hand comforing to her shape. Unfortunately, she was too sick to physically respond to what might otherwise have been thoroughly arousing. Her mind wasn't quite as debilitated.

"Sam?"

He kept the cloth moving slowly. "Hmmm?"

"Are you mad at me?"

"For being sick? Of course not. It's not your fault. I probably should have anticipated it, though there isn't a hell of a lot that can be done to prevent it."

"No. Not about this. About...before. I was worried that you were really mad at me."

"Dogs get mad. People get angry."

"Then were you angry?"

"Uh-huh."

"I'm sorry."

"Don't be. We have a basic difference of opinion, that's all."

He didn't sound angry, Chelsea decided. In fact, he hadn't sounded angry even when he'd first come to her. No, he'd been concerned and sympathetic and caring from the start.

"But it's okay," he went on, dipping the cloth once more and gently bathing her face. "Think of how boring it'd be if we agreed on everything."

For a fleeting instant, Chelsea thought of Linda, and of the boring couple she'd said she and Sam made. Did that mean there was hope for Chelsea and Sam? Did she *want* there to be hope? How did any of it fit into the scheme of things, considering that Chelsea was here on a mission? But she wasn't up to grappling with those questions or their answers, so she thrust them aside and wiped her mind clean of all thought. Well, almost all thought. She was still aware of how sick she felt, and that Sam was going to make it better.

Then she was being laid back on the hammock and Sam was getting up. "I'm going to get some pills and a fresh shirt. Be back in a second."

A fresh shirt. She ran her hand over her breasts. She was naked, save for her panties, and Sam had seen everything. But it was very dark. Did that mean she had some dignity left? And what was *he* wearing, she wondered vaguely just as he returned.

He hoisted her against him again and held a pill to her lips. She managed to turn her head away. "What is it?"

"Aspirin. Come on. Open up, like a good girl."

"But the water—"

"It's bottled. It won't hurt you."

"I don't know, Sam. I feel nauseous. What if it comes right back up?"

"Then I'll try again. We have to do something to get that fever down."

Unable to argue with his logic, she took the pill, but no sooner had it gone down when he was holding another to her lips.

"More?" she moaned.

"Um-hmm. You're a big girl. You need the second."

She opened her mouth, accepted the pill and washed it down. But he was back with a third.

"I've *had* two aspirin. What's that?"

"Lomotil. It'll put your digestive system to sleep for a little while. Come on, Chels. It'll make you feel better."

She grunted, but she took the pill anyway. "I think you enjoy playing doctor. How do you know so much, anyway? Isn't Lomotil by prescription?"

He shifted to put the glass on the floor and reach for the fresh shirt. "Um-hmm. And I know so much because I've been there. I remember *precisely* how bad it was, and I didn't even have someone to sponge me off."

"You? You were sick?"

"When I first got here, yes." He shook the shirt out and turned it in his free hand, trying to see what was where in the dark.

"I can't picture you sick. You seem so hale and hardy."

"You're forgetting the pictures you saw. When I got here I was pale and tired and overworked. Like you. Spending three days on my back was the cold-turkey withdrawal I mentioned. It was the buffer I needed between that life and this."

"Three days? I thought you said I'd feel better in one."

"*If* you don't fight it. I did. I was used to constant activity and couldn't seem to slow down, and there wasn't anyone to tell me to shut up and lie still. I was too dumb to listen to what my body was saying, so it got worse. Then I had no choice." He began to slip her arm into the sleeve, then reconsidered and pulled it out.

"What's wrong?"

"I think you could use a little streamlining here." With loud, prolonged rips, he tore off one arm of the shirt, then the other. "There. That's better." When he had the shirt on her, he eased her back in the hammock and fastened the buttons. "Close your eyes now and try to sleep. I'm going to sponge down your legs, then let you be."

Realizing that the rub-down had helped, Chelsea did close her eyes, but she had one thing to do before she slept. "Sam?" she whispered. "Thanks."

"For what?"

"For taking care of me and all."

He paused for a minute, and she knew he was looking at her. His voice was soft and sincere. "I should be the one thanking you. I've never had the experience of taking care of someone before. I think I like it."

Chelsea had no answer for that, so she simply nestled into the pillow and let the pleasure of his words and the cool touch of the cloth on her limbs lull her to sleep.

She was up twice more during the night, and each time Sam was there to bathe her heated skin. By the time dawn came, her stomach had settled. She still had a fever, and she felt weak and tired. But shifting experimentally in the hammock, she decided the worst seemed to be over.

Slowly she opened her eyes and directed them to Sam's side of the room. He was in his hammock, stretched out full-length with his legs crossed at the ankles and his arms folded beneath his head. He was wide awake and looking at her.

"You must be exhausted," she murmured, as though in the middle of an ongoing conversation. She guessed it had only been an hour or two since he'd last ministered to her. "I'm really sorry, Sam. You couldn't have gotten much sleep."

He swung out of the hammock. "If you say you're sorry one more time, I might give you something to be sorry for." He pretended sternness, but even that fell away as he approached her. "How do you feel?"

She took a minute to decide. "Better...I think."

He felt her forehead. By comparison, his skin was cool. "I'll get you more aspirin. Wait here."

She wanted to laugh. He kept saying that, as if she could actually go away. She wasn't going *anywhere!*

As soon as he'd left, she looked down at herself. The shirt she wore was loose and comfortable. She recalled how Sam had tended her, removing the wet shirt, sponging her body, redressing her, and she felt a blush warm her already warm cheeks.

"You still look flushed," Sam observed when he reappeared at her side.

"Blame it on the shirt," she grumbled. "If the armholes were any larger, it'd be obscene."

Sam chuckled. "That's okay. We're treating this thing clinically, aren't we?"

"Hmmph." In avoiding his gaze, she made the mistake of letting her own fall. "Sam? What are you wearing?"

He looked down at himself. "Shorts."

She continued to stare. Shorts, as in beach-type shorts? No, there was something missing, namely a fly. Or rather, there was something *there*,—a placket that lay flat enough to reveal the absence of either snaps or a zipper.

"*Boxer* shorts?"

"Heeey. Don't knock 'em. They're damned comfortable. Far cooler than those cotton things that cling to every—"

"I've never seen boxer shorts like those," Chelsea announced impulsively. "Aren't they usually baggy and kind of shapeless?"

"Depends on what shape's filling them," he responded with a grin.

Then she did raise her eyes, and her cheeks reddened all the more. She promptly pressed her lids shut, but the image remained. Sam's boxer shorts may have been more roomy than briefs, but not by much. They looked. . .marvelous. *He* looked marvelous.

"I *must* be better," she mumbled under her breath. Hours before she hadn't been able to conceive of anything the slightest bit sexual. Her body was still immune, but her mind sure wasn't.

"Hmm?"

"Nothing." She opened her eyes, but kept them trained well above his waist. "You have something for me?"

Sam closed his fingers around the aspirin and grinned. "You bet I do." His voice was enough of a drawl to convey the double meaning.

"Sam..."

He snapped his hand open and held out the water. "Okay." He bent forward and helped her sit up. "Here we go. Down the hatch." When she'd swallowed the aspirin, he dragged the table close and set the half-filled water glass on it. "Drink as much and as often as you can. You may be a little dehydrated."

She was up on an elbow, which was tricky because her elbow kept slipping through the open weave of the hammock, but she persisted. "You're not leaving me alone, are you?"

He was stepping into his pants. "Only for as long as it takes me to tell Tonia you're sick. She'll make you some *te de manzanilla*."

"It sounds alive."

"It's chamomile tea, and it's not alive.... Are you always this edgy?"

She sagged back into the hammock with a sigh. "I'm not used to being sick."

His eyes softened, as did his voice. "I won't abandon you, y'know."

"I know...but it's been years and years since anyone's taken care of me." His words of the previous night came back to her. "I think I like it."

Sam was quiet for a minute. He dug his hands into his pockets, which tugged the waistband of his pants down past his navel. Chelsea darted a quick glance there, then away.

"Were you always alone—once you left home to go to school?"

"There weren't any men, if that's what you mean."

"No men? Ever?"

She felt he had a right to know. She wanted him to know. It somehow compensated for what she *wasn't* telling him. "I've never been married, or even engaged. I've dated, and had some pretty deep relationships, but I've never lived with a guy—certainly not one who'd have been willing to take care of me this way."

"What *were* they like—the guys you dated?"

She thought for a minute. "They were nice. And intelligent. But shallow. Self-centered is a better word, I guess."

"You don't sound bitter."

She shrugged, feeling tired again. "I'm not. It wasn't as if I'd been in love. It might have hurt then, but it didn't." She closed her eyes, and her voice came softer. Her meager supply of energy had been exhausted. "There are other things to do in life. I keep busy..."

"Mmmm. Well, you're not going to today." He reached for his shirt and put it on, then stepped into his sandals and headed for the door. "See ya in five."

She raised a limp hand to wave, but he was gone, so she rolled over and went to sleep.

6

IN FACT, Chelsea's recuperation took two days, which, Sam claimed with an accusatory scowl, was because of the run-down condition she'd been in. The first day she felt ill enough not to mind the inactivity. By the second day her fever was down, but she still felt weak and tired. Her mind was back to full pace, however, and she might have grown restless had it not been for Sam's presence. He wasn't with her constantly—he took time out to chop firewood and do other chores around the *pueblito*—but he was always nearby, pampering her whenever possible.

They both enjoyed the pampering. He brought her tea, tea, and more tea. Then, when her stomach was ready, he let her try *pan tostada* or dry toast rusks. He sat with her for long hours, talking about the Maya as he knew them, telling her about things he'd show her when she was better and they could take off and explore. He spoke in great detail about the friends he'd made in Mexico, and his respect for them was as apparent as his fondness. Only once did he mention the disagreement he and Chelsea had had on the day preceeding her illness, and then it was in a gentle, almost beseechful tone.

"Please, Chelsea. Don't do anything to encourage Reni to leave."

"I wouldn't do that!" she countered quickly. She was hurt that he'd think she would, yet she supposed he had good reason, given the content of their argument that day. "It's not my place to try to sway her one way or the other. And I do see your side, Sam. There's a lot of beauty here, a centuries-old rhythm I wouldn't dream of disturbing. You may well be right, that Reni would suffer if she left. In the end, though, it's her decision to make, isn't it?"

"It is. I just don't want her helped along the way."

"What am I supposed to do when she asks questions? If she wants to know about movie theaters and posh restaurants and fancy clothes, should I lie?"

"Just downplay it. That's all I ask."

Chelsea didn't want to argue any more than he did. Things between them were too good. "Trust me. That's all *I* ask."

"I'd like to," he said even more softly. His gaze held hers in a searching kind of way. "It's just that I don't really know you all that well, do I?"

"You know more than most," was the only truthful answer she could give him. Then she felt guilty and unsure and filled with regret, so she forced a teasing grin. "It's not every man who's bathed me the way you did."

He sat back and gave her a punishing stare. "Hmmph. For all the good it did me. I hope you know that I'm suffering. You lie around here all soft and warm and tempting...it's not every man who'd exercise the control I have."

Chelsea reached out and patted his hand. "And I adore you for it," she quipped. "I do admit that you've been a saint."

Grabbing her hand, he pressed it to his thigh. He was wearing cutoffs again, favoring them, for the sake of coolness, over long pants when he was planning to be around the hut. "This saint is destined for a fall," he growled, then leaned forward and put his head close to hers. "It's just a matter of time. You know that, don't you?"

She felt a tingling in her breasts and knew she was definitely on the mend. But how to answer his question? "It frightens me."

"Frightens? Oh, no. It'll be beautiful."

"But then what? What after, Sam? I won't be here forever. At some point I'm going to have to go home, and you'll be here." At least, that was what he was supposed to believe at this stage. "What then?"

He shrugged off her worry. "You're a writer. You can be flexible with your time."

"Not as flexible as all that," she answered. She was thinking of the fall and of the graduate program she hoped to be enrolled in. She was also thinking of what she had to accomplish if she was going to be able to afford that program. She wondered if she should be prodding Sam more about returning to Boston, but instinct told her he wasn't ready for it yet. First, she had to cement their relationship.... Again she remembered his words—about it being only a matter of time before they made love. She sensed he was right, but she was still at war with herself. She could never sleep with him simply for the sake of the job she'd been hired to do. No, what made her want to make love with him went far beyond that, and she suddenly realized she might well have more at stake in securing Sam's return home than Mrs. London's payment.

"Well," Sam said, straightening with a sigh, "we'll deal with all that when the time comes. I'm just not up to worrying about the future."

"*You're* not up to it? I thought *I* was the one who was sick."

"But getting better by the minute," he said, eyes sparkling once again. "I may even let you eat something tonight."

"Oh, Sam. Won't I get sick again?"

"Hopefully this little bout will have built your antibodies. You can take it easy for a few days, but I think you'll be okay."

SHE WAS. By the next day she was able to join the rest of the villagers for dinner, and was warmly welcomed back. It appeared that the work she'd done with the women that first day had secured her acceptance among them, to the extent that they were disappointed when, several days later, Sam announced he was taking her to Chichen Itza.

Chelsea was thrilled. It wasn't that she didn't enjoy the women, or that she minded working alongside them. Rather, she wanted time alone with Sam. Since she'd recovered, they'd spent little more than evenings together, and those had been restrained as they both sought to temper the desire sparking between them. Chelsea wondered if Sam was pushing himself harder during the day simply to work off the sexual tension that built each night. For her part, she found him all the more attractive as the days passed.

They started off early in hopes of getting a head start on the heat. The sky was clear, and he insisted she wear her hat, which she held on to with one hand when the Jeep picked up speed on the highway.

"This feels strange," Chelsea commented when they were well on their way.

"The wind?" It was whipping through his hair, but he didn't seem to mind. Chelsea thought he looked marvelous that way, very free and relaxed and rakish. Of course, it helped that he'd worn his cutoffs and a T-shirt. His physique did justice to the outfit.

"No, no," she said. "Leaving the *pueblito*. It's like a little haven. You really get used to being there, don't you?"

"I have, but I'd been wondering if you felt penned up."

She turned down one side of her mouth. "Only when you kept me prisoner in that hammock."

"Whoa! The sickness did that. Don't blame me!" He was grinning, as was she.

"Don't you ever get restless? I mean, it's only been one week for me. You've been there for four months. Surely you think of home once in a while."

"I try not to."

"But...does it happen? Don't you ever wonder what's going on back there?"

"I get letters from the office, sent via Rafael. They tell me all I need to know."

"That the business is going well?"

"That I'm glad I'm here." His correction was accompanied by the reckless slash of a grin.

But Chelsea wanted to know exactly where she stood. "Do you think you'll *ever* go back?"

"I don't think."

"Sure you do."

"Well, not about that. I told you before. I don't want to go back to the kind of life I had."

She tried to sound as innocent, as nonchalant as she could. "But don't you miss *some* of the things? Your competitive instinct can't have just...died."

"There's no need for it here. I don't miss it."

"Do you think you will...two, four, six years down the road?"

"I'm not thinking that far."

She let out a breath. She was going to earn her money the hard way, that was for sure. Sam refused to think about the future. It was going to be up to her to *give* him reason to think about it.

In time.

WHEN THEY REACHED CHICHEN ITZA, Sam parked outside the Mayaland Hotel.

"This is beautiful," Chelsea said, climbing from the Jeep to look at the high, round arches leading into the large stone structure.

Sam came from behind, put his hands on her shoulders and reversed her direction. "Look there."

"Oh, my!" She saw another, more distant stone structure. It was domed, recognizable, but so obviously ancient that an involuntary quickening touched her pulse. It was a quickening that could well have been helped along by Sam's touch. "The observatory?"

"Right on. It's unbelievable. I'll tell you all about it when we get there." He released her to dip into the back of the Jeep for the bag he'd stowed there. "First things first." He fished around in it and presented her with a plastic bottle of insect repellent. Then a tube of suntan cream. Then a pair of worn sandals.

"*Huaraches*," he explained. "They're Tonia's, but she insisted you have them. They'll be easier on your feet than your own sandals. I happen to agree with her—" he arched a brow "—seeing as I was the one to doctor those blisters you had when you first arrived."

"Point taken," she acceded, though not without remembering how good he'd been at doctoring. "Y'know, maybe you should have gone into medicine," she teased reflectively. "You've got the bedside manner for it."

Sam twitched his mustache and pulled himself straighter. He was so close to her that she could all but feel the outline of his body. "You like my bedside manner?"

She took the insect repellent and squirted some on her arm. "On second thought, scratch the idea of medicine. You'd be in trouble with your lady patients." She looked him in the eye. "You're not clinical enough."

Suddenly he had his hand on the back of her thigh, then her bottom. She'd worn the shorts, which were very short, and the T-shirt, which was very long, but neither could insulate her from his heat. "*Do* you like my bedside manner?" he repeated softly.

"It's...okay."

His hand fell and he mocked injury. "'Okay'? Whaddya mean 'okay'? I thought it was damned good!" He threw up his hands and began muttering to himself as he took back the repellent and squeezed a glob onto his thigh. "'Okay'? Hmmph. Shows how much *you* know. 'Okay'? It was masterful...! Oh yuck..."

Chelsea, who'd been following his attempts to smear the repellent over his skin, burst out laughing. "Your legs are too hairy...and you squeezed too much...it's going round and round in circles...."

"I know that," he gritted. He reached into the Jeep once more and brought out a towel, which he used to wipe up the mess on his leg. "And it's all your fault. You distracted me."

She laughed again. "You look adorable when you're embarrassed."

"I'm not embarrassed."

"Then why is your neck all red? It does that, y'know, when—"

Suddenly she was pressed against the side of the Jeep and Sam was leaning into her. Provocatively.

"My neck is all red," he murmured close by her mouth, "because you're teasing and I'm hungry and in another minute I'm going to sling you over my shoulder and cart you up to one of those rooms and make love to you for the rest of the day." He moved his hips just enough to illustrate his point.

"What...what about the ruins?"

"Screw the ruins."

"Sam! That's an awful thing to say. You're the one who's been tantalizing me with them."

"Wanna take a room upstairs?"

"No."

"Why not?"

"I want to see the ruins."

"And you're teasing me because you feel safe here, is that it?"

Guilt was written all over her face, but she was struggling to keep from smiling. "I'm teasing you because it's fun. I'm in the mood to have fun. I haven't done it in ages. See what you've done to me? You've made me into a hedonistic—" She sucked in a breath when he moved against her again. "Sam!" This time it was a whispered cry, because she couldn't help but respond to his arousal. He felt so good against her; she hadn't felt him quite this way before. As though after a dry spell, he was storming her senses. All man. Wanting her.

"Kiss me," he murmured. His voice was thick, his breath hot against her cheek. "I held off while you were sick but it's seemed like forever. Kiss me, Chelsea."

She really had no choice in the matter. With a will of its own her head turned and her lips sought his. And then she didn't want any choice, because his mouth felt so right on hers and she'd missed it too.

Maybe she did feel safe in the setting. Still holding the tube of suntan cream, she slid her arms around his neck and clung to him while the rest of her melted. Her knees were suddenly weak but his body held her propped against the Jeep, and she yielded to the desire that had lain dormant and was now bursting at the seams.

Her lips molded to his, shifting hungrily. When he slid his tongue past her teeth, she sucked on it. Her breath came faster, and her whole body seemed to swell toward his.

"I'll get a room," he gasped, when at last he tore his mouth from hers.

"No...too fast, Sam...not yet..."

"You want it too, Chels. I can feel it."

She put her forehead against his chin and closed her eyes. "I know, I know. But I...want to wait."

"For what? Oh God, why?" His body still trembled with need, though she could sense he was doing his best to contain it.

"I can't explain, Sam. I just...I don't want it to be...I want it to be right."

"It's right now. I'd make it good, love."

She looked up at him then, letting him see her anguish. She couldn't explain what she felt, only knew that she'd too recently thought of Beatrice London and money and school, and she would have felt cheap letting Sam drag her into the nearest hotel.

"Please, Sam? *Please?*"

He took a long, ragged breath, and eased his weight from her. It was another little while before he straightened fully.

"I'm sorry, Chels. I guess I'm just impatient." He turned his head and looked off in the distance. "Maybe nervous."

"Nervous?"

"That you'll leave before I can...before we get around to..."

"Sex means that much to you?"

"Not that much," he muttered. "That wasn't what I meant."

"What did you mean?"

He brought his eyes back to hers. "There's something very powerful between us. You know that. We've talked of it before. I feel it's very...important that we see it through."

She swallowed hard, then said what she knew she had to say. "So do I. But there's no rush. I told you that I'd stay here for a while."

"You also said that you couldn't stay forever."

"I've only been here a week."

"For some, a week here is an eternity."

She put her hand flat on his chest. "Sam, I'm not leaving now. I have as much at stake as you do."

"Do you?" he asked, and there was an enigmatic cast to his eyes.

"I think so," she said, knowing it was the truth. In the mere week she'd been with Sam, he'd come to mean more to her than any other man ever had. Her heart was saying things, but she needed more time to interpret and understand and accept them. And all that was *before* she could begin to reconcile those heart-sounds with the future.

He sighed. "I guess I'll have to be satisfied with that...which is just as well because I think something just crawled across my foot."

Chelsea jumped away, her wide eyes riveted to the ground. "What is it! Where!"

Calmly Sam pointed to a small lizard as it disappeared under the Jeep. "Totally harmless.... Maybe he likes the insect repellent."

"Then I'm not putting any more on."

"Oh, yes, you are." His eyes narrowed. "Or would you rather I do it for you?"

"No. No." She held up a hand in refusal of his offer, which she knew would only get them in hot water again. "I can do it." Without further word, she took the plastic bottle and squeezed it against the arm she hadn't yet touched. She gave Sam a dollop when he held out his hand, then pouted. "I think there's a macho streak in you, Sam London. Would you really have slung me over your shoulder and carried me off?"

"Some day I will. Just wait and see." He cocked his head more thoughtfully. "There's something about life down here that brings out machismo. I never thought I possessed it, but it *is* kinda nice to feel strong and protective."

"And domineering?"

"That too. Well, maybe only a little."

"Your neck's red again."

His brows lowered. "That's how it all started before. Hurry up with that stuff, Chels, or take your chances."

She hurried. Not that part of her wasn't aching to take those chances. But the other part was more cautious, and she heeded its warning. Sex wasn't something she took lightly. As inevitable as the prospect of their lovemaking seemed at times, she wanted to be sure of what she was doing, particularly given the extenuating circumstances surrounding her presence in the Yucatán.

When they were both lotioned up, Sam took her hand and led her toward the ancient city. He stopped once when they passed a chicle tree and showed her the sticky white stuff that was harvested for gum. He stopped again when a colorful toucan flew past. Then he led her on, talking in such animated fashion of the history of the city that Chelsea couldn't help but be swept up in it.

That was only the beginning. After the approach on a long foot path, the jungle growth ended, and before them, rising from amid well-manicured grass, were the ruins of what had once been the center of Mayan civilization. There were only five or six buildings that Chelsea could see, but they were of such size and distinct shapes, and the air seemed filled with such a scent of antiquity, that she was awed.

"Incredible," she breathed. "It's one thing to read about them, another to actually *see* them."

"Wait till you see more." He led her toward the first and largest of the buildings, a pyramid-shaped one. "This is the central temple, El Castillo, the Castle of Kukulcan, the plumed serpent. It is *really* incredible, Chelsea." He pointed. "Look. See the steps running up the sides? There are ninety-one on each of the four sides, plus a single platform at the top. Sum total, three hundred and sixty-five. As in days of the year."

She barely had time to ingest that when he went on. "There are fifty-two carved panels, one for each week in the year. There are eighteen terraces—coinciding with the eighteen months of the Mayan calendar. There are actually two buildings there, one inside the other. The first was built by the Mayans and had straighter lines, much as the surrounding landscape is flat. The second structure, the one you're looking at now, reflects the Toltec influence. Originally the Toltecs came from the mountains, hence the more pyramidal shape."

"It's amazing that something like this could be built in those days!"

"People have always said the same about the pyramids in Egypt, and the only answer is through damned hard work. El Castillo took one hundred twenty years to build."

"But what was the incentive? I mean, the physical labor had to span three, maybe four generations. What kept the workers going?"

"Fear."

"Fear?"

"Uh-huh. Remember how you read that the ancient Maya were a dichotomous tribe, with the priests and scholars on the one hand and the workers on the other? Well, the priests and scholars conceived of the buildings. They were the mathematicians and architects. They actually used religion to get the workers going and keep them at it. For example, El Castillo is a temple for worship of the sun god. Miraculously, the scholars had been able to calculate when solar eclipses would take place. So they said to the people on the days of eclipses, 'Look. The sun god is angry. If he goes away, you won't be able to grow your maize and we'll all die.' The workers were terrified and went feverishly to work, and, lo and behold, the sun came out again."

"Clever. Very clever."

Sam was dragging her to another vantage point. "See the head of the serpent at the bottom corner of the main staircase? See how the terraces rise beside the staircase?"

"I see."

"Well, the Mayan astronomers planned this building so that twice a year, on March 21 and September 21, the spring and fall equinoxes, the shadow of the terraces against the staircase gives the impression of an undulating serpent whose coils perfectly join the head. Nowadays crowds gather on those occasions. It's an unbelievable sight—all three hours and twenty minutes of it!"

Chelsea was shaking her head in amazement. "Brilliant. I can't believe it."

"Believe it. I'd take you up the stairs, but since you've been sick—"

"I can do it, Sam!"

"Uh-uh. Not these stairs. Look at them closely. See how steep they are? There's a purpose in that, too. You see, the architects felt that, when climbing the temple of a god, one should always strike a pose of humility. Let me tell you, it's *impossible* to climb those steps standing upright. You all but have to crawl. Look. Someone's trying it now."

She grunted. "I see what you mean. He's holding the chain, but he's still pretty bent over."

"Coming down's even worse," Sam said with a grin. "Come. There are other steps you'll find easier."

They climbed the Temple of the Warriors, from whose top they could survey the entire section of the city. Sam stood behind Chelsea, with one hand on her shoulder and the other pointing out the various sights. He was a virtual treasure trove of knowledge, and she couldn't help but wonder if his study of the Mayan civilization provided him the intellectual outlet he might have otherwise missed.

Whatever the case, she was the beneficiary of his wealth of information. He was an enthusiastic and patient guide, answering her questions and sparking more. He seemed to take as much pleasure in showing her the sights as in seeing them himself. And he was forever solicitous to her physical state.

"Too much?" he asked when they'd first reached the top.

"Uh-uh," she panted. "I'm fine."

"Sun too strong?" he asked a little while later as they stood looking down on the Plaza of the Thousand Columns.

"I've got my hat," she said with a grin.

"Want to sit on Chac-Mool for a minute to rest before we go down?" he asked a few minutes later, pointing to the carved figure of the messenger to Chac, the rain god.

She accepted that invitation, not because she was tired but because she was reluctant to relinquish the feeling of reverence the spot at the top of the temple inspired. And because she didn't like the look at the stairway down.

"I can't do it, Sam," she wailed when the time had finally come. "The steps are too steep. I get dizzy looking."

He squeezed her hand, then let it go and demonstrated. "The easiest way is to wind down serpent fashion. Go diagonally. That way the steps don't seem so bad."

"You've just got longer legs. It's easy for you. I'm telling you, I'll keel over if I try that, and it's hard stone all the way down."

Sam had stopped about a quarter of the way down and was looking up at her in amusement. "I'd carry you, but my machismo doesn't go quite *that* far. I'd probably fall myself, and then we'd both be in trouble. Come on, Chels. You can't stay there forever."

Chelsea studied the steps for a long time, searching for the easiest route. In the end, she went down slowly, one step at a time, on her bottom.

Sam was the one to dust off her seat. "Cautious, but effective," was the way he summed up her descent. There was very little caution, sexually speaking, in his hand as it brushed off her bottom. But before she could comment on that, he was leading her down a long dirt road to the well.

"I understand there are wells like these all over the northeastern Yucatán," she said.

"Uh-huh. The topsoil in these parts is thin. Beneath it are layers of limestone, beneath them, natural springs. When the limestone caves in, wells like this are formed. Chichen actually has two such *cenotes*. The other, in the Old City, was used for drinking. This was the sacred well, where virgins were sacrificed."

Chelsea stared into the huge round pit. The water at its bottom was green and thick. "Looks like soup. Is it deep?"

"Not very."

"So why didn't the virgins swim?"

"They might have, if they'd been conscious."

"Ahhh. The books don't mention that. They weren't *willing* victims, then."

"Some may have been. But earlier in this century there were several attempts to dredge the bottom of the well. Artifacts were brought up, and bones and skulls, many of which were cracked or had actual holes in them. The Maya themselves were never a violent people. It's believed that the Toltecs introduced the concepts of warfare and sacrifice."

Drilling home his point, he next showed her the ball court. It was a large field with stone walls on either side, high on each of which was a round ring. "Two teams of seven players each. Seven was thought to be a lucky number, something to do with fertility."

"What?"

"What, what?"

"What did seven have to do with fertility?"

He shrugged. "Beats me. Do you know?"

"No. That's why I asked you." She laughed. "I think I'm getting sunstroke. This conversation's inane."

"Are you?"

"Inane? Not me. The *conversation*."

He glowered. "Are you getting sunstroke?"

"I don't know. What does sunstroke feel like?"

"Dizzy?"

"Nope."

"Nauseous?"

"Nope."

"I think you're just tired of hearing me talk."

"No, I'm not." If anything, the reverse was true. They'd passed other tourists from time to time, but Sam seemed to know more than any of them. He also happened to be far better looking, though, of course, that was Chelsea's own opinion. But wasn't it all that mattered, since she was the one he was with? She hooked her arm in his and diligently wiped the silly grin off her face. "Go on. You were talking about seven players?"

"Mmm. Sure you're feeling okay?"

"I'm sure. Seven players."

"Right. Well—" he raised one hand to point to the ring "—the goal of the game was to get a ball through that thing. By the way, the Maya were supposedly the first to use rubber balls."

She was studying the ring and its distance from the ground. "Higher than a basketball net, isn't it?"

"Slightly. And the players couldn't use their hands."

"What did they use?"

"Their knees or their hips."

"To get the ball up *there*?"

"Yup."

"That'd be impossible!"

"Not impossible. But very, very hard. Games sometimes went on for days, ending when the first goal was scored. Then—get this part—the best player of the losing team was decapitated by the best player of the winning team and his head was put on a post over there." Chelsea followed the pointing finger to a spot beyond the ball court. "The theory was that since he'd been such a valiant player, his blood would drip into the soil and make it fertile."

"Fertility again. Pretty gruesome, if you ask me."

"I agree. But...listen." He clapped his hands once.

"Echoes."

"Right. Now I'll do it again. This time count the number of echoes." He clapped. Chelsea counted.

"Seven?"

He grinned and nodded. She clapped again, listened, then walked forward a bit and tried it again. Seven echoes.

"How did they *do* that?"

"They were geniuses. Come." He had her hand again and was leading her closer to study the carvings on the walls of the court.

But something had happened to Chelsea along the way. Not sunstroke, though perhaps cultural saturation. She was suddenly far more interested in the way Sam traced the carvings with his long, tanned finger than with the carvings themselves. She was more fascinated with the strong arm he draped over the Wall of Skulls, and the way the muscles of his shoulder bunched when he did it, than with the actual carvings. She was more intrigued by the corded column of his throat as he looked heavenward through narrow openings in the observatory dome than by the fact that the ancient Maya charted the stars with astonishing precision. And when they climbed to the Nunnery, she was less interested in the fact that it had actually been a school than in the way Sam's legs flexed at the back of the thigh and calf as he led her onward.

She began to think that she must have sunstroke, for rational thought eluded her. She was supposed to be a writer, listening raptly to everything he said. Forsaking that, she was supposed to be subtly "de-programming" him, weaning him off his fascination with the Maya, so that she might eventually be able to convince him to return home.

Yet all she could think about was how spectacular he was and how very much she wanted to be with him, really *with* him.

By the time they returned to the Jeep, she wanted nothing more than to throw herself into his arms and beg him to ease the fire that burned deep in her belly. To hell with reason. Her senses had long since taken command.

"Are you tired?" he asked.

She was gazing into his eyes, mesmerized by their silver glow. "No."

"Hot?"

"Very!"

"Wanna cool off?"

"Do I ever!"

She waited for him to sling her over his shoulder and cart her into the Mayaland Hotel, but instead he opened the door of the Jeep and eased her inside.

"Where are we going?" she asked in dismay.

He slid behind the wheel and grinned. "To the caves."

"The caves?" All she could picture was a dirty hole in a cliff, with rattlers serenading and a slab of hard stone as a bed. Not quite the seductive scene she'd wanted.

He reached over and took her head. "You'll see."

Feeling clearly dejected, she turned her eyes to the road. She wondered if Sam sensed her mood, or her madness, and she glanced back at him. His features were at ease, his profile breathtaking. Dark, sweat-dampened hair fell over his brow.

His nose was straight, aristocratic but fitting. His mustache was full over his lip, and his chin was strong. A faint shadow of a beard touched his jaw and gave him a rugged look that meshed well with his deeply tanned skin.

He looked at her once, then did a double take. "Are you okay?" he asked, his voice deeper than usual.

"I'm fine," she answered softly. She was even better when he brought her hand to his thigh. His flesh was warm, textured by a virile spattering of hair. Unable to help herself, she shifted her hand slightly to better feel his strength.

"Chelsea?"

"I'm fine."

"Do you know what you're doing?"

"I'm not doing anything."

He moved her hand higher on his thigh until it brushed the ragged hem of his cutoffs. "I hope I don't go off the road."

"Should I help steer?"

"Uh...no. You're doing enough as it is." He didn't look at her, but she saw the telltale flush spread up his neck.

She felt no remorse. Hadn't *he* been the one to kiss her that first day? Hadn't *he* been the one to start it all?

"Where is this cave?" she asked impatiently. Hard rock couldn't be that bad. Of course, she could do without the rattlers...

"Not..." He cleared his throat. "Not far."

She wondered if it would involve a long trek once he stopped the Jeep. She wasn't sure she was up to that. "Is it really cool there?"

"You'll see."

"Sam...come on!" She wasn't in the mood for mystery.

He merely sent her a wicked half grin and moved her hand inward along the faded denim of his shorts.

She blew an exasperated breath up toward her hair, then, with her free hand, raked the long curls from her forehead. She put her head back against the seat and closed her eyes, hoping that blocking out the sight of Sam would somehow still her clamoring senses. It might have, except that her hand grew all the more sensitive and she could feel the edge of his hardness and it inflamed her all the more. She swallowed, then took a deep breath.

"Chelsea?"

"I'm fine, I'm fine. Let's get there, already."

"I'm with you," he said very softly. "Almost there."

They didn't talk then, and not even the wind eased the heat about them. Chelsea kept waiting for her body to calm, for its passion to cool. After all, the moment had passed, hadn't it? The drive in the Jeep should be like a bucket of cold water, shouldn't it? You couldn't prolong these things and expect them to stay at the same explosive level.... Could you?

It seemed an eternity before the Jeep turned off the main road onto a rutted one, a second eternity before it finally ground to a halt and Chelsea looked around. They were in a tiny clearing and there were no cliffs in sight. Only jungle.

Suddenly the image in her mind was revised and she pictured an earthy kind of cave buried somewhere deep in the wilds. Rattlers and hard rock were one thing; rattlers and jaguars and *garrapatas* and dirt embedded with God knew what other creatures were quite another.

"I don't think I'm going to like this," she mumbled under her breath.

Sam, who was fiddling in the glove compartment of the Jeep, chuckled softly. "You'll like it." He tossed his head toward what she made out to be a small path into the woods. "Come."

Chelsea followed, staying close behind him. She wrapped her arms about her middle and cast worried glances to either side, but Sam seemed fully confident in his stride, so finally she just concentrated on his back.

And it picked up right where it had left off, the admiration and the yearning. Droplets of sweat dampening his T-shirt between his shoulders. The fluid shift of those shoulders with each step he took. Well-formed arms swinging easily by his sides. Narrow hips barely twisting as he walked.

Chelsea decided that Sam had to be the most superb animal to ever walk through the jungle. All litheness and grace, he seemed fully in command, while she, on the other hand, felt distinctly out of control.

"How're you doin'?" he asked over his shoulder.

She was less than two feet behind. "I'm fine." Her voice sounded breathless, so she forced a more convincing tone. She had to swallow first. "You seem very familiar with this path. Do you come here often?"

"Whenever I can. It's a special place."

"I can't wait," she murmured, and saw his cheek bunch into a grin. "Much farther?"

"Nope."

A minute later he came to a full halt, and Chelsea barrelled into him. She left her hand on his back—as good as excuse as any to touch him—while the rest of her retreated several inches.

"See it?"

She stared at a large outcropping of rock ahead. It wasn't terribly high, certainly not high enough to harbor a cave, at least not one a human could fit into. "No."

He reached around, took her hand from his back and drew her forward. "Don't look up. Look down. There. At the bottom of the rock."

"It's a hole."

"It's the start of a tunnel."

She took a step back but came up against his sturdy form. "Uh, Sam, I'm not sure about tunnels."

He put his cheek to her temple and spoke softly, soothingly. "You weren't sure about the descent from the Temple of the Warriors either, but you made it, and it was worth it, wasn't it...? Well, wasn't it?"

"Yes," she replied hesitantly. "But that was wide open. This is different. What if I get claustrophobia?"

"You won't. The entrance is the only tough part, and we should be grateful. If it were any wider, more people would know about it. It would be an invitation to every tourist around. This way we'll have it to ourselves."

She leaned back into him, finding reassurance in his strength. At that moment she was almost willing to have him take her on the jungle floor.

"Relax," he murmured encouragingly. "Once we pass the entrance, the whole thing opens up."

"Opens up...to where?"

He straightened and took her hand. "You'll see. Come on. I'll go first so I can help you down."

Before she could protest, he was slipping feet first through the hole. To her surprise and immense relief, the hole appeared larger close up. Sam had no trouble levering himself through with space to spare. Then his hand reemerged and he was tugging her ankle.

"Sit down and slide. I'll catch you."

With an unsteady breath she sat down, eased her legs through the hole and slid into his arms. She was astonished to find that he was standing upright. Clutching his arms, she very cautiously looked around.

"Are there bats or any squirmies in here?" she whispered.

His grin was just visible through the light from above. "Nope. Just us."

"And this is your cave?" All she could see was rock and darkness.

"This is the beginning." He reached into the pocket of his shorts, drew out the small flashlight he'd taken from the glove compartment, and clicked it on to reveal a passageway. It was narrow, but high, and nowhere near as threatening to Chelsea as the entrance had been.

Holding tightly to Sam's hand, she walked carefully behind him. The rock made a steady descent, with steplike inclines at points, steeper drops at others. At each of the latter he turned to help her, lifting her comfortably down, then proceeding. Twice the tunnel curved sharply. The light from the entrance had long since disappeared.

"This is spooky," she whispered, quickening her step so that she was even closer to him. She wrapped both arms around his free one and hung on fiercely.

"It's just dark. Wait—watch your step—here's the last drop." He helped her over it. "And a final turn."

They followed it around, and then the tunnel was behind them. Before them was an open cavern whose roof arched into a dome thirty feet above and whose sides exceeded even that in width.

Sam snapped off the flashlight and returned it to his pocket. "Well? Whaddya think?"

Chelsea was standing with her mouth open. "I think it's absolutely beautiful!" she breathed in awe. Around one side of the cavern, leading off from where they stood, were random wide slabs of stone. Beyond was a crystal-clear pool, lit by a natural spotlight that beamed down from an open hole in the apex of the roof and bathed the entire cavern in an aura of blue. Huge stalactite formations hung into the pool on one side, their tapering tentacles perfectly visible through the still water. "How did you ever find this place?"

"I didn't. A pig did."

"A *pig*?"

"A farmer not too far from here noticed that his pig was wandering off for hours at a stretch. One day he followed it— right into this cave."

"Unbelievable!" Chelsea whispered, taking in the silence, the serenity, the spirituality of the place.

When Sam moved forward toward the largest and flattest of the stone slabs, she followed. Once there he turned to her. "Want to swim?"

Her eyes widened, hesitant. "Can we?"

"Why not?"

"This cave has probably been here for hundreds and hundreds of years. It seems somehow...sacred."

"I've swum here before. The water is wonderful. Filled with calcium, they say. Your skin feels marvelous when you get out."

Chelsea's gaze skipped from Sam to the water. It looked inviting. And she was sweaty. A slow smile curved her lips. "I bet it'd feel great." Then the smile faded. "But...we don't have suits..."

His chiding look told her exactly what he thought of that problem. When he reached down and tugged up his T-shirt, her eyes widened all the more.

" Sam?" She felt it all, back in full force. What had been momentarily suspended during the descent into the cave surged back with a vengeance to set her insides aquiver. Her pulse began to race when, with a very natural but nonetheless sensual twist of his torso, he pulled the T-shirt over his head and dropped it onto the rock.

His gaze was suddenly more intense as, deliberately but without haste, he covered the small space between them. His broad chest loomed before her, bronzed and patterned with a manly coat of hair, muscles rippling ever so slightly when he reached out to caress her shoulders.

"Don't be shy, love," he murmured hoarsely. "Here. Let me help you." Very slowly he ducked his head and whispered a kiss on her cheek, then her nose. Assailed by suddenly shaky knees, Chelsea grasped his waist, but the feel of him, all warm and hard, weakened her all the more. She closed her eyes when his lips touched them, loving the feel of his mustache against her lids, loving the shimmer of his long fingers spreading over her back, loving his heat when one of his hands fell to the small of her back and pressed her intimately close.

She knew then that there was no turning back, that the inevitable was about to happen and that it would be wonderful. And she knew that, regardless of the rhyme or the reason or the ramification, she was madly in love with Sam London.

7

HE KISSED HER with a slow growing force, titillating, persuading, inflaming her until she was breathless. It was precisely the help she'd needed, because by the time he tugged at her T-shirt she wanted it off as badly as he did.

Tossing the shirt aside, he ran his hands lightly along her arms, but his attention was focused on her breasts, swollen and aching for his touch. He'd begun to breath more heavily by the time he met her gaze, and his voice was hoarse. "You're perfect, Chelsea. Absolutely perfect."

He'd seen her before, she knew, but under very different circumstances. Now, with the setting unbelievably romantic and her sensual awareness nearly electrical, she felt proud and pleased and more hungry than ever.

"So are you," she whispered, laying her palms flat on his middle and inching them upward. While part of her felt a dizzying urgency, another wanted the pleasure of the moment to last forever and beyond. So she fought for slowness, splaying her fingers, acquainting them with the leanness of his ribcage, the gradual broadening swell of his chest, his shoulders.

He moaned softly and closed his eyes, but his hands mimicked hers, climbing, smoothing, exploring, arousing. When at last he cupped her breasts and began to caress them, she was the one to moan then shiver, as he grazed her nipples and seconds later rolled them with the warm, faintly abrasive pads of his thumbs. She dug her fingers into his shoulders and whimpered softly.

"Feel good?"

"Oh...yes..."

"C'm'ere."

He had his arms around her then and was crushing her to his chest. The feel of his strength, his warmth, his texture against her breasts sent tremors curling to the tips of her toes. His breath was coming in ragged spurts by her ear, and it seemed only natural, only right when he slid his hands into the back of her shorts to lower them to her hips. Then, while one hand pressed her bottom, the other slipped to the front and found the special warmth that branded her woman.

She caught her breath and would have retreated had not his hand on her backside prevented it. "Sam...oh..."

He continued to caress her, gentling her as he moved ever deeper. "It's okay, Chels. Don't be afraid."

"I'm not...it's just—it's like fire..."

He lightened his touch, but only momentarily. And wisely so, for she quickly found she wanted everything he did, harder, deeper.

"Better?" he murmured softly.

Her answer was a shuddering sigh, but her fingers were suddenly restless. No longer content with clutching his shoulders, they sought the solid musculature of his back, then his waist, then the fastening of his cutoffs. She worked blindly, her face buried in the hollow above his collarbone, and she was taking in shallow little breaths. The scent of his skin drugged her, making her feel light-headed while, lower, his gentle stroking brought her to an even higher pitch.

Impatient, she abandoned his waistband and moved her hand over the front of his shorts. Fully aroused, his sex was a straining force against the denim and her hand. He arched into her palm, then quickly retreated and unzipped himself.

"Touch me, Chels," he rasped. "I need to feel your hands...I've dreamed of it...touch me..."

Chelsea would have done so even had he not asked it. She'd seen all of him but this, and even aside from any prurient curiosity, she felt a driving need for the intimacy, the power, the satisfaction. He'd once said that "good" was relative, that it was achieved only to then be redefined into something more. So it was with physicality. Where once "good" had been holding his hand or kissing him then touching his chest and his shoulders and his back, now it escalated further. It was like sugar in the bloodstream; a hefty dose gave instant results but when the craving returned it was worse than before.

Right now she wanted the joy of touching Sam, of bringing him joy with her touch. Splaying her fingers over his waist, she eased them into his shorts and found what she sought. All man. Large, hard and throbbing.

"Oh, Chels," he moaned, his body convulsing. With low murmured words, he urged her on. "That's it...yes...God, yes..." His own hand had fallen still, but she didn't mind because his heat was surging through her fingers, up her arms, into her breasts and then down to her belly. If anything she felt more aroused than she had before, and from his aching response, as her fingers caressed every private inch of him, Sam very obviously was in a like state.

Then he stilled her hands and was setting her back so that he could rid himself of the shorts that barred their final satisfaction. His eyes were wide, smoldering with desire, and Chelsea watched helplessly as what her touch already knew so well became known to her gaze. Almost absently she slipped out of her own shorts, not once taking her eyes from Sam's aroused body.

Reaching for her hand, he led her toward the edge of the pool and turned her to him. "You're not scared, are you?" he asked very gently, just the faintest bit uncertain. His fingers were unsteady as they smoothed her hair behind her ears.

She met his gaze. "A little," she whispered. "But I want you so badly."

He framed her face in his hands, and his voice was scarcely more than a throaty breath. "I'm scared too, if it's any consolation. I want it to be good for you, but it's been a long time for me—"

She stilled his words with her fingertips, then stroked the soft bristle of his mustache. "You don't have any cause for worry," she said with a soft, very feminine smile. "Haven't you seen me drooling all week?"

"If I'd seen that, I'd have worried you'd contracted rabies," he teased, but none of the light left his eyes and his body retained its impassioned state.

"Not rabies. You." Standing on tiptoe, she replaced her fingers with her lips and for the very first time her full nakedness meshed with his. A tiny gasp flowed from one mouth to the other, its source unknown and unimportant, for the electricity was real and mutual and their kiss quickly developed into one of unbearable need.

When Chelsea thought she was ready to die, and happily at that, Sam swept her into his arms and walked the few steps to the pool's edge. Their lips were melded together, and later she was to realize that it had been a miracle he hadn't fallen. But it must have been their day for miracles because he moved easily into the water, down one submerged step, then a second and a third, until, very gently, he let her body break the rippling surface.

His mouth left hers for only an instant, when he gracefully dove over her and circled beneath to reemerge before her once again. Then he was half out of the water, braced back against a ledge, and he was lifting her, wet and shining, high above him. Taking one of her dripping breasts into his mouth, he drew on it avidly.

Any chill Chelsea might have felt from the water was negated by the fire that Sam's lips, his tongue, his teeth and hands stoked. Her fingers wove into his hair and she arched her back, urging him closer, wanting him to take and take until she dissolved into his being.

Hands on her sleek hips, he raised her higher, mouthing his way down her stomach, then up again to treat her other breast to the hot suction of his mouth. She cried out in delight and need, and tugged at his hair until his mouth was free to rescue hers from what seemed utter desolation.

"I want you, Chelsea," he moaned against her lips. "I want to be there...now...." His hips had begun a slow undulation, and his hardness prodded boldy. "Do you want me inside?"

"I do, I do," she breathed. "Hurry, Sam. Please!"

"Put your legs around me, love." He guided her thighs as they spread over his. "Now look at me, Chels. Open your eyes and look at me."

She did as he asked, and what she saw was more than enough justification for what they were doing. She loved him, and the very first day they'd met he'd jokingly said he loved her. But now...the look of sheer adoration on his face...well, if it wasn't love it was as close as some people ever came to it.

She felt his hands spread over her bottom, pressing her forward and down. Slowly, tenderly, as was his way, he penetrated her. Her own expression must have held wonder then, because when she felt his fullness deep, deep inside, an incredible sense of being, of oneness, of beauty surged through her.

He let out a long, shuddering breath and was smiling even as he took her lips. Melting into his kiss, she wrapped her arms around his neck and let him lead her in a slow, rocking motion that soon grew faster, then wilder. He seemed to know just what she needed and when, as though his body was so finely tuned to hers that it could anticipate each shift of desire and satisfy it. If he'd had any doubts about his ability to make it good for her, they were laid to rest by her soft moans and smiles and pleasure-gasps.

The water around them rippled in a flowing rhythm. The walls of the cavern absorbed their muffled sighs and fevered whispers. Pale-blue light shimmered all around them, lending an ethereal cast to their lovemaking, but they were oblivious to it, so enveloped were they in their own very private world of passion.

When Chelsea felt her climax near, she helplessly cried Sam's name. Never had she felt anything remotely akin to the pleasure about to burst, and the sheer force of it frightened her.

"Let go, love," he whispered. "Let it come...."

The sound of his voice by her ear, the feel of his arms around her back—they were the reassurance she needed that he'd be there to hold her when she relinquished that last bit of control. And it went then—the control, the clear thought, the awareness of all things physical and emotional—and she was catapulted into a realm of pure ecstasy, brilliant and pulsing.

Sam followed her quickly, joining her, lingering behind when she'd begun the descent to reality. His large body was quaking, but all the while he held her surely, telling her without words that she was precious and rare.

At last, when his body grew slack in the aftermath of the storm, he loosened his hold and smiled down at her. He didn't speak then, as though words would only sully what had been so breathtakingly beautiful. But he kissed her, and his lips were more eloquent in expressing delight and gratitude and, yes, love than the sweetest of poems.

"Very, very special..." Chelsea murmured when he'd released her lips and she'd finally found the breath to speak.

He held her tightly and rocked her until they'd both more fully recovered. Then, with only the faintest of smug chuckles to forewarn her, he flipped them both back into the water. She came up sputtering, throwing the hair out of her eyes, but she was grinning.

"That was a dirty trick, Sam London."

"We came here to cool off, didn't we?" He was grinning, too, and when she splashed water at him he simply submerged, resurfacing with his head back so that his hair lay flat against his skull. "Ahhhh. That felt good."

"The water or me?"

"Both. You're like a fountain of youth. I haven't felt this great in days."

"Aren't you supposed to be totally drained at this point?" she teased, treading water a few feet away.

"I *am* totally drained, but, man, do I feel *great*!" With one stroke he was before her, wrapping her in his arms. His legs, treading steadily, were strong enough to keep them both afloat. "You're wonderful, Chelsea. Do you know that?"

She had her arms coiled about his neck and was looking down into his face. "Sure I do. But it's nice to hear it from someone other than myself for a change." Actually she heard it quite often—from grateful parents to whom she'd returned a lost child—but that world was unreal here, and unwanted.

"Then I'll say it again, more softly and with feeling." He took a breath. "You're wonderful, Chelsea."

She tipped back her head and laughed, taking in a mouthful of water as he released her and she sank. When she came up she promptly spit it at him but he'd taken off to the far side of the pool, stroking smoothly, turning, floating on his back, then rolling over and stroking again. Following his lead, she swam for a bit, but she tired before he did and was waiting on the rock when he finally hauled himself from the water.

"You look like a god," she said.

"Naked and dripping."

She grinned. "Right."

Bracing with one hand, he lowered himself to the rock, then stretched out on his back beside her and tugged her down. "How do you feel?"

She, too, lay on her back, her head turned to face him. "Wonderful."

"Glad we came?"

"You bet."

"You're not upset that I rushed you—after this morning and all?"

"You didn't exactly force me into anything."

He gave a mischievous grin. "I didn't, did I?" Then he grew more serious and his eyes took on the same intensity she'd seen in them so often. It was an intensity that seemed to dig beneath her surface and probe. "What made you do it, Chels? I know you wanted to wait."

For a split second she felt guilty. She knew he had cause to probe, knew that she had been less than forthright with him. But this wasn't the time or the place to go into that, so she chose her words with care, striving for honesty without upset. "I guess you were right when you said it was inevitable." With a smile, she glanced down his body. Long. Perfectly made. As manly in repose as in arousal. "And after spending the entire day looking at your damned gorgeous physique, I figured the waiting was absurd."

"Looking at my—you mean, you didn't see anything I showed you at Chichen?"

"Of course I did. All that...and more." She rolled until she was propped against him with her arm resting on his chest. "Let's just say that I underestimated my, uh, my appetite."

"As in sexual?"

"Bingo."

He chuckled and hugged her, then set her away and sat up. "We'd better get dressed. I don't want to be here when the pig arrives."

"The *pig!*" She whirled toward the cavern's entrance and covered herself in a belated spurt of modesty, which made Sam laugh aloud. "You didn't say that the pig still came! I thought we had this all to ourselves!"

He relented then. "I was teasing. No more pig. But...aren't you grateful to him?"

Chelsea took a calming breath as she reached for her clothes. "That, I am...most definitely. That, I am."

THEY RETURNED TO THE JEEP arm in arm, and through dinner in Valladolid and then the drive back to the *pueblito* they touched and kissed at will. With their lovemaking, a barrier had dissolved. Public decorum was the only restraint they observed.

It was late when they finally turned off the highway onto the narrow path, then parked the car and ran through the dark to the hut. They were smothering laughs, feeling something like children sneaking in after curfew, and Sam didn't bother to turn on a light as he ushered Chelsea toward the back room.

"Go change and get ready for bed," he said softly. "I'll get us some wine."

"'Get ready for bed.' There's a phrase from your past, Sam," she teased. "Wouldn't it be more correct to say, 'Go change and get ready for hammock.' This isn't a bedroom; it's a hammock room."

"On second thought, I think I'll skip the wine. You sound a little high."

"I am." Grinning, she snatched the shirt from the end of her hammock. "Be right back."

By the time she returned, Sam was stretched out in his hammock wearing the boxer shorts she surprised herself by so admiring. Well, it wasn't so much the shorts she admired as the way they fit him. In either case she stood for several moments looking down at him in the dark. When he held out a hand, she hesitated.

"We've never tried two in a hammock," she warned.

"Sure we have. Remember when you were sick and I bathed you?" He grasped her wrist and tugged her in. Her landing wasn't the most graceful, but with a little maneuvering she was comfortably nestled, spoonlike, with her back to his front. He wrapped his arms around her middle and rested his chin on the top of her head. "Tell me about what you were like as a kid, Chelsea."

His request had been offered quietly, in keeping with the serenity of the night, and Chelsea readily acquiesced. "I was pretty lucky, actually. I had two loving parents and grew up in a close, warm home. We were always struggling to make ends meet—my dad was a laborer and my mom, well, women didn't think of working at that time."

"Are your parents still alive?"

"Oh, yes. They live in the same house where I grew up. Dad is retired now, which is nice because otherwise my mother would be lonely." Her heart skipped a beat and she anticipated his next question even before it came.

"Were you an only child?"

"No. I had a younger sister."

She'd tried to keep her voice even, but something in it must have given her away. Or maybe Sam was as attuned to her thoughts, which at the moment were shadowed, as he was to her body.

"'Had?' Did something happen?"

She took a deep breath and found her hand seeking his. "Susan was seven years younger than me. When she was sixteen, she ran—or was taken—away from home. We haven't seen her since."

Sam's arms tightened around her. "God, Chels, I'm sorry! There's been no word at all, no sign?"

"Nope."

"Did the police look?"

"After a fashion. They wouldn't officially list her as missing until she'd been gone for twenty-four hours, and after that, well, they went through the motions, but that was about all."

"Your parents must have been crushed."

"Me, too. I'd been away from home for five years at that point, and I blamed myself for not keeping in closer touch with Susan. We were never that close, because of the age difference. She was always a quiet kid."

"Do you have any idea why she left—if in fact she did it on her own?"

Chelsea shook her head against his chest. Its solidity was a comfort. "I've spent six years trying to figure that out, but

I just don't know. I mean, *I* was happy at home. Sure, I went away to school and then lived away when I started to teach, but that was because I went where the job was. I can't believe there was anything about either of my parents that could have alienated Susan so that she'd run away. They're both very quiet, soft-spoken people. If anything, my mother was more meek than she might have been, but never once could we doubt that she loved us."

"There are organizations to help look for—"

"Not at that time. I tried, Sam," she cried. "I did everything I could to find her. I saw that her picture was distributed in every major city. I put notices in newspapers. I made phone call after phone call to friends of friends of friends she had, but I *still* came up empty-handed."

His hand was on her brow. "Shhh. Don't torture yourself now. It wasn't your fault. You know that."

She sighed and forced herself to relax. "I think I'll always blame myself for not having been closer to her. But in the final analysis there's not much more I can do. I still make inquiries, but if Susan's alive today I doubt she looks anything like the pictures we have. We've accepted that she's gone, as much as any family can. We still hope and pray, and it still hurts, particularly for my parents, who have a lot more time to sit and brood than I do. I try to see them as often as possible."

"Do they know you're here?"

"I called them before I left to tell them I'd be in Mexico. I really should drop them a note." Anxious to shake off the discouragement she always felt when thinking of Susan—and to shift the focus of the discussion from herself—she tipped her head back. "Tell me about you, Sam. What was your childhood like?"

He hesitated a minute, as though reluctant to leave the subject of Chelsea's life. She wondered then whether she'd said too much, whether some little word or tone might have given away her present occupation. For whatever his reasons, though, Sam gave in.

"Very privileged. Very proper. Very programmed."

"Sounds exciting."

"To some, I suppose."

"But not you."

"No. I was like my father. I always enjoyed applying myself to things—projects from school or camp, finally work. I could easily have done without the rest—the parties and the cruises and the receptions. In the end they drove my father crazy. No, on second thought, I think it was my mother who finally got to him."

Chelsea might have expressed surprise but it wouldn't have been truthful. So she held her tongue, and Sam went on anyway. He seemed more than willing, even determined to talk, as though he wanted her to know what made him tick. She had no argument with that.

"My mother is a very difficult woman. I love her because she's my mother, but I steer clear of her as much as possible. She's cold and domineering. She runs the lives of those around her with a steel hand. My father and I both had our share of ambition, but my father, well, he was softer about it. When my mother pushed, he tensed up. When she bullied, he simply shied away."

He paused for a minute, his chin resting more heavily on her head. Chelsea caressed his hand both in comfort and encouragement. A little voice in the back of her mind wanted to ask questions and to urge him on, but it was overruled by the woman in her who loved him and knew that he needed to take his own time.

"After I graduated from the B School I went into the family business. I felt I might be the ally my father needed, and God knew there was enough work to challenge me. Then I ran into my mother the businesswomen, and saw things, really *saw* them, from the inside. She was in and out of the office, nagging, commanding, sticking her finger in every pie, criticizing when she didn't think we were doing enough or when she thought she saw a promotional scheme or a new business prospect we weren't following up on. After a couple of years I knew I couldn't take any more. I went to my father, near to bursting, and told him what I felt—that I had to leave, that *he'd* be wise to get out before she drove him into the ground. He was already failing; I could see that. I mean, there's only so much tension a person can take!"

That was the disagreement Beatrice London had mentioned to Chelsea, the one whose specifics the older women had never known. Now Chelsea could begin to understand why Sam's father had kept mum. "What did your father say when you told him all this?" she prodded gently.

"He said that he couldn't leave the business, that he couldn't leave my mother. He loved her. Hell, so did—do—I, but I was damned if I was going to let her rule my life." He let out a long breath. "So I left to start my own firm, and Dad continued downhill. Several years ago he had a massive coronary and died instantly. It was probably a blessing. She'd never have let him slow down, much less retire."

Chelsea ran her hand up and down his forearm. "Do you feel guilty for having left?"

"Guilty? I suppose. I feel bad for having *had* to leave. It's my family's business, after all. I really didn't want to desert my father that way, but it was a matter of survival." His voice lowered and grew dry. "At least, that was what I thought at the time. Of course, I didn't do much better on my own."

"But you've been wonderfully successful!"

"Sure, but at a cost. Tension. Constant worry. Headaches from thinking about all the *other* things I should be doing. Don't you see, Chelsea? Instead of my mother holding the knife at my throat, I started holding it myself. I think that's one of the things I've come to understand since I've been here and had time to think."

"I thought you didn't think," she teased.

He kissed her ear softly. "About the future...about the future. I have thought about the past, and I've realized that there's a helluva lot of my mother in me after all."

"Come on. You're not cold and domineering." She was very careful to use his own words, rather than ones representing the opinion she'd herself formed after meeting Beatrice.

"Maybe not that, but the endless ambition, the insane drive—I got to the point where nothing in life was fun anymore. Anything and everything I did had to have a purpose."

"Isn't that the way we all are?"

"Not in the extreme, as it was with me, and not when the only goal in life is doing more, better and faster."

With the effort and determination the hammock demanded, Chelsea squirmed around to face him. "You've broken the pattern, living down here as you have. Isn't it possible that you can go back, maybe consolidate your business interests, or somehow limit your role in them?" She brushed her knuckles lightly against his cheek. "Understanding the problem is half the battle. If you were to go back to Boston with the express intent of keeping things in perspective, of *finding* things to do for the sole purpose of having fun, of making a clear demarcation between work and pleasure—wouldn't it work?"

His eyes held hers and he wrapped a blond curl around his finger. "I don't know."

"Wouldn't it be worth a try?"

He leaned forward and kissed her cheek. "I don't know."

Chelsea growled with a mixture of frustration and playfulness. "You are exasperating. Whenever we get to the good part, you fade out."

He gave her a lopsided smile. "What do you expect, turning around on me this way? It's bad enough when I don't have to look you in the eye, but when I do, there's no way my mind can function properly."

She knew very well that he was avoiding the issue, but he *was* looking her in the eye and he wasn't the only one affected. She shouldn't have turned around, but she'd wanted to, and his body was so long, so warm, so hairy and firm.

He sought her lips then, kissing her sweetly. When he kissed her a second time, it was with greater feeling. By the third time, he was positively hot, but she didn't mind because she had her arms around his neck and was fueling his hunger with her own.

They kissed more, and touched, and Sam found her breasts through the huge armhole of her shirt. His stroking and taunting had her quickly straining closer.

"Let's get this open," he murmured against her lips and deftly dispensed with the buttons. "There," he crooned as he ran his hand from one breast to the other. "So firm and full..."

"You make them that way," she whispered. She caressed his chest, found one taut nipple and brushed her finger back and forth over it. He groaned and she grinned. "Only fair..."

He gave a low growl, but he was shifting, lowering his shorts, and his voice was thick with desire when he nudged her legs apart. "Put your thigh over mine...that's it..."

She was breathing harder. "I thought you said...you couldn't do it in a hammock."

He pressed her closer and easily, so easily because she was moist and warm, slid into her. "I said...mmmmmmm...I *wondered* if you could...oh, God, Chels, you're...so perfect for...me..."

They didn't talk then, because there were too many other ways to say what they felt. On their sides in the hammock, each had only one arm free, but it was put to good use in the leisurely sensual exploration they'd been too heated to fully appreciate that afternoon. Between those hands, lips that nibbled and tasted and drank, and the sexual persuasion of their loins, the fever rose.

Sam thrust slowly and smoothly, but his effect on her was as explosive as if he'd been loving her with unleashed force.

She found it unbelievably exciting to mate this way, peacefully, almost religiously. It was, she realized, totally appropriate to the setting.

With her leg braced around his thigh, her hips met his, retreated, sought again. In time the tempo quickened until, with every muscle straining, they climaxed in near-unison.

The panting that followed was less well-timed and far more ragged than anything that had come before. Only later, after Sam had resettled her close to him in the hammock, did Chelsea wonder if it was a harbinger of things to come. For, just as she couldn't help but glow with the love she felt, she couldn't help but feel duplicitous. She had accepted money, half of which was already in her bank account, to "lure" Sam home. He didn't know about that, or about her business, or about the plans she had for going back to school in two short months. In time it all had to come out—but when? And would the repercussions be ragged and jarring?

IN THE DAYS THAT FOLLOWED, Chelsea heeded Sam's example and did her best to push all thought of the future aside. She knew she was being selfish, but for once in her life she didn't care. She loved him to distraction, and she simply wasn't willing to do anything that might spoil the happiness of the moment.

Quite cleverly Sam managed to manipulate the women of the village so that Chelsea could be with him as much as possible. She lent a hand with him in harvesting long, silver-green, bayonetlike leaves from the arrow-straight rows of henequen. She knelt with him to admire the statue of a Mayan god, which was being carved out of wood by one of the elderly villagers. She joined in the joking and easy laughter that took place when he and several other of the men took to sawing planks from a log to make a new door for one of the huts. She watched in astonishment when, in the ancient Mayan manner, they made an addition to the beehive rack by hollowing out a section of a log, sealing its ends with mud and punching a hole in its side to permit the bees access.

And each night she wrote it all down in her notebook. The first time she did it, she felt as though she were perpetrating a hoax. After all, she'd told Sam she was a writer, and he'd been the one to ask if she oughtn't to be taking notes. But she quickly found that she enjoyed the writing. She'd seen so much, all of it fascinating, and she wanted to remember everything. Moreover, she took to writing her feelings for Sam, so the notebook became an intimate kind of diary. Subconsciously, perhaps, she hoped he'd sneak it out one day and read it, but she suspected that he was too straightforward for that.

One week passed after their trip to Chichen and another began, and Chelsea adapted to the rhythm of Mayan life as though it was the only one she'd ever known. Each day was more relaxing, more interesting, more rewarding than the last. And Sam was always there, enthusiastic and caring by day, loving by night.

After she'd been with him for three weeks, though, something very subtle began to happen. For a fleeting moment here, an instant there, her thoughts turned homeward. She determinedly chased them away, but they returned, each time at a shorter interval than the last. Moreover, she sensed that Sam was suffering from the same affliction, because from time to time she'd catch him with a troubled, faraway look in his eyes.

She should be grateful, she told herself. It was her job to make him think of home. But she was frightened of the unknown to follow, and she was terrified that one of those would tear them apart.

She'd actually begun to wonder if some part of Sam was growing restless when, one day in the middle of that third week, he suggested they drive into Cancun. She readily agreed. The thought of returning there with Sam excited her, and, of course, there was the matter of her suitcase—not that she had any need of it. Sam had been right about that, but she was half-worried that the hotel had given up on her and the bag would be lost once again.

Chelsea with her faithful carry-on bag and Sam with his suitcase—he hadn't opened it yet, and it was a strangely ominous presence—drove directly to the Camino Real and checked in, intent on spending several nights there before returning to the *pueblito*. To Chelsea's relief, her errant suitcase had indeed been safely stored for her, though there was something threatening about it too as the bellboy carried it to their room.

"Funny," she mused when at last they were alone and she stood staring at the bag, "I thought I was going to be lost without it, but I almost hate to open it now."

"I know what you mean," he said quietly, then took a breath as if for courage. "But it's hot, and it's not raining, and since it's siesta time and everything else is closed down, it might be very nice to go to the beach."

He was looking at her and she sensed in him the same unsureness that she felt herself. It was something about the room, the hotel, the other Americans they'd passed in the lobby. They were back in civilization, where they'd never before been together, and it remained to be seen if the magic that had bound them in the Mayan lowlands would remain.

Sam took the first step. Curving his hand very gently around her neck, he spoke. "It's been a very long time since I've been here, and so much has happened to me since I left that I'm feeling a little shaky right about now. Will you help me, Chels? Stay close beside me and tell me I'm doing the right thing by coming back here with you?"

In that instant she knew the magic remained, because she felt such a rise of tenderness that her throat grew tight. She brought his hand to her cheek and tilted her face into it. "Of course I'll help. I need you too."

Wrapping his arms around her then, he held her tightly. There were no sexual implications in the hug, and it was perhaps all the more meaningful for that reason. She felt warmed all over in an emotional kind of way, such that when he set her back and opened his bag, she followed suit without another thought.

Fifteen minutes later they were on the beach, alternately basking in the sun and cooling off in the waves, ordering piña coladas and then laughing at their decorative delivery, which seemed to them the height of extravagance after life in the *pueblito*.

When they'd had enough of the sun, they returned to the room where they indulged in long, hot showers—separately, together, separately again, together again—until they felt sure the management would be knocking on their door to complain. Then almost shyly they dressed in clean clothes from their suitcases. Chelsea blow dried her hair and put on a pink-and-white shortall—a one-piece short and top outfit—with fresh sandals to match. Sam put on a pair of white shorts, a crisp yellow short-sleeved shirt and a pair of deck shoes. Almost shyly they looked at each other, then burst out with simultaneous compliments and ended up laughing.

Light-headed, they left the hotel and headed for the shops, but Sam steered her clear of them at the last minute.

"Where are we going?" she asked as he ushered her further down the main street.

"I have a sudden urge," he said, so passionately that she wondered for a minute why he was moving *away* from the hotel. "I want," he stated deeply and distinctly, "a cheeseburger."

She laughed. "So you *have* missed something."

"Nope. Out of sight, out of mind. But I saw this little burger place on the way in, and my stomach is suddenly like a little kid, tugging and whining, 'I wannit! I wannit!'" He shot her a sheepish grin. "Sound okay?"

"Sounds great!"

It tasted great, too. Thick cheeseburgers with lettuce and tomato and onion and ketchup—Sam had three to Chelsea's two, and they were both sighing with satisfaction by the time they hit the street again.

Browsing leisurely, they wandered through the shops, but the carvings in the art stores seemed inferior to those the old man at the *pueblito* had made and the Mexican dresses hanging in stalls looked gaudy in comparison to the *huipiles* embroidered by Julia and Tonia.

Chelsea was fascinated by two things, each of which Sam insisted on buying her. The first was a round carving of the Mayan calendar, made in different shades of wood. She couldn't decipher it, though Sam was able to explain several of the markings, but she loved the idea of hanging it in her apartment.

The second was even more special, more personal. It was a ring made of sterling silver, with a flat, straight surface across the top. After much conferring over patterns they liked, they picked an elongated oval one, then watched, delighted and fascinated, as the young Mexican craftsman cut the oval and, within it, Chelsea's initials from the silver. It was beautiful, sleek and shiny, and she couldn't keep from lifting her hand to look at it every few minutes.

When they returned to the hotel they sat in the lobby, playing tourist, listening to a concert being performed by a group of singers and guitarists. The music was typically Mexican, largely love songs with an upbeat tempo and a mellow haunting quality. Sam took her hand in his and she felt something pass between them—something dear but strangely sad, as though they were clinging to a fleeting dream.

After the concert they went for a swim in the pool, then showered again, then went out for dinner. This time Chelsea wore a pale-blue shirtdress with padded shoulders and the collar raised in back. She'd put on makeup and heels, and was feeling eminently self-conscious until she took a look at Sam.

For a minute he looked strange, almost foreign to her, and she felt frightened. He wore a broad-striped mauve-and-gray shirt, open at the neck, and a pair of gray linen slacks and black loafers. His hair was neatly combed, and the faint scent of after-shave lingered in the air about him.

"You look very chic and cosmopolitan," she said nervously.

"So do you," he said in like tone. "But you're beautiful."

"And you're handsome."

"Then I guess they'll allow us into the restaurant," he quipped. Then he smiled, which was all Chelsea needed. If she could block out all else—his clothes, their surroundings—he was still the man she loved.

When he offered his elbow, she hooked her arm in it and together they left the room and found a cab. Maxime's proved to be an elegant French restaurant set in the former home of the mayor. The food was delicately prepared, the service without fault, the atmosphere calm and relaxing. They laughed about how weird it was to be waited on, how they'd probably get sick because the food was so rich and bacteria-free. They talked of light things—other vacation spots each had either seen or wanted to see, favorite and not-so-favorite restaurants at home, the Boston Common at Christmastime.

But in between there were awkward times, actually not so much awkward, Chelsea mused, as pensive. Times when their thoughts were their own and not to be shared, and that was sad in itself.

When they returned to the hotel, she wasn't sure what to expect. She stood on the balcony looking out over the Caribbean, wanting desperately to be back at the *pueblito*, in the hut where everything seemed so simple and right.

Sam stood no more than three feet away but something kept her from reaching for him, though she was lonely and aching.

"We'll make it," he said, so softly that she wondered if he was talking to himself. She looked over at him. His features were lit by the pale moon shimmering across the water, and she saw that his jaw was tense. She sensed then that his words had been more a prayer than a statement of fact, and she remembered how, earlier that day, he'd asked for her help. Yet she'd been so wrapped up in her own worries that she hadn't been thinking of the qualms he must be having about returning to civilization, if not about their relationship itself.

Love was a balm then, overpowering her fears, and she broke the distance between them and wrapped her arms around him. "We will, we will," she murmured, pressing the softest of kisses to his throat. Her reward was in the feel of his arms going around her, tightening, crushing her until she had to gasp for breath.

"Come." He released her and led her into the room, where in unspoken agreement they quickly undressed. With each item of clothing that fell aside, she felt better. When they were naked before each other, she felt even better. For, after casting off the trappings of the outer world, they were as they'd been before. Man and woman. Familiar and safe. Inexorably drawn to each other.

Their lovemaking was intense and prolonged. It was their first time on a bed, they joked, and they made the most of it, rolling and writhing without fear of injury or physical upset. Sam used the freedom to thoroughly explore every inch of Chelsea's body. He twisted around to kiss her toes, flipped her over to lave the backs of her knees with his tongue, returned her to her back so that he could intimately kiss that part of her he'd never tasted before.

In a brief moment of sanity, Chelsea recalled that Samuel Prescott London was supposed to be inhibited. *Inhibited?* No way! And she was no more so, finding sensitive spots all over his body, inciting them with her hands, her lips, her tongue.

They brought each other to fulfillment once, then shifted and began again. When Chelsea thought she was totally exhausted, Sam proved her wrong. When Sam swore he'd never move again, Chelsea made him eat his words. At one point, supposedly between bouts, when she was in her familiar spoonlike position against him, he entered her that way and she was stunned.

He was forceful but ever gentle, demanding but ever giving, and by the time they finally drifted to sleep some time near dawn, she thought she'd never love him more.

THEY SLEPT WELL INTO THE MORNING, then went for a late breakfast buffet, where they gorged on pancakes drowned in syrup, croissants and sweet rolls rich with butter and jam, and all the other little treats that they hadn't had in so long. Lying on the beach later was a necessity. Their stomachs were so full they couldn't have moved even if their limbs hadn't been aching from the night's activity. So they soaked in the sun and eased their weary bones in the sea. From time to time Chelsea would look at Sam and glow at the sight. Relaxed flat out on his lounge chair, he was long and lean, bronzed and virile. His swimsuit was a modest though trim-fitting blue and white job that reminded her of his boxer shorts, which in turn reminded her of the nights they'd spent together at the *pueblito*. Then her mind would wander further and she'd brood about the future.

Tomorrow they'd be headed inland again, but how long could she stay? She went round and round trying to decide if she should be pressuring Sam more about returning, wondering whether indeed he'd follow her if she were to announce that she was flying home. Oh, yes, she wanted him there. She cringed at the thought of life without him. She believed that he loved her, but was that love strong enough to see him through the adjustments he'd have to make in his life to make the city palatable to him? Was it strong enough to see him through the explanations he'd have to hear from her?

She cursed Beatrice London in one breath, blessed her in another. Had it not been for the woman, she'd never be in the untenable position she was. On the other hand, had it not been for her, she never would have met Sam.

Sam must have been doing his own share of soul-searching, for by afternoon he seemed as ready for a diversion as she was. When he suggested that they go to the bullfight, she jumped at the opportunity. He'd been to one before, but she hadn't, and she was curious and eager. If she found it vaguely brutal, there was consolation in Sam's understanding.

When the spectacle was over, he took her for a soothing drive through Cancun city. It was a young city, barely ten years old, and had been built up at the same time as the island—which was really unrecognizable as an island because the causeway to the mainland was so short. Aside from shops and restaurants built for the tourists, the city housed workers from the local hotels.

Sam pointed out various monuments commemorating one event or another, then, on the drive back to the hotel, showed her intricate formations in the median strip shrubbery that she hadn't noticed before.

That night they ate dinner at Bogart's. The high ceiling fans were reminiscent of *Casablanca*, but the decor was thoroughly modern and the food international. Chelsea enjoyed it as much as she was able, given the fact that she felt an odd premonition about the night. It was to be their last in Cancun, and she felt unsettled.

Sam was unusually quiet at dinner. She wondered if he shared her uneasiness, particularly when he took her in his arms the instant they entered their room and proceeded to make love to her with an intensity verging on fear. Her own response was no less frenzied, for it bore the sense of desperation she felt.

There were no words this time, no gentle urgings and soft endearments. But when it was over and Sam was asleep, Chelsea whispered her love to him, over and over until at last she too heard no more.

The next morning, when she stirred against his warmth, she sensed an unmistakeable tension that had nothing to do with passion. Opening her eyes, she raised her head to look up at him. Wide awake, he met her gaze, and she knew that the moment of truth had come.

8

"DID YOU MEAN IT?" he asked. He was propped against the headboard of the bed, and there were shadows beneath his eyes. His expression was shuttered, but the taut set of his neck and shoulders spoke volumes.

She swallowed. "Mean what?"

"That you love me."

"You heard?" she whispered, and at his nod hastened to confirm it. "Yes. I meant it. I do love you, Sam. More than I ever thought I could love another human being." She felt it imperative that he know, beforehand, the precise state of her heart. "But there's more I have to tell you."

"I know," he stated quietly, his eyes never once leaving hers.

She hadn't quite expected his statement. Her brow furrowed and she sat up, dragging the sheet around her as she faced him. "You *know*?"

He stared at her wordlessly for a minute and her heart began to hammer. When at last he spoke, it was in a low, even tone.

"Jason Ingram has been dead for three years, Chelsea. He was killed in an automobile accident. I read about it in the alumni publication."

Jason Ingram *dead*? Jason Ingram. . .her alleged contact. . .and Sam had known from the very first day. "Why didn't you say something?" she breathed unsteadily. "Why didn't you accuse me of being a fraud?" One part of her wished he had; then the truth might have come out long before and she might never have stayed around long enough to get to know Sam, to fall in love. Or she might still have stayed around and their love would have been that much freer and sweeter.

"I didn't say anything because I didn't want to know. I very successfully pushed it out of my mind."

"Until now."

"Until you said you loved me."

"I do, Sam," she cried urgently. "You have to believe that. I *do* love you!"

The muscle in his jaw flexed. "That's a pretty strong claim, and you've got to know you're playing with fire. I think you'd better tell me the whole story. The truth, Chelsea. All of it."

He was angry, carefully controlled, but angry, and she didn't blame him. It hurt, because she loved him so, but simultaneously she felt a sense of relief that at last she could bare her heart and mind.

"Everything I told you about my childhood is true," she began, begging with her eyes, her voice, the intensity of her pose. "I grew up in a New Hampshire mill town, went off to college and then taught for a year. And yes, I was frustrated with my work, but that wasn't the main reason I quit after the year."

"What was?"

"Susan's disappearance. For several months I worked fulltime looking for her. I was frustrated beyond belief because it seemed that there wasn't anyone who could help me. But I discovered that there were scores of other families in similar situations, and in the course of looking for Susan I managed to locate several other of those missing children." She spoke quickly, her voice at a high pitch, pleading for Sam's understanding, his trust. When his expression said nothing, she rushed on.

"So I decided to devote myself to doing that—looking for missing children—because I was already forming contacts and God knows I was dedicated to the cause."

"I can understand that," was his terse reply.

"I've been doing it for six years, Sam, but the last three of those years I've been saving every penny. I worked at Icabod's at night to earn extra money. I'd decided that I wanted to go back to school to get a Ph.D. in counseling so that I could help prevent some of those runaway situations."

"That's fine," he said, obviously waiting for the connection between what she'd done in Boston and what she was doing here.

That was the hard part for Chelsea, but its time had just about come. She clutched at the sheet and took a steadying breath. "Early in June I got a call from your mother. I met with her in Wellesley and she said she wanted to hire me."

If Sam's face had been expressionless before, it was no longer so. His every feature hardened—eyes darkened, nostrils flared, jaws clenched and lips thinned. "You met with my mother," he gritted. "With my *mother!*"

"You must have suspected it."

He was too angry to even shake his head. "You did say you phoned her. But I thought maybe one of the guys at the office sent you. I *never* would have believed you'd been tied up with *her!*"

"I went to her house not knowing what to expect. After she told me what it was she wanted—"

"What *did* she want? Exactly."

"She wanted me to find you and bring you back."

"Damn it! What *business* was it of hers?"

"That was what I asked her, though not in as many words. I said that you were old enough to make your own decisions. But she's your mother. She thought she knew what was best."

"God *damn* it!"

"I didn't want to take the job, Sam," she pleaded. "I told her that I didn't usually do this type of thing."

"Wait a minute. I thought you just said that you did."

"She wanted me to get you *back*. That was part of the deal! I was to find you and," she took a breath, "in your mother's word, 'lure' you back to Boston."

Sam bolted from the bed and stalked across the room before whirling to face her again. He was stark naked, but neither of them noticed. He was too angry, and Chelsea was too embroiled in what seemed somehow a fight for her life.

"And you went along," he snarled in disgust.

"I *had* to! She'd hired an investigator. She knew exactly where I'd come from, what I was doing, how much I earned, even how much I paid in taxes!"

"So? What different did it make if she knew those things? If she was up to blackmail, she'd have had to have something else on you. What was it, Chelsea?" He glared at her, a white line of fury between his brows. "What else haven't you told me?"

"Nothing! You know it all!"

"But you said you *had* to do it. Why, for God's sake? How could you cheapen yourself by agreeing to seduce a man?"

He didn't understand any of it, and she was frantic. Her voice was high and trembling. "I *didn't* agree to seduce you. When I thought that was what she was suggesting, I told her I wouldn't do it."

"But you did. You did it, Chelsea."

She was shaking her head jerkily. "No. What happened between us happened because I'd fallen in love with you."

"Bull! You conspired with that witch. Coldly and deliberately."

"That's not true!"

He had his fists on his hips and his head was thrust forward so that the veins in his neck stood out prominently. "If it isn't, then way—did—you—do it?"

"I told you. Because I love—"

He cut her off with the sharp wave of his hand. "Why did you *accept the job*?"

In hindsight, Chelsea would have chosen different words, but at the moment she was disconsolate and perilously close to tears. "Because I needed the money, damn it! I wanted the money! She offered me the one thing she knew I couldn't refuse! You have to understand, Sam. She knew that I wanted to go to grad school. She knew how long I'd have to go, and that it would take me years more to save up enough money on my own. She knew *exactly* how long the program was, and how much it would cost. And she offered it all to me, if I'd come down here and somehow get you back."

"You couldn't have needed the money that bad. Haven't you ever heard about scholarships?"

"I went through college on a scholarship. But five years ago my mother's brother died and left Susan and me a trust fund, so technically I don't qualify for a scholarship."

"If you've got a trust fund, why would you need it? Why in the hell don't you just use your own money to pay your tuition?"

"Because until I'm thirty-five I can only use the interest, and *that* I give to my parents every month to supplement the little they get from dad's retirement fund." Even Beatrice London hadn't known that, but Chelsea was too distraught to feel any satisfaction.

She caught her breath and swallowed hard, but Sam showed no sign of softening. "I wanted to go to school," she said brokenly. "I wanted it more than anything, and she was dangling it right there in front of my nose. She even offered to get me admitted!"

"I'm sure she did," he snapped. Spinning around, he dug in the dresser for his shorts. "You were never a writer. You'd done some research on the Maya, but beyond that it was all a lie."

"No—"

"And you sold yourself for the highest price. I have to say," he muttered, yanking on his cutoffs, "that's *one* way to get ahead in the world. I just wouldn't have expected you to stoop to it."

Tears were trickling down her cheeks but she was oblivious to them. "You don't understand! You won't listen! At the time I thought it might all work out. I pictured you so very differently. I never *dreamed* I'd be attracted to you—"

"Which makes it all the worse," he interrupted, tugging his T-shirt over his head. "You'd have given yourself to a man you didn't even like. You'd have wound him around your little finger and then led him home by the nose. That's disgusting, Chelsea. Really disgusting. I mean, I wouldn't have put it past my mother, but *you*?" He ran an angry hand through his hair. "God, I really thought you were different."

"I *am* what you thought. I've been me for the past three weeks—where are you going?" she cried in alarm.

"Out."

"Don't go! Please! Stay and help me work this through!"

"You can stay if you want. See if you can find peace with yourself. I know that I sure as hell won't be able to!"

"Sam, don't—"

But the door slammed on her words and Chelsea was suddenly and utterly alone. She stared at the still white barrier, hoping that it might open again and he'd be back. But its only movement was caused by the blurring of her vision. Soft sobs erupted from her throat and grew louder, more heart-wrenching, until at last she crumpled onto the bed and cried.

She clutched the pillow—his pillow—and hugged it to her, but all it brought back was the scent of him and memories. Beautiful memories that tore into her, cut her apart, left a gaping void in the vicinity of her heart.

She cried until she was exhausted, until her sobs lengthened into breathy hiccoughs. And she continued to lie where she was because nothing seemed to want to function—not her arms or her legs or her mind.

It was the knock of the maid wanting to clean the room that finally roused her from her paralysis. She sat up in bed and called to the girl to come back later, then slowly looked around and forced herself to think.

Blotting her tears on the backs of her hands, she climbed from the bed, showered and dressed. Then she sat in the upholstered chair and waited. Surely Sam was just out walking, giving himself a chance to cool off. Surely he'd see her side. He *had* to. After all, he loved her.... Or did he? Not once, looking her straight in the eye, had he said the words. He'd kidded that first day, but she had to take that at face value. He'd called her "love" from time to time, but it was an endearment people often used, and it wasn't the same as a flat out, "I love you."

But she'd *seen* it in his eyes, *felt* it in his body. Or had she been wrong? Had she simply seen something she'd wanted to see? If he loved her, he'd be back. She knew it.

So she waited. And waited. As the minutes dragged into hours—she put the maid off twice more—she began to despair, for she forced herself to look at his side of the situation, and what she saw was bleak.

Sam felt betrayed. He felt used and manipulated. And if he loved her, things were even worse! He'd never been a man to easily give his love, and he was probably cursing himself for a fool!

Chelsea wrung her hands, stared at the walls, the ceiling, the small clock on the dresser. Her stomach was a mass of tight knots, but her limbs felt rubbery. Noontime approached, and when he hadn't returned, she began to wonder if he was sending her a message. She realized that when he'd stormed out he'd been wearing his denim cutoffs and familiar T-shirt. Not his "resort" shorts and shirt. Perhaps he didn't intend to come back at all. Perhaps he was already back at the *pueblito*!

Feeling as if she were living a nightmare, she quietly got up and began to pack her things. One thought was predominant in her mind—she'd brought him the pain, the tension he'd come down here to escape. That thought brought her

even more anguish, loving him as she did. If leaving, returning to the States would free him of it, so be it.

Her suitcase was closed and she was repacking her carry-
on bag when she came across the small notebook she'd used
as a diary. She picked it up, smoothed her hand over its cover,
turned it, then held it suspended for a minute. She could leave
it for Sam, she realized, let him read for himself what she felt.
But no. She tucked the notebook in the bag and zipped it
closed. If he hadn't believed her spoken words, the diary
would be worthless.

She'd reached the end of the line. Breathing raggedly,
trying not to start crying again, she slung the carryon over
her shoulder, lifted her suitcase and rushed from the room.

A taxi was waiting in front of the hotel and had her at the
airport in no time. She was able to get a last-minute seat on
a plane bound for New York, from where she could easily take
a shuttle to Boston. Ironically, given the waiting she'd had to
do when she first landed in Cancun, she was airborne within
an hour of leaving the hotel. Another message, she told herself. She should have listened all along!

But the only thing she could hear, as the plane banked and
headed north, was the pained beating of her battered heart.
And she knew it would be a long, long time before it eased.

IT WAS LATE THAT NIGHT before she finally unlocked the door
of her small apartment and dropped her things inside. The
air was stale and hot, and not much relief came from opening the windows. It seemed that July had been cruel to the
city—or was it the other way around? The same tempera-
ture, she knew, wouldn't have been as oppressive in the Yucatán, but then, there was nothing suffocating about the
Yucatán...

She didn't want to think. She was tired and heartsick.
Tossing her clothes in a heap, she threw back the coverings
of her bed and sank down on the sheets. They were clean and
fresh-smelling and...sterile. She closed her eyes and tried to

blot out all that had happened since she'd left, tried to imagine she'd *never* left and that this was just another hot July night like so many she'd spent here in past years.

It didn't work. Her mind kept returning to Sam's face during that last confrontation—the fury, the disgust, the disillusionment. And though she thought she'd been too drained she started to cry again, which made her all the more hot and uncomfortable.

There was nothing she could do, though, but let her sorrow vent itself. When her sobbing finally waned, she got up and took a cool shower. It only served to remind her of the primitive showers she'd taken behind the hut, and the tears returned with a vengeance.

At last she fell asleep, waking in spurts when one dream or another—her mind had refused to leave the Yucatán, it seemed—wrenched at her. Memories crowded in, overlapped, came in flashes that were quickly followed by despair. By morning she knew that her only salvation would be in nonstop activity.

So she quickly dressed and ran to the post office, to pick up her mail and arrange to have its delivery resumed; the supermarket, to restock her empty refrigerator; the bank, to withdraw what she'd deposited of Beatrice London's retainer. The only part of the money she'd keep, she decided, was what she'd already spent on the trip. That seemed fair. As for the rest, it was tainted. After what Sam had said, she knew she'd feel dirty until she'd returned every remaining cent. The sooner she got it out of her possession, the better.

Determinedly, she put in a call to the Wellesley Hills estate as soon as she returned to her apartment. Beatrice London, quite appropriately, was at work. So she looked up the number of the London Corporation and dialed, only to learn that the woman was in conference and would have to get back to her.

Frustrated, Chelsea hung up the phone. She stowed the food she'd bought in the refrigerator and thumbed through the mail that had collected during her absence. It was small solace to find a letter of acceptance into the doctoral program at Boston University; she wouldn't be going this fall, that was for sure.

Tossing the rest of the mail impatiently onto the table, she paced her apartment, glaring at the phone each time she passed it, willing Beatrice London to call her back. She knew that she'd never be able to think about resuming her own work until this last bit of business had been cleaned up, and in the meanwhile she was restless and distressed.

Her apartment was home, but it wasn't. It was empty. She was empty. She felt lost, at loose ends and oh, so weary. She had to *do* something. She had to keep busy.

But still she waited on Beatrice London's call.

At long last she sank onto the sofa and, in an attempt to curb the self-pity that shadowed her, took stock of exactly where she was and what she had in life. She had her apartment here in Cambridge, with its relatively reasonable rent. She had a business that only awaited her go-ahead to spring back to life. At Icabod's she had a friend in her boss, who'd told her she'd have a job if she wanted it. She even had the admission letter from BU, an admission that she was sure could be deferred for a while. It was even remotely possible that, given the nature of the work she'd been doing for the past six years, the proper university personnel might be able to arrange for some kind of fellowship to see her through. And if that didn't happen, she would continue on as she'd been doing before that fateful June day when she'd been summoned to Wellesley Hills. She'd work, save, and eventually get to grad school as she'd planned.

So what had she lost? One month…and a hefty chunk of her heart. Her eyes watered again. She missed Sam so! It was bad enough today not waking to his commanding presence, not talking with him, not helping him work. But thought of the days and weeks and months to come without seeing him, without feeling his arms around her and knowing his warmth and caring and the kind of gentle protectiveness he'd shown her...made her feel hollow and positively destitute.

The phone rang and she jumped. Dashing the tears from her cheeks, she ran to the kitchen and snatched up the receiver.

"Hello?"

"Miss Ross. This is Beatrice London." The tone was colder, more imperious than ever. "I understand you called me."

Chelsea pressed her fingers into the folds of her skirt. "Yes. I'd like to meet with you as soon as possible."

"And I you, Miss Ross," the other woman stated indignantly. "My office is at One Boston Place. Be here in half an hour."

"That's fine," Chelsea answered boldly. If Beatrice London was angry about something—presumably that Chelsea was back and Sam wasn't—she was no less so. Without another word, she hung up the phone, picked up her purse and headed for the subway.

She walked at what seemed to her a clipped pace, though it was no faster than everyone around her was walking. She assumed she was simply used to the more casual pace of Mexico, and when that thought brought a hard lump to her throat, she forced herself to swallow. Gritting her teeth, she focused on her upcoming meeting with Mrs. London.

By the time she emerged from the subway in Government Center and headed down State Street to One Boston Place, she was incensed. She'd told Beatrice London that Sam was a grown man and had a right to make decisions for himself. What right did the woman have in meddling? Didn't she realize that it was her interference that had alienated Sam in the first place? How could she continue to make him miserable? He'd done nothing to deserve it, nothing at all!

While the elevator carried her to the thirtieth floor, Chelsea took deep breaths to calm herself. Beatrice London was no longer a client, but there was still some propriety to be observed. The last thing Chelsea wanted was to show that she'd been out of her league this time around.

Walking straight and tall, she approached the receptionist and announced herself. It was exactly half an hour since she'd hung up the phone, but she half suspected Mrs. London would keep her waiting purely as a show of power. When the receptionist immediately directed her through the wide doors and into the inner sanctum of the London Corporation, Chelsea was frankly surprised. But she kept her composure and smoothly glided through the doors and down the corridor until she reached Beatrice London's secretary.

"Mrs. London is expecting you," the young woman said coolly. "Please go in."

The door to the office beyond was open, but not for long. Chelsea had no sooner stepped over the threshold than Mrs. London, who was sitting behind the large desk with her elbows on the arms of her high-backed chair, spoke.

"Close the door, Miss Ross. I don't care to have my employees hear what I'm about to say."

Chelsea closed the door, then turned to face the woman. Beatrice London was as perfectly dressed and coiffed as she'd been at their last meeting, though there was a pinched look around her nose and mouth that spoke of pure anger.

"Please sit down," she commanded quietly.

"I think not," Chelsea responded, willing herself to appear poised and self-assured—neither of which she was feeling, since the woman before her was thoroughly intimidating. The aura of regality she'd worn that first day had metamorphosed into one of tyranny. Chelsea well understood why for sheer survival Sam had broken free.

Reaching into her purse, Chelsea drew out the money order she'd had the bank draw up. She'd clipped a list of her expenses behind it. Both she placed on the desk. "Here is the retainer you gave me, less what I spent for plane fare, taxis and car rental. You'll find a detailed list of those expenses on the second sheet. I want no part of this job, Mrs. London. You'll have to hire someone else to do your dirty work."

Beatrice London's eyes were hard as charcoal. "It's a little late for that, Miss Ross. I should be suing you for damages, and I may yet, so if you've got your heart set on that graduate degree of yours, perhaps you ought to think again."

Chelsea hadn't known what to expect, but it wasn't this. "I'm...I'm not sure I know what you mean."

"Samuel called me last night, Miss Ross. He was absolutely furious, and, frankly, so am I! I thought I told you that you weren't to let him know I had any part of this."

Sam had called? He'd called his mother. It took her a minute to ingest the information. "There were extenuating circumstances," she offered at last, but her voice sounded decidedly meek, so she cleared her throat and tried again. "I was with Sam for over three weeks. It was only at the end that I felt I had to tell him the truth."

"And now the whole thing is ruined," Mrs. London railed. She sat forward, placing her hands on the desk. Her fingers tightened until her knuckles were white. "Thanks to you, he blames me for everything! There's no way he'll return now, and there isn't a chance in the world that he'll trust anyone else I might send. You've done that, Miss Ross. You've made a bad situation even worse!"

Chelsea didn't know what to say. "I—I'm sorry. I never intended that."

"And just what *did* you intend, Miss Ross? It appears you managed to get under Samuel's skin. Did you hope to hook a wealthy man and have your future made?"

On the one hand Chelsea was appalled by the suggestion. On the other she wanted to laugh. "If you could see the way Sam's been living, you'd never be saying that. During the time I was with him, it never once occurred to me that he had more, monetarily, than I did."

"Then what *did* occur to you? You were there for three weeks. Were you just vacationing? Along for the ride? It must have become apparent after a time that Samuel didn't want to come back. Why on earth did you stay after that?"

Chelsea chose her words with care. With even greater care she struggled to contain her anger. That this woman was making *her* out to be the villain was incredible! "You hired me to do a job. You told me to take as long as I needed. It wasn't simply a matter of going down there, telling Sam he ought to come home and expecting he'd comply. At the beginning he wouldn't talk about it at all. As we got to know each other he opened up more. He has some very strong feelings—"

"I know that, Miss Ross. I was the one who had to hold the phone a foot away last night while he thundered on. And I'd like to know exactly what *you* did to make him so angry at me."

"I told him that you'd hired me. That was all."

"You sided with him, didn't you? You told him he'd be a fool to come back."

"I did not! I'd never have done that! I wanted him back too!"

"Yes," the older woman stated, her eyes narrowing. "You wanted the rest of your money." She sat back suddenly. It was the most abrupt movement Chelsea had seen her make and it said something for her composure. "But now you've returned most of what I gave you in the first place, Miss Ross. And I have to ask myself why. The only conclusion I can reach is that you know you've done wrong and you're trying to buy your way free and clear. Is that it, Miss Ross? Are you wallowing in guilt?"

Any thoughts Chelsea had of remaining composed fled then. Her legs had begun to shake and she was clutching her bag for dear life. She felt that she was raw, and that the odious woman before her was rubbing salt on the wound. "Yes, I feel guilty! But that isn't why I'm returning your money. I'm returning it because it's dirty and it makes me feel that way too. No, Mrs. London, I feel guilty because I kept your filthy secret for three long weeks, and during those weeks I fell in love with Sam. It began to gnaw and gnaw at me that he didn't know everything, because I think he loved me too and still I was keeping things from him. I was frightened of telling him the truth, and rightly so, as it turned out." She took a shuddering breath. "I think that I hurt Sam very, very badly. *That*'s what I feel guilty about!"

Beatrice London stared at her with those coal-dark eyes for a minute. When she spoke, her tone was scathing. "Very touching, Miss Ross. You fell in love with my son. And you thought Samuel loved you? Did you honestly believe that a girl like you could appeal to a man of my son's station? Did you honestly think it would ever really work?"

"It was working in Mexico. I hadn't thought of the future. We both avoided it."

"Well. That was intuitive, at least."

"Not intuitive," Chelsea argued, feeling her anger coming to the fore. "It was the way things were down there. We lived day to day, enjoying the present without brooding on the future. At least, it was that way till the end, when both of us began thinking more. I had to get over the hurdle of telling Sam the truth before I could begin to think of a future with him. As for Sam, I honestly think he was beginning to consider coming home."

"Until you told him about me."

"I told him the simple truth. He was angry, and he stormed off. I love him, and I hurt him, and because of that I'm hurting too. Very badly."

"So now you're back here, with a broken heart. And that's two of us, Miss Ross. That's two of us."

"No, Mrs. London," Chelsea stated distinctly. There were several things she wanted to make very clear before she left. "Don't ever make the mistake of putting us in the same boat. I love Sam, love him with all my heart. I don't *have* to love him. He's not flesh of my flesh. He's not my 'responsibility.' I don't love him because of what business he's in or who he knows or because he makes just the right appearance at very proper social functions. I love him because of *him*, because of the beautiful person he is inside. With every single trapping of civilization stripped away, I love him."

She took a quick breath, then raced on. "It really is ironic that you'd suggest I might be after his money. The man you described to me in June, the man I went looking for didn't appeal to me at all. I didn't believe Sam was who he said he was at first, because he was different in every conceivable way from what I'd come to expect. And all monetary considerations aside, it's possible that if he *had* come back with me, I might have found him to be a very different man from the one I'd fallen in love with."

She turned to leave, feeling that if she didn't soon she was sure to explode. She was so hurt, so angry, so lovesick, so utterly distraught that her nerves were strung tight. She didn't even care when her eyes flooded with tears. "I want you to know one last thing. You son happens to be the finest, the warmest, the most caring person I've ever met in my life. He's intelligent and witty. He's thoughtful and giving. And he's strong, so much stronger than either you or me, because he was able to see something desperately wrong with his life and take steps to change it. I respect him for that. Respect him, and love him. I'll always love him, Mrs. London. And I'll always pray that he finds the peace and happiness he deserves."

She was breathless when she finished, and it was all she could do to stumble from the room, run down the corridor, get into the elevator and reach the ground floor before she was reduced to a quivering mass of misery. Getting Beatrice London off her back had been the final severance of her link with Sam. Not that her heart would listen, but her mind did and her body did and she felt bereft.

Dragging a pair of oversized sunglasses from her purse, she put them on to mask her grief from the world. Then she started walking up over Beacon Hill, down to the Charles and along the river path toward Cambridge. She'd never have dreamed of walking the entire way home, but the thought of being contained in an airless subway car, with people milling about, was anathema to her. And more than anything, she wanted to exhaust herself so that when she finally reached her apartment she'd be numb.

Which she was. Numb. And tired. She crawled into bed, heedless of the fact that it was early afternoon and that she was still fully dressed. She was hot and sweaty, yet she pulled the sheet to her ears; there was a chill inside her that no amount of heat seemed able to ease.

She fell asleep for several hours and awoke, if not feeling rested, then at least feeling she'd put some distance between herself and the scene in Beatrice London's office. Sam was another thing, because she couldn't put distance between herself and him. She remembered every little thing they'd done together as though it had been yesterday, rather than a week, ten days, two weeks ago. She lay in bed wondering what he was doing at the moment, picturing him at the *pueblito* working among the men, eating at Tonia's hut, sleeping in the hammock they'd shared.

She took the Mayan calendar from her suitcase and fingered it lovingly because Sam had touched it. She looked at her ring and knew she'd never take it off because he had bought it for her and helped design it. She put on the shorts and the "Cancun" T-shirt, and even the styleless underpants he'd picked up at the store in Valladolid.

And she sat on her bed dressed that way and hugged the round wood carving to her breast while she wept at the knowledge that she couldn't have Sam, that she'd never have him again.

THE FOLLOWING MORNING she fetched her car from the garage where she'd stored it and drove to New Hampshire to see her parents. She felt a desperate need to go home, to remember all that had been good there, the warmth, the love.

She hadn't intended to weigh her parents down with her tale of woe, but within hours it was spilling out anyway. She supposed she'd needed to share her heartache with people who cared. That, subsconsciously, this was one of the reasons she'd come. And it helped some, telling her parents how much she loved Sam, feeling their arms around her as she cried, hearing their gentle words of consolation.

But they had no miracle glue to repair her broken heart. She knew she'd be the only one who could tend to it.

So, after two days, she returned to Cambridge. She still hurt. Every time she thought of Sam she hurt. But the wound wasn't quite as raw anymore, so she was able to do what she'd originally intended, to throw herself back into her work, make up for lost time, move on.

After a handful of phone calls, she had several children to find. With another call, she was back on the payroll at Icabod's. Her life returned to the pattern she'd known before she'd left for the Yucatán, and she was in demand and busy. And excruciatingly tired.

She couldn't seem to sleep, not well at least. She'd lie awake for hours trying not to think of Sam but failing. She'd awaken in the middle of the night and imagine he was with her, only to be disillusioned when she opened her eyes and realized where she was and that she was alone. Then she'd lie on her back, staring at the ceiling, hashing and rehashing what had happened, wondering if there had been any other way, if she might somehow have been able to salvage their relationship. Once or twice, in moments of overpowering distress, she contemplated flying back to Mexico and begging, but she knew Sam wouldn't want that. She kept seeing the disdain in his eyes that last day, and she knew she couldn't bear to face it again.

So she rationalized. Beatrice London was right. Chelsea and Sam came from different worlds. Their relationship would never have survived the return to Boston. He'd be back in his office, wearing his tense face and glasses, and she'd die a little each day because he'd be so embroiled in his rat race that she wouldn't be able to reach him. So she'd watch as he very slowly drove himself into the ground, and she'd feel guilty for having dragged him back from the Yucatán, where he'd been so healthy, so vibrant, so happy.

It was better this way, she told herself. But that didn't mean she felt any better about it, because regardless of what she did or how busy she was in the course of a day, she was lonely. Always lonely. She wanted to tell Sam about her work, but he wasn't there. She wanted to stretch out beside him when she was exhausted, but he wasn't there. She wanted to hold him and tell him how much she loved him and somehow vent the feelings that seemed at times to be choking her, but he wasn't there.

She was constantly tired, because she worked too hard and too fast with too little rest in between. She was often weak, because she couldn't bear the thought of eating, much less eating alone. Her tan faded. She lost weight. If she hadn't known better, she would have thought she was pregnant. But she did know better. The IUD she'd never bothered to have removed precluded conception.

She wished she *were* pregnant. To have some part of Sam living in her would have been a solace. But it wasn't so.

Her problem was a broken heart. And there wasn't a single, solitary thing she could do about it—except hope that in time it would mend, that in time she'd begin to care, really care about living.

The day was hot and muggy and Chelsea was thoroughly enervated by the time she returned to her apartment. She'd spent the morning running around interviewing people on behalf of one client. She'd spent the early part of the afternoon on the phone, then had dashed out again to speak with a welfare worker who thought she had a lead on a second case. The lead proved to be a dead end, which Chelsea discovered only after she'd visited three more people in the neighborhood where the child had supposedly been seen.

Chelsea had been back from the Yucatán for two full weeks. She felt twenty years older.

A loud clap of thunder rent the air and she put a hand over her heart to still its sudden leap. When a knock came at her door with nearly as much force, she whirled around. Feeling dizzy, she grasped the back of the sofa. Whoever it was would go away. She simply wasn't in the mood to converse with another human being. Not when she was feeling like a soggy paper bag, worn and useless, threatening to tear with the smallest input. And she had barely an hour to somehow get herself together before heading for Icabod's!

The knock came again and she groaned. Wiping a forearm across her clammy brow, she steadied herself for a minute, took a deep breath, walked to the door and drew it open.

She might have been all right if it had been a matter of simple fatigue or overheating. Had it been her landlord, or her neighbor, or the postal carrier, she might have made it. Seeing Sam standing at her door, though, was the straw that broke the camel's back.

For the first time in her life, Chelsea Ross fainted dead away.

9

CHELSEA CAME TO SLOWLY. She was vaguely aware of someone slapping her face, calling her name. It sounded so like Sam's voice, so filled with warmth and worry, that she knew she must be dreaming, so she kept her eyes closed and let the dream go on.

But her cheeks felt another sting and the stark reality of it brought her lids up with a snap. She stared, then blinked, then swallowed, sure she was hallucinating.

"Chelsea? My God, Chelsea, are you all right?"

It *was* Sam, bending over her with a concern so reminiscent of that he'd shown the night in the *pueblito* when she'd gotten sick. Confused and frightened, she wanted to cry. Tears smarted behind her lids, though she could have sworn there had been none left.

Disoriented, she jerked her head around. She was lying on the sofa, with Sam sitting on its edge and leaning close. She quickly struggled to push herself up, but when she reached her feet she swayed. He dragged her down, tucked her head between her knees and firmly massaged the back of her neck.

"Take it easy. Breath deeply." He sounded as though he were taking his own advice. There was a long pause, then a soulful, "What have you *done* to yourself, Chelsea? You look awful!"

She would have laughed hysterically had she not been preoccupied controlling her dizziness. Her head was spinning in more ways than one. When she was finally able to sit up, she stumbled away from Sam and made it to the side chair before her legs gave out. He was half off the sofa to rush to her, but she warded him off with a shaky hand, and he sank back.

"What's the matter with you," he asked hoarsely.

"What are you doing here?" she whispered, eyes wide as she clutched the arms of the chair. She was shaking all over and couldn't seem to stop.

"I came back."

"But what are you doing *here*? You don't belong here! I don't know you!" Though her reaction was in large part the result of shock, there was some truth to it. He was wearing a dark business suit, a crisp white shirt, a striped tie and conservative cordovans. His mustache was still there, and his tan, but his hair had been trimmed and there was a tautness over the bridge of his nose and across his jaw. He looked every bit the aggressive businessman, and that thought made her tremble all the more.

As though sensing her fear, he forced the tension from his features. "You know me, Chels," he said more gently. "I may be dressed a little differently, but I'm the same man underneath."

She was in dire pain, dire emotional pain, and she was bewildered. "But why are you here?"

He came forward again, then stopped when she flinched. But nothing could stop his words. "I came to tell you that I love you. I do, y'know. I have since the first day we met."

She had her hands on her ears and was shaking her head. "Don't say that! Anything but that!"

His arms moved, as though about to encircle her. When she cringed, he clutched his hands between his knees. "It's the truth. Why shouldn't I say it?"

"Why *now*, Sam?" she screamed, feeling as though she were in hell. The tears that had welled moments before began to slide down her cheeks. He was cruel, she thought. How could he do this to her? She'd wanted and wanted, then convinced herself that it would never work. How *could* he?

Anguish brought her from the chair. Her every muscle was taut, which was a blessing because otherwise she would never have been able to stand. Her bones felt like powder, and she was crying openly. All the more gut-wrenching was the sadness she saw in his eyes when he looked at her.

"Better late than never—isn't that what they say...? Don't cry, Chels. Please?" He was on his feet, taking a step closer. "Something's terribly wrong. I don't understand—"

"It hurts!" she cried, sobbing. "It hurts so much!" Wheeling around, she fled into her bedroom and collapsed not on the bed but in a corner of the floor. She huddled there, hugging her knees, with her forehead pressed to them.

Sam's footsteps tapped softly across the wood floor, but she didn't hear through her misery. Then he was hunkering down, stroking her head, murmuring, "What have I done? Dear Lord, what have I done?" He put an arm around her shoulder. "Don't cry. Please, Chels, don't cry. I'll make it better, whatever it is. I promise. I'll make it better."

When he drew her closer, she resisted at first. But with her eyes closed she could only hear him and smell him and feel his warmth, and it was so familiar, so dear that the part of her that needed him so badly ruled. Unable to help herself, she continued to cry, but her sobs were muffled against his suit and soon she was clutching its lapels, brokenly whispering his name.

His arms tightened and he pressed her face to his chest until, at long last, the storm abated. Then he settled with her on the floor and began to talk softly, gently, soothingly.

"I was a fool, Chelsea, but I was hurt that day. I knew you'd been hiding something. I assumed someone had sent you, but I really did manage to push it out of my mind, because I adored you and I didn't want to think it might be true."

He paused for a minute to stroke her back. She was quiet, listening. Only an intermittent hiccough broke the silence until he spoke again.

"When you said you loved me, I felt that my entire future was at stake. I wanted to ask you to stay with me always, but I had to know the truth then. Hearing it from your lips was like a knife thrust." He pressed his head protectively over hers. "I know I overreacted. I'm human, and imperfect. I think I was so damned scared because I've never felt this way about a woman, and then to learn that you'd been lying, that *she*'d sent you...something snapped in my mind, I guess."

Chelsea sat against him without moving. It all made sense, what he said, but still she was tortured because she'd come so much further since that awful morning.

"I walked around Cancun all day, Chelsea, not knowing what to do. After a while I realized how wrong I'd been, but then I got defensive." He shifted his cheek against her hair and his voice grew softer. "Men do that when they're feeling vulnerable, when they hurt. And I was hurting.

"I kept asking myself why you hadn't told me sooner, why you'd let it go on so long. You had to know I loved you. I wanted you with me every minute, and it wasn't only the physical thing. I found pleasure in showing you all about life down there, a life I'd begun to take for granted. And that stunned me, because I hadn't realized I was taking *anything* for granted. But I guess all of life is that way, whether it's here or in the Yucatán. Being able to share, to see things through another person's eyes, makes them fresh and new and special." His breath fanned her temple. "Are you listening, Chels?"

Unable to speak yet, she slowly nodded her head. He seemed satisfied with the wordless response.

"Those last few days I'd begun to think more about where we were headed, what I was going to do. I knew you wouldn't stay in Mexico forever, and suddenly I wasn't sure if I wanted to either. I kept remembering the things you'd said about making adjustments here, setting priorities I could live with. But I didn't think I could do it alone. I wanted you. I *needed* you."

He pressed a soft kiss on the top of her head before returning his cheek there. "I thought about all those things while I wandered around Cancun. My anger wore itself out. The hurt faded. And I knew you'd been right, that I should have stayed and talked it through with you. By the time I got back to the hotel you were gone. I called the airport and found that you'd flown out hours before. I was stunned—both because you'd left and because I realized that through that entire day I'd only been thinking of *me*."

He rubbed his hand up and down her spine. It was a gesture of comfort rather than sensual awareness. "I sat in that hotel room and relived the argument we'd had. I heard myself, the ugly words I'd used, the accusations I'd known weren't true but which had come out in the heat of anger. I was a bastard, Chelsea. I should never have said those things, because they weren't true and they hurt you."

His voice was less steady when he went on, as though he were back there again, suffering. "My first thought was to go after you. But then I realized that you needed time, that *I* needed time. There was still the other issue for me. I'd been away for nearly seven months, and I had to be sure I'd come to terms about returning. I didn't want to chase you back here and then find myself reverting into a man you'd despise. I had to be convinced that I was doing the right thing for both of us.

"So I went back to the *pueblito*. Five days was all I needed. Maybe I'd outgrown it. It had served its purpose, given me a total break, a chance to get my head together. It wasn't the same there without you, but I tried not to think about that because I didn't want to be running home for that reason alone. At the end of the five days I just knew I was ready."

He paused, but Chelsea remained silent, so he went on. "I wish I could say that in the nine days I've been back I've solved all my problems, but I can't. I've talked things over with David. We both know there have to be changes. We may split the business up and go our separate ways, or I may just take charge of one limited section. I may even sell the whole thing to him, but I've got to think more on that. I've been following your advice, though, leaving work at the office, making time to do things just for the fun of it. I've taken up running, and I've gone for drives to the beach, and the mountains." He whispered a sad laugh. "Only thing is that I keep thinking about you and about how much more fun I'd be having if we were together. I was going to give you more time, Chelsea, honestly I was, but I couldn't. I've driven by this place every day for the past week, and I just couldn't wait any longer." His voice thickened. "To have you open the door looking like you haven't slept or eaten, and then to have you pass out—God, Chelsea, say something. Tell me what's wrong!"

Chelsea took a long, shuddering breath. She felt more tired than she had in her entire life. "It wouldn't work," she ventured weakly.

"What wouldn't work?"

"Us."

"Why ever not?"

"Because our worlds are different, yours and mine."

"Only as different as we make them."

"But there's been too much anger and hurt."

"If I could turn back the clock and erase all that, I would, Chels. You have to believe that!"

"But you can't," she said dully. "Things were said. I'll always remember and wonder and be afraid."

"You don't have *anything* to be afraid of. I love you. I'll spend the rest of my life saying it and proving it if you'll only let me."

She brushed her cheek against his chest. Though she'd intended it to be a headshake, it came out more like a caress. "I'm so tired," she murmured. "You're wrong, but I can't fight with you just now."

Her muscles had grown slack, which made it that much easier for Sam to lift her and carry her to the bed. "You lie there while I get some things together."

"What things?"

He was opening her closet, rummaging beneath the clothes. "Overnight-type things.... Have you got a bag in here?"

"I'm not going anywhere with you. I have to work."

"You can't work. You're too tired."

"I have to work. My boss expects me."

"I'll call him and tell him you're sick."

"I'm not sick. Just tired. I'll sleep tonight."

"Damn right you will," he said purposely. "What's his number?"

She raised herself up by stages until she was sitting. "You're not calling."

Sam pressed her back quickly, holding her shoulders with a firm but gentle hand. "No more than half an hour ago you passed out. You're run down, overtired and undernourished. You need rest, Chelsea, and I intend to see that you get it."

"But my job—"

"Your job can just wait."

"It waited while I was in Mexico. Sam, I've got to go—"

"And stand on your feet for hours pouring drinks? I can't let you do that, Chelsea. If it's a matter of money, I'll be glad to reimburse you—"

She bolted up, her eyes filled with sudden fire. "I don't want your money! I've *never* wanted your money! Can't you understand that?"

Stunned by the vehemence that seemed to have erupted from nowhere, he pulled back. "I'm not sure where that came from," he said very quietly, "but it's one of many things we'll have to talk about. First, though, you need rest."

"I can rest here."

"It's hot as hell here."

"Is it much different from the *pueblito*? The heat didn't bother you there. See, you've changed, Sam," she challenged, eyes flashing.

Striving for patience, he pressed his lips together, briefly closed his eyes, eventually took a deep breath. "Yes. I've changed. I've come to realize, just as you were trying to tell me, that life isn't black-and-white, all or nothing. Just because there are some things wrong with my life here doesn't mean I have to chuck everything. I don't need high blood pressure and tension headaches, so I intend to reorganize my life to prevent them. But I earn a good living and I can afford to have luxuries like a nice car and clothes and air-conditioning. Besides," he scowled boyishly, "you know damned well that the heat down there is totally different from the heat up here."

"It's that stuffy suit you're wearing."

He shot a glance toward the ceiling. "Are you going to give me the number at Icabod's, or should I call directory assistance?"

She gave it to him simply because it seemed dumb for him to bother an operator. But she hadn't moved to pack her things when he returned to the bedroom.

"I told him you'd call him in the morning to let him know about tomorrow night. He wasn't surprised, Chelsea. He said he'd been worried about you."

But Chelsea was worried too. "I'm not going with you, Sam. I'm staying here."

"Come on, Chels. I thought we settled that."

"You did. But we're not in Mexico anymore. I'm on my own turf here. And I want to stay."

"You're scared. Just like you were down there."

"You're right."

He came to sit beside her then, taking her limp hand in his. His gray eyes were warm, his expression beseechful. "I won't hurt you again, Chelsea. Please, please believe that. I love you, and I want things to work out for us. But the only way that can happen is if we spend time together, talk everything out, get to know each other here, just like we did there." He brushed her damp cheek with the back of his hand. "Right now you're not feeling well, and I want to help. I want you to come to my place because I think you'll be more comfortable there. And I want you to see it. It's my home. It's not all that bad."

Chelsea pictured that Wellesley Hills estate and shuddered.

"It's not *like* that," Sam insisted, seeming to have read her mind. "And the only way you'll be able to see for yourself is by coming with me. I won't force you to do anything. For now, I just want to take care of you. That's all."

Giving her hand a light squeeze, he stood and went back to the closet. Chelsea wondered if he'd been afraid to wait for her answer, but she was just as glad he hadn't waited. She didn't know what to say. She wanted to be with him. So much of what he said made sense. But there was still the hurt, the fear of further hurt. And, damn it, she felt so weak....

Stretching back on the bed, she threw an arm over her eyes. She heard him pull her overnight bag from the back of the closet, felt its light weight settle on the end of the bed, heard him open one drawer then another, removing clothes, putting them in the bag.

"Do you want to change before we leave?" he asked softly.

Letting her arm fall back, she stared at him for a minute. But in lying quiescently while he'd packed for her, she'd given him her decision. "I suppose I should," she murmured at last.

He lifted the bag and headed for the living room. "I'll be waiting here. Come on out when you're ready."

Peeling off her sweaty skirt and blouse, she took a quick shower and put on a fresh sundress. Sam had a smile for her when she joined him, but it was a sweet, nonsexual smile that was without threat of any sort. So she let him guide her out of her apartment and into his car, where she promptly put her head back and closed her eyes.

"You really are beat, aren't you?" he asked as he started the car and headed toward Boston.

"Mmmm."

"Haven't been sleeping?"

"Uh-uh."

"Because of the heat?"

"Mmmm." She knew that he knew it wasn't the whole truth, but she wasn't up to elaborating or, for that matter, baring her heart.

"Is it too cool in here for you?"

"Oh, no."

He chuckled but she was glad he didn't say anything. Her earlier comment on air-conditioning had been snide, as had been the one about his suit.

Again he seemed to read her mind. "It's not really 'stuffy'...is it?"

"No." In fact, it looked pretty good on him. She didn't have to open her eyes to remind herself of that fact.

Sam left her to rest while he drove. When he pulled into a parking space alongside a row of waterfront condominiums, he gently touched her arm. "We're here, Chelsea."

She opened her eyes then and looked around. She was too logy to take in much more than a three-story building, long and either newly built or recently gentrified. It was attractive, but she'd known it would be.

"Which is yours?" she asked softly.

"Come. I'll show you."

He slid out of the car, slinging the strap of her bag on his shoulder, then came around to help her out. Chelsea wasn't one to await chivalry, but her legs felt weak and she appreciated the supportive hand.

He led her to the door closest to his car, unlocked it and gestured her inside. She found herself in a large living room, done in blues and browns, contemporary in style and far simpler than anything she'd imagined.

If Sam noted her surprise, he refrained from commenting on it. "There's a kitchen and dining area off the living room," he said, but he was already guiding her upstairs and toward the largest of the two rooms there. "This is my bedroom. There's another one next door, but I think you'll be more comfortable here." Setting her bag down on a modular-type chair, he crossed to the platform bed and began tugging back its quilt. "I want you to lie down and rest now. Sleep if you can; if not, just close your eyes. I'm going down to see about getting something solid in for dinner. I'll be back up to check on you in a little while.... Okay?"

Chelsea felt that she'd run out of gas and was gliding on fumes. She managed to nod, to watch him leave the room, to take in enough of her surroundings to know that Samuel Prescott London had good taste in an understated kind of way. Then she climbed between the fresh cool sheets of his king-sized bed, put her head on his pillow and promptly fell asleep.

"CHELSEA? Wake up, sweetheart.... Chelsea?"

Chelsea returned to consciousness slowly, first taking in the voice, then the hand gently shaking her shoulder, then the cool dry air in the room, then the bed. She raised her head and looked around, wondering how long she'd slept. The room was naturally bright, though direct sunlight no longer poured through the windows. And there was Sam—*Sam?*—smiling by her side. He reached to brush her hair back from her face, and she noticed that he was still wearing a suit, but it was different, a lighter blue tweed, and a solid beige tie hung down the center of his fresh white shirt.

She frowned. "What time is it?"

"Eight forty-five."

"But...so bright?"

His smile widened. "It's morning... How do you feel?"

"Morning?"

"Uh-huh. I'd have let you sleep longer but I've got to get to work. I didn't want you to wake up and think I'd abandoned you."

"Morning?"

"I've left cereal and bananas and croissants in the kitchen. Help yourself to anything else. How about if I come back at one and we can go somewhere for lunch?"

"Lunch?" She struggled to sit up. "God, Sam, I can't believe I slept this long!"

He adjusted the pillows at her back. "You needed it. You look better already... Chels?" His smile faded, though his expression remained exquisitely soft. "I know that you probably feel you've got to rush home and work, but I really want you to stay. If it'll make you feel better, I'll drive you to your place later and you can pick up any papers you need. You can use the phone here just as well as your own. But what you can really use is another day of rest. You've done a job on yourself this time around."

She chanced a meek smile. "You're forever picking up the pieces, aren't you?"

"Maybe this time it was my fault. Not that I mind picking up the pieces, but I'd much rather see you strong and together.... Promise me you'll wait here till I get back?"

She snuggled more comfortably against the pillow. "I don't think I'm up to going much of anywhere just yet. I may fall back to sleep as soon as you've gone."

"Get something to eat first, huh?" Without waiting for her answer, he kissed her lightly on her forehead and left.

By the time Chelsea heard the downstairs door close, she'd realized several things. The first was that she felt happier than she'd felt in ages; she knew there were still many things she and Sam had to settle, but her heart was light and she was actually looking forward to the day.

The second was that she was wearing her nightgown. God bless Sam. He'd undressed her and tucked her back into bed when, very obviously, she'd had no intention of waking.

The third was that she was hungry. Ravenously so.

Tossing back the sheet, she stood quickly, then sank back to bed when a flash of dizziness reminded her of the ordeal she'd been through in the past two weeks. More slowly this time she pushed herself up and went downstairs to find that Sam had set a place for her at the island counter—woven placemat, linen napkin, silverwear, glasswear and all. A tall box of Wheaties stood beside it, and beside that a ripe banana. And there was a note.

"I'd have put everything in the dish but the banana gets yucky if you don't eat it soon after it's peeled. There's cream in the fridge, and butter and jam. The croissants are in the bag on top. If you want them warmed, put them in the microwave for fifteen seconds each. If you feel like eggs or cottage cheese, help yourself. I'll see you later. Love, Sam."

"DID YOU EAT?" was his first question when he walked in the door at one.

Chelsea grinned. "Slightly. I had the cereal and bananas, both croissants, two scrambled eggs and a slice of cheese." She rubbed her hands together. "Now. Where are we going for lunch?"

Sam laughed and gave her a hug. "I think I've let loose a food freak, but I love it, I love it." He held her back. "And you look three hundred percent better. You've even got color in your cheeks, and don't tell me it's blusher because I know the real thing when I see it."

Her color deepened. She liked it when he looked at her. She felt attractive and appreciated. "Thank you for hanging my dress up. I put it in the bathroom while I showered to get rid of the last of the wrinkles."

"My pleasure." He curved her arm through his elbow. "And as for lunch, we've got reservations at Jasper's. Ever been there?"

"Nope."

"I think you'll like it."

She did, though it went without saying that Sam's company was the highlight of the meal. He didn't jump into a heavy discussion of their relationship, seeming to realize as she did that they needed a brief healing time before tackling it. Rather he kept the conversation lighter, asking her about the work she'd done since she'd returned, telling her about his own.

In a way it was as meaningful a discussion, in terms of their relationship, as the other would have been, for they'd never before discussed their "real" lives, and Chelsea, for one, was fascinated to listen and gratified to share.

Sam explained the organizational structure of his firm and outlined the major projects it was presently involved in. He told her of the specific options open to him for cutting back, their pluses and minuses, and he genuinely welcomed her input.

In turn, she found him to be deeply interested in her work. He asked intelligent questions, expressed due concern over one particularly sensitive case or another, demonstrated a kind of insight that suggested new directions, new leads.

By the time they left the restaurant, Chelsea felt invigorated, so much so that she was slightly appalled when, after Sam had returned her to his condo with a promise to be back at six, she fell asleep for another two hours.

"I can't believe I did that," she exclaimed as he drove her to Cambridge that evening.

"You were tired."

"That's the understatement of the year."

He arched a brow as he turned onto the Anderson Bridge. "I'd have put it more strongly. I really did a job on you, didn't I?"

She cast him a hesitant look. "Yes."

They both knew they'd be talking that night, that they *had* to talk that night, but the sun was still up and there was more immediate work to do. When they reached Chelsea's apartment, she packed a large suitcase of clothes and a smaller one of papers and notes. At her own initiative she'd already called Icabod's to say that she wouldn't be in. Fortunately, her boss adored her and didn't say 'boo.'

Back at Sam's place, she unpacked her things while Sam ran across to a seafood restaurant to bring in dinner. He'd told her to take one of the third-floor rooms as an office, and she had no argument. It was a small room, cozy and bright, with a full wall of windows and a balcony overlooking the harbor.

"I probably won't get anything done here," she teased when Sam joined her to see how her unpacking was coming. "I'll sit and watch the harbor all day, or the marketplace, or the airport."

"You'll work," he retorted knowingly. Then he led her downstairs, poured them each a glass of wine and proceeded to ply her with thick lobster stew and corn on the cob and salad and rolls until she was begging for mercy. So they retired to the living room, where they sat quietly until, at last, Sam took her hand in his.

"I have to know one thing, Chelsea. One thing more important than any other." His gaze was intense, with need and vulnerability vying for prominence. "Do you love me? After all I said and did, do you still love me?"

There was no way she could be anything but truthful, either to herself or to him. "I do."

He closed his eyes for a brief instant, and she could see his body relax. He'd changed into jeans and a sport shirt before dinner, and he looked so much more like the Sam she'd known in Mexico that a wave of tenderness flowed through her.

Eyes open again, he was studying her hand, rubbing his thumbs over her knuckles, gently back and forth. "That's got to be our basis then. We love each other. So now we've got to look at the other things in our lives and see if they'll mesh." He lifted his eyes to hers. "What are you doing about school?"

"I've been accepted at BU, but I'm putting it off until I can save enough money to pay for it."

"Mother said you'd returned what she'd given you."

So he'd spoken with her since he'd been back. Chelsea had wondered about that. She was glad he had, glad that he'd learned about the money from Mrs. London. Chelsea hadn't wanted to tell him herself.

"You didn't have to do that, Chels. You deserved that money—that and the second half. You got me back."

"No, *you* got you back. And I didn't want the money. Not after what you said."

"Then you returned it for my sake?"

"No. For my sake. If we hadn't become emotionally involved, I might have felt differently. But after having fallen in love with you, I did feel cheap keeping that money."

"I'm sure my mother told you what a noble gesture it was." Sarcasm was heavy in his voice, leaving no doubt as to his suspicions.

The last thing Chelsea wanted was to add to the friction between mother and son. "Nobility had nothing to do with it," she stated quietly. "It was a matter of self-respect. I want everything to be clean, honestly earned. My getting that degree has come to mean more to me than I ever imagined it would. When I first decided to go for it, my motivation was purely to be able to counsel, to help people. Then, when I felt stronger about it, I realized that having a Ph.D. under my belt was the solid proof I needed that I'd come up in the world."

"You don't need to 'come up.' You're already there!"

Chelsea was quick to counter him. "You can say that because you were born on top. I can be more realistic. My parents, wonderful as they are, were both uneducated, and I firmly believe that because of that they never came near to fulfilling the potential their intelligence would have allowed."

"But you've got a college degree—"

"And who was it who said that you reach one goal, only to find another on the horizon?"

He shrugged and looked suitably guilty. "Touché."

"So that's the other reason why getting this degree means so much to me."

"I can put you through school—"

"No—"

"But I'd *love* doing it! Hell, Chels, I've got the money. If I can't spend it on things that matter to me, what should I do with it?"

"Invest it, give it to charity—just not mine."

"Is that it? You feel I'd be giving it to you just to be noble? You're wrong, Chelsea. I'd be doing it because I love you and because I know that going to school will make you happy, and because if that happens I'm the one to benefit from it as well. See, there are selfish motives involved too."

"But it's *my* life, *my* education. I have a certain pride."

"Y'know, if we were married, what's mine would be yours. You could take the money from our joint checking account—"

"We're not married."

"I want to be. *Will* you marry me, Chelsea?"

"No. Not...yet."

"You're not sure our love will last?"

"It'll last, at least mine will. But one of the things I realized in the past two weeks is that it takes more than love to make a binding relationship." Beatrice London's words haunted her, had haunted her since they'd been uttered that morning in her office. "You and I come from totally different stock. We met and fell in love in Mexico, in an atmosphere that was a far cry from the one we'd be living in here. Our tastes might turn out to be different. You might hate my friends; I might hate yours. You might bury yourself in your work again; I might do the same. And despite our good intentions, we might find that our relationship takes second place. That would cause friction and distance, and then what would we have?"

"That wouldn't happen!"

"Can you be sure?"

"Life doesn't come with guarantees, Chelsea."

"But I want them! Well, one part of me does, at least. Where my heart's concerned, it *is* either all or nothing. I want all your love, all your warmth, all your caring—or I'd just as soon settle for nothing, which was what I'd acclimated myself to doing before you showed up at my door yesterday."

Sam was silent for a time. He turned her hand in his and studied her palm, as though the lines there might give him a clue as to what the future held. At last he looked up.

"I can tell you that I love you with all my heart, and that I'll spend a lifetime giving you every bit of myself that I'm able to—but you still won't be sure. What if we give ourselves time. What if we stay together, get to know each other, consciously look at all those things you see as potential barriers. I won't rush you into marriage. I won't even rush you into sex, though God knows I want that because it's another way I can tell you how much I love you. But I'll be patient.... What do you say?"

He was offering a stepping stone to heaven. She knew she might stumble and fall off, and that thought terrified her because the more she saw of heaven the more she wanted to be there. But she *did* want to be there, and that made the attempt worthwhile.

She took a deep breath, then slowly smiled. "I say that you make an awful lot of sense." She lifted his hands to her mouth and kissed first one, then the other. "I do love you, Sam. And I want it to work."

"It will, love. I *know* it will."

AS THE DAYS PASSED, Chelsea increasingly believed he might be right. She was happy, even happier than she'd been in Mexico. Though she'd resigned—again—from her job at Icabod's, she kept at her missing-persons search. She worked out of Sam's condo using the extra telephone line he had specially installed for her—he'd said that he wanted to know he could get through to her at any time of day. She found no fault with his thinking because she was delighted when he called and would have otherwise been loath to keep the line tied up.

She and Sam ate breakfast together every morning, dinner every night and lunch whenever he could get away from work, which he made a point to do at least once or twice a week. They spent their evenings together, sometimes quietly at home, other times going to shows or simply walking around the waterfront. On weekends they were inseparable.

Lovemaking—Chelsea hadn't been able to resist any more than Sam had—became the highest expression of their love. It took the words and the smiles and the more innocent and frequent touching one step farther. It had its place, though, for there were many nights when they fell quietly asleep in each other's arms, and those were beautiful as well.

Gradually Sam introduced her to both his business associates and his friends, and though she liked some more than others she found them all to be far more approachable and welcoming than she'd feared. Linda Huntington she felt especially comfortable with. Likewise, some more than others, Sam took to her friends. He was ever adaptable to new topics of conversation and seemed as much at ease sitting at a time-worn table in a Brighton duplex as in a designer dining room high atop Devonshire Place.

They talked often of their Mayan *pueblito*—at one point Sam even surprised her by saying that if Reni was determined to travel north, he'd oversee her welfare himself. But the crux of their thoughts were on the present and the future.

Indeed, things seemed to be working out. After much soul-searching and discussion with Chelsea, Sam decided to leave London and McGee intact but to limit his role, by contract, to the particular division that dealt with shopping malls. He felt comfortable with that, and even before the papers had been formally drawn up he was limiting his hours. Healthy and strong and relaxed, he told Chelsea time and again that it seemed he'd found his touchstone in her. She was, he insisted, precisely what the doctor ordered.

After living with Sam for a month, Chelsea was more in love than ever. She'd begun to picture life as it would be months and years down the road—married life, with the house in the country Sam spoke of and the children he wanted—and she found herself unable to contemplate any other kind of future.

Only one thing stood in the way of her total bliss. Only one thing she really couldn't discuss with Sam. Only one thing niggled in the far recesses of her mind. Realizing that Sam knew her inside and out, she wasn't surprised when he raised the subject himself.

"I spoke with my mother today," he told her one Thursday when he arrived home from work. "I've invited her to have dinner with us tomorrow night."

No, there wasn't surprise, but there was trepidation aplenty. "Oh, Sam, I don't know. Do you think that's such a good idea?"

"It's got to be done sooner or later."

"But...she and I parted on pretty poor terms. I'm surprised she even accepted the invitation."

"I didn't give her much of a chance to refuse."

"Then she's probably *doubly* angry.... Maybe we should just wait awhile. We could do it later in the fall."

He drew her close, gently working the tension out of her shoulders with his strong hands. "She's the only thing that stands between us, Chels. You haven't said a word about her, or about what she said to you during those two meetings. I know you're doing it to protect me, and I respect that. But I know her, and I can easily imagine what she said. Her tongue can be pretty cutting."

"And what if she uses it to put a wedge between us?"

"She can't do that, because there's no wedge she could possibly use that would have any import. I'm not susceptible to her, Chelsea. Nothing she can say would change my feelings about you, so if that's worrying you, forget it. I declared my independence when I walked out of that house years ago, and I've stuck to it. It hasn't been an effort either. I know exactly what my mother is and what she'd do, given a chance. We're immune to her. Haven't we proven how well our lives mesh? Haven't we?"

"Yes."

"Then I think we should have dinner with her and let her see our conviction."

"I don't know...wouldn't it be better to just let things ride?"

"I can't do that, Chels! I want you to marry me, and I want it soon, and, damn it, she's standing in our way!" Hearing his own raised voice, he tempered his tone. "You're afraid of her, and that bothers me. I don't want her to forever be a threat in the back of your mind. Don't you see? We'll be presenting her with a fait accompli. She'll see for herself that we love each other, and you'll see for yourself that she can yield when she has to."

"And if she doesn't? If she resists?"

"Then that's her problem, and I'll wash my hands of it. I told you once that I love her because she's my mother, but I refuse to let her rule my life. If she can't accept the fact that I'm happier now than I've ever been before, well, then she's got her priorities screwed up and I pity her."

Chelsea's face was rife with uncertainty. "Do you really think seeing her now will help?"

"It can't hurt. Trust me, Chels. I know what I'm doing."

10

"I KNOW WHAT I'M DOING," he'd said.

Chelsea tried to convince herself of that through an agonizingly slow Friday. She had her doubts, but in many respects Sam was right. Beatrice London, ironically the instrument of their introduction, *was* the only thing standing between them now. Just a shadow, sometimes fading out altogether, but a recurring presence nonetheless. Phrases flitted through Chelsea's mind—a girl like you...a man of my son's station—and they planted doubts that Sam succeeded in quashing only temporarily.

Chelsea wasn't sure what she hoped for. Mrs. London wasn't about to take back the words she'd said. But perhaps, just perhaps she'd show some sign of acceptance. Though Sam had said it didn't matter to him either way, Chelsea wanted it for his sake, if not her own.

She dressed carefully that night, choosing a dress she'd bought when she'd been shopping with him the weekend before. It was pink silk, sleeveless and V-necked, gathered in blouson folds to a low waist before straightening to the knee. A wide sash, tied around the hips, gave her a look of fashionable slimness.

She stood before Sam's dresser staring at herself in the mirror. Her hair was just right. Her makeup was just right. She held a strand of pearls to her neck but they got lost in the V of her dress. She replaced it with a costume piece of brightly colored beads, but they were too casual.

"Why the frown?" Sam asked softly. He crossed the room to stand slightly behind her, but she could see how handsome he looked in his dark suit and tie.

"These necklaces aren't right. I should have thought to pick up something else this week, but I'm not a good shopper. I didn't know we'd be going out, and with your *mother* no less."

Sam studied her reflection, his eyes growing uncertain. He looked down, then cleared his throat. "I've got something you can wear. It'd be just right with the dress."

"You have something?"

"Mmm." He reached around her to pull open his top drawer and remove a long, flat box. "Here. Open it and see what you think."

Chelsea stared at the box, then shifted her gaze to Sam. "You bought something for me?"

"Is that so strange?" he asked quietly, a faint smile on his lips. "I want to buy things for you. It was pure fun picking it out."

"I've never gotten a gift from a man before."

"I'm not just any man. I'm your husband-to-be. Go on, Chels. Open it."

Pleased and excited, she snapped off the elastic ribbon, opening the box only to find another box , this one velvet, inside. She removed it, slowly opened it, then caught her breath.

"Sam! It's beautiful!" Very carefully she lifted the necklace, a wide serpentine chain with a sparkling diamond set at its center.

"You like it?" He still seemed unsure. "I saw some things that were more glittery, more elaborate, but this one was simple and elegant, like you."

"I *love* it!" Holding tightly to the necklace, she threw her arms around his neck. "Thank you, Sam. It's perfect!" Without another word she disengaged herself and put on the necklace. It nestled against her skin, its diamond eye sparkling. It couldn't have suited her better had it been custom designed.

"It looks great," he said, his voice thick with appreciation.

Smiling, she sighed. "That it does." She turned and hugged him again, but he was reaching behind her.

"Here. These go with it."

Startled, she drew back to find him offering her a second, smaller box. Her eyes went from the box to him, then back. Unable to resist, she opened it quickly. Inside were a pair of earrings, wide gold crescents with, again, a diamond embedded in each tip. Her eyes were as glittery as the diamonds when she looked up at him.

"I feel like it's Christmas, but Santa never brought gifts like these!"

He was removing the earrings and carefully clipping them to her ears. When he was done, he cupped her neck with both hands, tipped her chin up and smiled. "They look marvelous." Then he turned her so she could inspect herself in the mirror.

The earrings were just visible through her hair, their diamonds casting an almost mysterious glint. They went perfectly with the necklace, and both went perfectly with the dress. She felt more special than ever. Putting one hand to the necklace, another to an earring, she looked at Sam in the mirror.

"I don't know what to say!" she whispered.

"Don't say a thing until you see the last."

"The last?"

"Mmm." For a third time he reached into the drawer. This time the box he withdrew was even smaller, suspiciously so. She hesitated, her pulse racing. "Go on," he urged her. "Open it."

Very slowly she slid the band off the box and lifted its lid. Very slowly she removed the velvet box inside and, hands trembling, opened it. This time the glitter of the diamond she saw was made all the more so by the tears welling spontaneously in her eyes.

"Oh, Sam," she whispered.

He took the ring from the box and slid it onto the third finger of her left hand. "I want you to wear it, Chelsea," he said hoarsely. "I want the world to know that we *will* be married one day soon." He brought her beringed finger to his mouth and kissed it. "I love you. God, I love you so much!" Taking her in his arms, he crushed her close.

"I love you too, Sam," she managed, though her throat was tight with emotion. "And the ring is exquisite! Thank you!"

He kissed her once, then a second time. Then, framing her face with his hands, he held her back. "I bought it last week, but I wanted to wait for the right time to give it to you. This seemed like that time, but I want you to know that I'm not doing it for my mother's sake. I'm doing it for mine, for ours."

"I know," she whispered, filled with such unbelievable happiness that she felt near to bursting. Sam London was more handsome, more wonderful, more loving than any man she might have conjured in her fantasies. That he was real, that he was *hers* was incredible!

He cleared his throat. "If you keep looking at me that way, we may just keep mother waiting an hour."

She sobered instantly. "Oh, no. We can't do that." She grabbed his wrist and peered at his watch. "Seven-fifteen? The reservations are for seven-thirty!"

He chuckled at her alarm. "Locke-Ober's is all of three minutes by car. If we weren't so dressed up, we could walk it in ten, but then we'd be sticky and sweaty and how can I do that to you when you look fresh and absolutely gorgeous?"

"You're good for my ego, Sam."

"And you mine, sweetheart.... All set?"

Chelsea took a last look at herself in the mirror, picked up her small purse and linked her fingers with Sam's when he held out his hand.

It was her right hand he held, which was good. She wanted her left hand free so that she could look at her engagement ring. It gave her courage, and she needed that. As wonderfully as the evening had begun, she was not looking forward to the second act.

CHELSEA AND SAM had been seated at their table for five minutes before Beatrice London appeared in the wake of the maitre d'. She walked slowly, with a certain regality, but it suddenly struck Chelsea that her pace might well be due to her age. Though she remained the image of fine breeding, old wealth and corporate superstardom, she seemed, strangely, less intimidating to Chelsea.

"You okay?" Sam murmured.

She nodded, her eyes following Beatrice London's approach. "I'm okay."

He grinned and squeezed her hand, releasing it only when he stood to greet his mother. He kissed the older woman's cheek, then turned to the table.

"Mother, you remember Chelsea."

Mrs. London nodded. "How are you, Miss Ross?"

Chelsea smiled as warmly as she could. She saw no sign of antagonism on Beatrice's face, which was encouraging. "Chelsea, please. And I'm fine, thank you."

Sam seated his mother, then returned to his own chair. It was a table for four. The two women sat opposite each other, with Sam in the middle. He promptly waved over the wine steward and ordered champagne.

"A celebration is in order," he explained when the man had left tc fetch their bubbly. "Chelsea and I are engaged. We wanted you to be the first to know."

Chelsea wasn't sure who gasped first, Mrs. London or herself. She'd known the woman would eventually see her ring, though her left hand was clenched in her lap. But she'd never dreamed Sam would take the bull by the horns and spring the news so bluntly.

"Engaged?" Mrs. London looked from Sam to Chelsea, then back. If her composure had been momentarily shaken, she quickly regained it. "Isn't this sudden?"

Sam was beaming. He took Chelsea's right hand and brought it to his thigh. "We've known each other for over two months now. Since I've been back I've had a lot of convincing to do, but she's finally agreed." He looked at Chelsea with such glee that she couldn't help but blush and smile.

"Then congratulations—to you both," Mrs. London offered gently. She didn't smile, but her graciousness was commendable, and Chelsea found herself admiring it.

"And there's news about work, too," Sam went on. He launched into great detail about the changes he'd made at London and McGee, pausing only when the champagne arrived to propose a toast. "To Chelsea," he began, love and pride shining in his eyes, "who's taught me so much about myself and has brought me happiness and contentment." He sipped from his glass, then winked at her over its rim.

She smiled and shook her head. He was naughty. Positively naughty!

If Beatrice London thought so, she didn't say. And rather than choke on her champagne, which Chelsea knew she had every right to do, she remained eminently poised.

When Sam resumed the discussion of his work, Beatrice seemed genuinely interested. When he politely inquired about the latest happenings at the London Corporation, she went on at length about an entertainment complex the Corporation was taking over in Atlanta.

Food came and went. Chelsea ate and listened quietly to the conversation, asking questions from time to time with the confidence that had come from hours and hours of talking with Sam about his projects.

At one point Mrs. London quite civilly asked how her own work was going. Chelsea answered quickly, feeling self-conscious until Sam prodded her into greater detail. He'd always respected her work, and she loved him for that too. Though she was aware that his mother gave little more than gratuitous nods as she spoke, she appreciated how much even those small gestures must have cost the woman. Perhaps Sam had been right. Perhaps it *had* been wise to meet at this time. Warmth, even excitement at their engagement was too much to expect. Chelsea was satisfied to settle for simple tolerance.

Then Sam deserted her. They were waiting for the arrival of their desserts when he broke off from the conversation. "I believe that's Malcolm Whane sitting over in the corner. I really should say hello." He put his napkin on the table and rose. "If you ladies will excuse me for a minute..." And he was gone.

Nervously Chelsea followed his retreating form. She swallowed once, then dropped her gaze to the linen tablecloth.

"He did that on purpose, you know," Beatrice London observed. "He wanted to give the two of us a chance to talk alone."

Chelsea darted her a timid glance. "I think you're right."

"About this, yes. Not necessarily about everything, though."

Slowly, uncertainly, Chelsea again met her gaze.

"I have to be honest with you, Chelsea. I would have picked a very different sort of woman to be my son's wife. I won't apologize for anything that happened between us in the past. I meant everything I said."

Chelsea's expression grew pained. "I'm sorry you feel that way," she said softly. "The last thing I want is for Sam to be hurt. You two may have had your differences, but you're his mother and he does love you."

"But he loves you too, doesn't he?"

"I—yes."

"And you very obviously love him. That was the one thing that stood out most clearly in my mind after our last meeting. The things you said to me right before you left—telling me what kind of a man Samuel was—they were very beautiful. As a mother, I wasn't immune to your compliments."

"I hadn't intended them as compliments, Mrs. London. In my mind I was stating facts. Given the chance, I'd state them all over again, and even add a few."

"I'm sure you would. Tell me. Your schooling. Are you starting this fall?"

Chelsea tipped her chin up. "No. I don't have the money saved yet."

"Surely Samuel has offered to put up your tuition."

"He has, but I refused. Regardless of what you believe, I'm not marrying him for anything monetary he might offer me. That's one of the reasons I held off his proposal of marriage for so long."

"But you gave in."

Chelsea shrugged, then smiled shyly. "I do love him. I want to be with him. I need him, and I think he needs me." Her tone slowly gained confidence. "I may not have the breeding of the woman you would have chosen for him. I may not have the money or the class or the social experience. But I think I can make Sam happy, and in the end, that's all that counts, isn't it?"

Beatrice London looked at her for a long minute. "I never thought I'd be saying this, but you may be right there. Samuel looks better than he has in years. Oh, I can do without the mustache, and his hair's still too long, but he very clearly is happy." She arched both brows. "I still don't understand what made him miserable before. But something did, to such an extent that he took off and stayed away for nearly seven months. It's very possible that he would still be in Mexico had it not been for you. So in a way, dear, you did earn that money. I could still—"

"No!" Chelsea burst out, then lowered her voice. "Please. Not another word about that."

Beatrice gave her pseudo-shrug. "As you wish... But getting back to what I was saying, I've come to the conclusion that I'd rather have Samuel here, with whomever and doing whatever he chooses, than to have him in self-imposed exile." When she looked at Chelsea then, there was the faintest glimmer of surrender in her dark eyes. "I want you to know that I won't stand in the way of your marriage, Chelsea. If this is what Samuel wants, I'll give him all support I can."

Chelsea knew that Beatrice had said all she wanted to. No, she hadn't offered an apology, or extended a welcome or put on a show of warmth. But Chelsea didn't want that. At least now she knew where she stood.

"Thank you," she said quietly, sincerely. "I'd appreciate that."

To her surprise, Mrs. London ventured a half smile. "I have to admit that, between the two of you, you'll make beautiful children."

Chelsea blushed. "I think so too."

As though on cue, Sam returned, sitting down at the table with a nonchalance Chelsea would later chide him on. Oh, he was crafty, but she loved him. Lord, how she loved him!

SEVERAL WEEKS LATER Chelsea and Sam lay curled snugly against each other in bed. It wasn't the double bed in her Cambridge apartment, or the platform bed in his waterfront condo, but the four-poster bed in the rustic country home they'd passed papers on several days before.

"Like it?" he asked softly.

"The bed? I love it."

"The cabin. Do you like the cabin?"

"I love it!"

"It needs lots of work."

"That's Samuel Prescott London talking. *My* Sam knows that if we'd wanted something modern and elegant we'd have bought it. We have modern and elegant enough in the city. This place is a weekend retreat. It's perfect. Unimposing, relaxing, serene. Isn't that what you said when you first saw it?"

"Mmm. I just want to make sure you're happy with it."

"How could I not be happy?" She propped her chin on his chest. "I'm with you, aren't I?"

"For better or for worse." He kissed her nose, then let his head fall back to the pillow. "But this place is pretty primitive. Some people would consider it 'for worse.'"

She grinned. "Not me. A *two*-seater outhouse is pure luxury."

He chuckled. "By comparison, I suppose you're right."

"Is that why you fell in love with this place—because it reminds you of the *pueblito*?"

"Not really. But it represents many of the things I had and felt there. Peace. Freedom. Yes, serenity. It'll give us a place to escape to." He ran his hand down her spine, then tightened his arms around her. "Every weekend. I'll like that."

"*I'll* like it when it gets cold up here. That Franklin stove looks great! And," she tacked on in a drawl, "I loved watching you chop wood today."

"Hmph. I didn't get as much done as I'd hoped. You distracted me."

"I've always wanted to make love outdoors. And in our own woods—what could be better?"

"It was pretty good, wasn't it?"

"Mmmm." She thought back to that passionate interlude. It never failed to amaze her that things between them could get better and better. "You've really come a long way, haven't you?"

"In lovemaking?"

"In relaxing. No more tension headaches?"

"Nope."

"No more high blood pressure?"

"Nope."

"You're as fit as you were in Mexico.... Now if we can only do something about those pin-striped suits...."

He tickled her ribs and, laughing, she tried to escape his fingers, but he wouldn't let her go. "Stop that, Sam-u-el!"

"Oh, God, you're not going to call me that, are you?"

"Only when you misbehave."

"I'm not misbehaving. At least, not yet."

Grinning, she tipped up her head so that she could see his face. He was looking down at her, eyes half-lidded, lips relaxed. "I do like it when you misbehave," she said more softly. She touched his face with fingers that trembled slightly. "I love you very, very much. But then, you know that, don't you?"

His mustache twitched at one side as he gave her a crooked grin. "It's okay. Say it as often as you want. As often as you want."

She did.

Six exciting series
for you every month...
from Harlequin

Harlequin Romance·
The series that started it all

Tender, captivating and heartwarming...
love stories that sweep you off to faraway places
and delight you with the magic of love.

◆

Harlequin Presents·

Powerful contemporary love
stories...as individual as the
women who read them

The No. 1 romance series...
exciting love stories for you, the woman of today...
a rare blend of passion and dramatic realism.

◆

Harlequin Superromance®
It's more than romance...
it's Harlequin Superromance

A sophisticated, contemporary romance-fiction
series, providing you with a longer,
more involving read...a richer mix of complex plots,
realism and adventure.

Harlequin
American Romance™
Harlequin celebrates the American woman...

...by offering you romance stories written about American women, by American women for American women. This series offers you contemporary romances uniquely North American in flavor and appeal.

◆

Harlequin Temptation™
Passionate stories for today's woman

An exciting series of sensual, mature stories of love...dilemmas, choices, resolutions... all contemporary issues dealt with in a true-to-life fashion by some of your favorite authors.

◆

Harlequin Intrigue™
Because romance can be quite an adventure

Harlequin Intrigue, an innovative series that blends the romance you expect... with the unexpected. Each story has an added element of intrigue that provides a new twist to the Harlequin tradition of romance excellence.

Harlequin Books·

PROD-A-2

Just what the woman on the go needs!

BOOKMATE

The perfect "mate" for all Harlequin paperbacks!

Holds paperbacks open for hands-free reading!

- **• TRAVELING**
- **• VACATIONING**
- **• AT WORK • IN BED**
- **• COOKING • EATING**
- **• STUDYING**

Perfect size for all standard paperbacks, this wonderful invention makes reading a pure pleasure! Ingenious design holds paperback books OPEN and FLAT so even wind can't ruffle pages—leaves your hands free to do other things. Reinforced, wipe-clean vinyl-covered holder flexes to let you turn pages without undoing the strap...supports paperbacks so well, they have the strength of hardcovers!

Snaps closed for easy carrying.

Available now. Send your name, address, and zip or postal code, along with a check or money order for just $4.99 + .75¢ for postage & handling (for a total of $5.74) payable to Harlequin Reader Service to:

Harlequin Reader Service
901 Fuhrmann Blvd.
P.O. Box 1325
Buffalo, N.Y. 14269

MATE-1RR

Offer not available in Canada.

Can you keep a secret?

You can keep this one
plus 4 free novels

FREE BOOKS/GIFT COUPON

Mail to Harlequin Reader Service®

In the U.S.	In Canada
901 Fuhrmann Blvd.	P.O. Box 2800, Station "A"
P.O. Box 1394	5170 Yonge Street
Buffalo, N.Y. 14240-1394	Willowdale, Ontario M2N 6J3

YES! Please send me 4 free Harlequin Superromance® novels and my free surprise gift. Then send me 4 brand-new novels every month as they come off the presses. Bill me at the low price of $2.50 each—a 10% saving off the retail price. There are no shipping, handling or other hidden costs. There is no minimum number of books I must purchase. I can always return a shipment and cancel at any time. Even if I never buy another book from Harlequin, the 4 free novels and the surprise gift are mine to keep forever.

Name _____ (PLEASE PRINT)

Address _____ Apt. No. _____

City _____ State/Prov. _____ Zip/Postal Code _____

This offer is limited to one order per household and not valid to present subscribers. Price is subject to change.

MSSR-SUB-1R

Take 4 novels and a surprise gift FREE

FREE BOOKS/GIFT COUPON

Mail to **Harlequin Reader Service**®

In the U.S.
901 Fuhrmann Blvd.
P.O. Box 1394
Buffalo, N.Y. 14240-1394

In Canada
P.O. Box 2800, Station "A"
5170 Yonge Street
Willowdale, Ontario M2N 6J3

YES! Please send me 4 free Harlequin Temptation® novels and my free surprise gift. Then send me 4 brand-new novels every month as they come off the presses. Bill me at the low price of $1.99 each — a 13% saving off the retail price. There are no shipping, handling or other hidden costs. There is no minimum number of books I must purchase. I can always return a shipment and cancel at any time. Even if I never buy another book from Harlequin, the 4 free novels and the surprise gift are mine to keep forever.

_____
Name   (PLEASE PRINT)

_____
Address   Apt. No.

_____
City   State/Prov.   Zip/Postal Code

This offer is limited to one order per household and not valid to present subscribers. Price is subject to change.

ILHT–SUB–1R